The Ghost of Christmas Past

Also by Rhys Bowen

The Molly Murphy Mysteries

Time of Fog and Fire
Away in a Manger
The Edge of Dreams
City of Darkness and Light
The Family Way
Hush Now, Don't You Cry
Bless the Bride
The Last Illusion
In a Gilded Cage
Tell Me, Pretty Maiden
In Dublin's Fair City
Oh Danny Boy
In Like Flynn
For the Love of Mike
Death of Riley
Murphy's Law

The Constable Evans Mysteries

Evanly Bodies
Evan Blessed
Evan's Gate
Evan Only Knows
Evans to Betsy
Evan Can Wait
Evan and Elle
Evanly Choirs
Evan Help Us
Evans Above

The Ghost of Christmas Past

Rhys Bowen

 Minotaur Books New York

This is a work of fiction. All of the characters, organizations, and events portrayed in this novel are either products of the author's imagination or are used fictitiously.

www.minotaurbooks.com

The Library of Congress has cataloged the hardcover edition as follows:

Names: Bowen, Rhys, author.
Title: The ghost of Christmas past / Rhys Bowen.
Description: First edition. | New York : Minotaur Books, 2017.
Identifiers: LCCN 201702485 | ISBN 978-1-250-12572-9 (hardcover) | ISBN 978-1-250-12573-6 (ebook)
Subjects: LCSH: Murphy, Molly (Fictitious character)—Fiction. | Women private investigators—New York (State)—Fiction. | GSAFD: Mystery fiction.
Classification: LCC PR6052.0848 G48 2017 | DDC 823/.914—dc23
LC record available at https://lccn.loc.gov/2017024853

ISBN 978-1-250-19067-3 (trade paperback)

First Minotaur Books Paperback Edition: October 2018

10 9 8 7 6 5 4 3 2

This book is dedicated to my fellow author Barbara Hinske and her great-great aunt Florence Lind, who has now been immortalized as a character in this book. As Barbara wrote to me, "My great-great aunt Florence was a maiden lady Latin teacher. She lived with my grandmother and died at the age of 103. Precise, demanding, articulate, and strong, she was in control until the very end. The day she died, she ate her usual breakfast, wrote her morning's correspondence, walked a half mile to the mailbox to post her letters, and then had a heart attack and died. When she was in charge of my cousins and me when I was young, she'd make us sit up straight and play Scrabble—with the dictionary at hand (not that she needed it) and NO cheating."

As always my thanks to my team at Minotaur, my team at Jane Rotrosen Agency, and my family.

One

New York City, December 1906

It had been a year of losses. Losses and uncertainty. Of a darkness I couldn't shake off. Daniel's job with the New York police still hung in the balance although a new commissioner was due to take office in January—a commissioner we hoped would be less in the pocket of Tammany Hall. Daniel had avoided the unpleasantness of a corrupt department trying to find a reason to get rid of him by accepting assignments from Mr. John Wilkie, head of the U.S. Secret Service. The first assignment had taken him to San Francisco, and nearly cost us everything we held dear. He had subsequently been summoned to Washington on several occasions, but still hadn't made up his mind whether to accept a permanent position there. This was probably because of me. Because he knew that I worried terribly when he was away and I relied on the support of dear friends in New York. And frankly I needed that support at the moment.

You see, I was not quite myself after we returned from San Francisco. I had told myself that all was well and I could get on with my old life again, but all was not well. I had been wounded both physically and mentally. Pushed to the edge, actually. And the result was that I lost the child I had not known I was carrying. A miscarriage after three months, just when I had told myself that all would be well. The doctor had made light of it: a good percentage of pregnancies end in a miscarriage, he had told me. It was just nature's way of making sure imperfect babies didn't come into the world. But I was essentially a healthy young woman. Nothing to stop me from having another baby right away. He talked of it as if it was only a matter of discarding one dress and choosing a new one. But I mourned that baby and I was overcome with guilt. If I hadn't been impulsive and gone out to my husband in San Francisco, I was sure the baby would have been all right. I'd have been giving birth right about this time. A Christmas baby. I tried to remind myself that if I hadn't gone out to San Francisco, I might have lost a husband, but nothing I could say or think could bring me out from the darkness that threatened to swallow me.

I went about my chores, took care of my son and my husband, pretended to enjoy my friends' attempts to cheer me up and make me laugh, but in reality it felt as if I was looking at the world through a black veil. And just when I felt that I couldn't handle one more piece of bad news, ever, it came anyway. In October we received a telegram to say that Daniel's mother had been taken to the hospital, stricken with pneumonia. She was so sick that we thought we'd lose her. I have to confess that I had never been that fond of Mrs. Sullivan, as I still called her. I had always felt that she saw me as a disappointment; that she had wanted her son to make a better marriage and rise higher in society. But it hurt me to see Daniel so distraught at the thought of losing his mother. I suppose the bond between mother and only son is a fierce one.

Amazingly she came through the worst, and I took our son, Liam, up to Westchester County to help the elderly housekeeper, Martha, look after Daniel's mother as she recuperated. My young ward, Bridie, I left with my neighbors Sid and Gus, so that she could continue her schooling. She was blossoming into a confident and cultured young woman and I didn't want to interrupt her education. Giving me a challenge like that was probably a good thing. It took my thoughts away from my own current state. In fact as Christmas approached I found myself actually looking forward to it. Daniel would be coming home from Washington, then he'd bring Bridie up to Westchester to join us. I pictured us cutting a big tree from the nearby woods. Mrs. Sullivan would not be up to baking, but she could teach me to make her favorite recipes. And Liam was now two years old and big enough to help with decorating the house. In fact we'd already been through the woods collecting pinecones and holly.

Then two weeks before the holiday, Mrs. Sullivan received a letter. Her face lit up when she saw who it was from.

"Why, it's never Florence Lind," she said, looking up at me. "She and I were bosom friends when we were growing up. We've kept in touch ever since, although our lives have taken such different paths. She always was a headstrong young girl and she became a strong woman. She never married, but she became a leading voice in the suffrage movement. Not that I approve of that, mind you. I've always believed that a woman's place is in the home and it's up to the men to run the country. But Florence was passionate about it. That is until her favorite sister died tragically, leaving two young daughters. Florence immediately abandoned her cause and went to raise her sister's children."

She paused and I could see her reading the letter. "Oh, how nice," she exclaimed. "That is thoughtful of her."

She looked up again. "It seems that she also hasn't been well recently and has gone to live with one of her nieces. Not far from here as it happens. Scarborough. Do you know it? On the Hudson. Some fine mansions in that neighborhood." She gave a satisfied nod. "The house is called Greenbriars, apparently. Florence says it's most comfortable. I remember she told me that the girl had married well. Cedric Van Aiken, from one of the old Dutch families, you know. Anyway Florence has now moved in with them and this is what she says: 'I hear from mutual friends that you have been quite ill, Mary dear. My sweet niece Winnie has told me I should treat her house as my own and invite whatever friends I wish, so I thought of inviting you to come to Greenbriars for Christmas. It would do you a world of good. Big roaring fires and good food and we two old ladies can chatter away to our hearts' content. It will be just like old times, won't it? Do say you'll come. And if I must confess, it would be a boon to me as well. I am still feeling a little like a fish out of water here, away from my old life, and would dearly welcome an old friend. They will send the carriage for you whenever you wish to come. Your affectionate friend Florence.'"

There was an excited smile on her face when she folded the letter. "Isn't that a surprise? Being invited to an elegant house party at my age. I wonder if I have anything suitable to wear? And you'll be able to go back to your little house in the city. I know you were only planning to spend Christmas here to humor an old lady, and now you can be with your friends and spend another merry holiday."

"Will you be well enough to go?" I asked. "You are still quite weak, you know."

"I'll take Ivy with me to help me," she said. "You'll take good care of me, won't you, my dear?" And she reached out to pat the hand of the young girl who had just come into the room with a cup of chamomile tea for her mistress. She was a skinny little thing with big dark eyes. She looked younger than her true age, which must have been around thirteen. Somehow she epitomized the word waif.

"Yes, ma'am. Of course I will." The girl's voice was scarcely bigger than a whisper and she gave a shy smile.

"She's working out well, don't you think?" Daniel's mother asked as Ivy left the room again. She had recently acquired Ivy from an orphanage in New York City, and the girl was being trained by Martha in all things domestic. From what I had seen she had proven herself a fast and willing learner. But since my mother-in-law had formerly taken in Bridie to train her for a similar domestic position, only to become so fond of her that Bridie was never destined to a be a maid, I wondered if Ivy would have a similar future.

"And what will I have to do at Greenbriars, except sit and be waited on?" Daniel's mother went on, still smiling. "And it will be such a tonic to be with dear Florence."

I could hardly say that I had been quite looking forward to Christmas in the country with her. Now I would be back at my house on Patchin Place in Greenwich Village and my neighbors would have lively parties and shower us with gifts, and I would make an effort to look as if I was enjoying myself.

I helped my mother-in-law decide what to take with her, suitable for a grand house party. We discussed what sort of gifts to buy for her friend and niece.

"I don't think I can be expected to bring gifts for the husband and his family, can I?" she said. "Since I have never met him and don't know his taste."

"A box of chocolates for the family, or crystallized fruit is always acceptable," I suggested.

She nodded. "Good idea. That shows willing, doesn't it? But I must think carefully about what to get for dear Florence. She is not the type of woman who will be thrilled with frou-frou. A book or a journal maybe."

In the end she sent me off into White Plains, where I chose a leather-embossed journal for her friend Florence Lind as well as some French soap for the niece. "Who doesn't like French soap?" as Mrs. Sullivan put it.

On the appointed day the carriage came—a grand-looking affair with a pair of perfectly matched grays and a coachman in black and gold livery. The coachman helped the old lady into her seat, then Ivy helped with the luggage before climbing in beside Mrs. Sullivan.

"Have a wonderful Christmas, my dears," Daniel's mother called to us. She blew a kiss to Liam, who had to be restrained from joining them. He loved anything on wheels, just like his daddy. We waved as they set off, then packed up our things and rode to the station on a far less glamorous wagon driven by the handyman, Josh. A trace of snow had fallen the night before, the first of the season. It made the trees and fences look quite festive as they sparkled in the sunshine. As the train approached the city I vowed that I would make sure my family had a lovely holiday and that I would force myself to snap out of my black mood. I looked forward to seeing my friends again, and my dear Bridie, not to mention my husband, whom I had only seen on brief visits for over a month. We'd be reunited for a lovely Christmas. All was going to be well.

Two

I confess my heart was beating quite fast when I was helped down from the hansom cab at the entrance to Patchin Place. My little side street was a backwater of calmness against the rush and hubbub of Greenwich Avenue and the Jefferson Market opposite. It was barely wider than an alleyway but quite charming with a row of warm brick houses on either side, bay trees growing in pots outside front doors, and cobbles underfoot. Cabs never attempted to come all the way to my front door as the street was too narrow to turn a vehicle and horses do not enjoy being backed up.

"You'll be all right the rest of the way then?" the cabby asked as he lifted down my bags.

"Oh, yes, don't worry. My friends will help me bring in the luggage," I said. In truth there was only one large valise and my carpetbag, since I didn't own many clothes in the first place and had only taken the bare minimum up to my mother-in-law's.

Liam stood looking around, assessing where he was. A month is a long time in the life of a two-year-old. Then he broke into a big smile. "Bwidie!" he exclaimed, looking up at me. "Go see Bwidie."

"Yes, darling. We're going to see Bridie," I said. "But she won't be home from school for a little while. Shall we go and visit Auntie Gus and Auntie Sid instead?"

"A-Gus. A-Sid," he agreed and set off wobbling over the cobbles toward the far end of Patchin Place. My house faced that of my dearest friends Augusta Walcott and Elena Goldfarb, otherwise known as Gus and Sid—names that completely defied the convention of their upbringing, to go with a lifestyle that also defied convention. They played by their own rules and play they did, from flitting off to Paris to study art to transforming their living room into a Mongolian yurt. One never knew what one would find when their front door opened. That was half the joy of it. The other half was that they were the kindest and most generous of women. I loved them like the sisters I never had.

I left the big suitcase and hurried after Liam in case he tripped on the uneven and slippery cobbles. I took his hand and we went up to Sid and Gus's front door. Liam gave me a look of excited anticipation. I nodded and rapped with their door knocker. We heard the sound of footsteps coming downstairs and the door was opened by Gus, her arms full of clothing.

"Molly?" she exclaimed. She sounded pleased but surprised. "What are you doing here? Is something wrong?"

"Not at all. Change of plans for Christmas. Daniel's mother has been invited to a swank house party and so we've come home. Here, let me take that from you," I added as the top of the pile of clothing began to teeter. "Have you been doing the laundry or are you weeding out garments to give to the poor?"

"Neither," she said. "We're in the middle of packing. Come in. Come in. Only watch your step. The hallway is rather crowded, I'm afraid."

I noticed then that there were several trunks and suitcases stacked in the front hall. "You're going away?" I asked as Gus put down the pile on top of a half-packed cabin trunk, swept Liam up into her arms, and started to carry him into the front parlor.

She nodded, turning back to me. "We received an invitation from an old Vassar friend. A group of former classmates are reuniting at a place on the Hudson, not too far from our dear alma mater. And we thought you'd be away for Christmas, so there was nothing to keep us here."

"Oh, I see," I said flatly. I glanced up the alleyway to where my bag sat, unattended. "I'd better go and retrieve my suitcase before some urchin thinks that Christmas has come early for him."

"I'll help." She put down Liam. "Stay there like a good boy while Auntie Gus helps your mommy fetch the bags, and then we'll go and find something good to eat, all right?"

Liam nodded. We walked up Patchin Place then carried the heavy bag between us, not saying a word. In truth I couldn't think of what to say that would not betray my disappointment that they wouldn't be around when I needed their support, and I suspected that Gus felt awkward about it too.

Liam was waiting at her front door, watching us with an anxious look. Gus picked him up and carried him through into the front parlor, where a big fire was burning in the hearth. She motioned me to sit and perched opposite on a high-backed chair with a squirming Liam on her lap. "I suppose you want to get down, young fellow," she said. "My, how big you've become. Off you go then. Go and explore." Liam needed no more urging. He was already headed for the stuffed bird under its glass dome, his favorite.

"So when are you leaving?" I asked, trying to keep the tone of my voice light.

Gus toyed with the fabric of her skirt. "We were planning to leave as soon as Bridie's school term ended and Captain Sullivan arrived home to take her up to his mother's house." I could see the embarrassment on her face as she said the words. "I'm so sorry, Molly. If only we'd known, we'd never have accepted."

"Don't be silly." I managed a bright smile. "There is no way you should have turned down an invitation like that, even if you had known we were going to be home. Go and have a wonderful time. We'll be fine here. It will be good to have Daniel around for a while and I'm dying to see what Bridie has been learning."

I saw a spasm of concern cross Gus's face.

"She is all right, isn't she?"

"Bridie? Oh, yes. Never better." It was her turn to fake a bright smile. "Doing so well at school. The teacher says she's at the top of her class and we've already promised to speak to our former professors at Vassar when the time comes. . . ." She let the end of that sentence trail off.

"Who is it, Gus?" came Sid's clear voice down the stairs and Sid herself appeared in the doorway, looking remarkably conventional and understated for once. Sid's normal attire ranged from gentlemen's smoking jackets to Chinese brocade trousers. Today she was in a dark skirt and white shirtwaist—the normal attire of most New York women. She spotted us and leaped down the last few stairs. "Well, I never. It's Molly and Liam, come home to us. We didn't expect to see you until after Christmas! We have your presents all wrapped up in one of those bags. We were going to come over and surprise you at Mrs. Sullivan's house. We won't be staying very far away." She paused, a look of concern on her face. "Oh, dear. It's not bad news, is it? Daniel's mother is all right?"

"She's recovering nicely, thank you. So nicely that she's accepted an invitation to a house party over the holiday. A childhood friend, apparently. She went off in a very fancy carriage while Liam and I hitched a ride home on the farm cart with the cabbages." I attempted a carefree laugh, but my friends knew me better than that.

"And now you'll be home alone here for Christmas?" Sid asked.

"Not alone. With my family around me."

"We could still cancel our arrangement." Sid shot Gus a glance.

"Don't be so silly," I said. "Of course you must go. You know you want to see your old classmates. We'll be just fine. We may entertain. Miss Van Woekem, for example. She loves to see Liam. And poor Mrs. Endicott. And we'll all be back together in the New Year."

"Yes. Back together in the New Year," Sid said and again she and Gus exchanged a glance.

"Bridie should be home from school soon," Sid said. "She's been doing very well. You'll be proud of her. And she's grown too. We are so fond of her, in fact we'll hate to lose her. . . ."

"Why should you lose her?" I asked. "She's only across the street. She can visit you anytime she likes."

"I spoke out of turn," Sid said hastily.

I looked from one face to the other. "What is it?" I asked. "Is something wrong with Bridie? She's not sick, is she?"

"No, never better," Gus said, not taking her eyes off Sid's face. "It's just that . . . She's had some news. We'd better not spoil it for her. She wants to tell you herself."

"Good news?"

There was a pause. "Yes, I suppose you could say it's good news," Gus said. "Just not for us."

"Then for God's sake tell me," I blurted out. "Don't keep me in suspense. If it's bad news, I'd rather know. In fact I'd rather know in advance than hear it from Bridie's lips."

"It's her father," Gus said slowly.

"He's been confirmed dead?"

She shook her head. "Quite the opposite. Apparently he has been making good money working down in New Orleans and now he's on his way back to New York. He's coming to reclaim Bridie and take her back home to Ireland."

Three

Of all the news I could have received, this was the most unexpected. It caught me like a punch in the gut, winding me so that for a long moment I couldn't speak. Thoughts and images flashed around inside my head: little Bridie snuggling up against me as I brought her to America in the hold of a ship, the time she nearly died of typhoid, and then watching her become the big sister, learn to knit, play with Liam, rescue two orphan children. . . . She had been part of my life for so long now that I truly thought of her as my daughter. I couldn't even picture life without her.

"Why is he going back to Ireland?" I asked. "I thought he hated it there. The injustice. The oppression."

"I can't tell you that," Sid said. "You know he never was the greatest of letter writers. . . ."

"You can say that again," I said angrily. "How many years went by when the poor child didn't know if her father was dead or alive, down there in Panama?"

"It appears he was very sick for a long while," Gus said, again looking at Sid for confirmation. "He had yellow fever and was in a hospital for months. Then his boy got some kind of tropical disease. But they both survived, and what's more they prospered." She turned to me. "We should be glad for her, Molly. She'll be going back to her own family."

"But I'm her family." I heard the catch in my voice. "We are her family. He can't give her what we can."

"You don't know that," Gus said softly. "He may remarry, a kind and nice woman. He may have the money to send her to a good school and a university. She may be looking forward to a splendid life. We can't begrudge her that."

I got up. "I should take my suitcase over to my house," I said. "It's in the way of your packing."

"We'll come and help," Sid said. As we walked to the front door she put an arm around my shoulder. "I know it's a big shock, Molly. It was a horrible blow for us too. In fact we'd even discussed adopting her. You know how fond we've grown of her and we could afford the best of education. But we have to believe this is for the best."

"How can it be for the best?" I blurted out, amazed at my own vehemence. "Seamus is an uneducated lout. When he went off to Panama to build that canal he was quite prepared to put Bridie into service when she was just a little mite. How will he ever see that she deserves an education?"

We picked up the heavy suitcase between us, pausing to smile as Liam struggled to carry the carpetbag. *I have Liam*, I told myself. *I still have Liam. I will have more children. The doctor says so.* But a little voice at the back of my head whispered that Daniel had been an only child. Mrs. Sullivan had told me once that she'd had such a difficult time with Daniel that doctors warned her against having any more children. Would Liam be an only child too?

We carried the bags to my front door. I located the key, unlocked it, and stepped into a cold front hallway. I hadn't been thinking that Daniel had been away and Bridie had been living across the street, the house had been unoccupied for some time. So of course there had been no stove or fires to keep the place warm. I fought to master my emotions, but the damp cold of that front hall felt like a mirror of the cold around my heart. "Look, Liam, we're home again," I said. "Mommy must light the stove and warm up the kitchen and then we'll find all your toys."

Liam didn't seem to care that the house was scarcely warmer than the street outside. He was already running ahead of me into the kitchen looking for his blocks. Sid gave me a worried glance. "Why don't you come and stay the night with us?" she said. "It won't warm up in here for ages. And you've no food in."

"If you're sure I won't get in the way of your packing," I said. "It's like an icebox in here. I'll get the kitchen stove started right away and then I should go out and do some grocery shopping. If Daniel hasn't been here for a while, there will be nothing in the larder. I'd better make a list. . . ."

I could hear myself babbling on. Sid put a hand on my shoulder. "Plenty of time for that tomorrow," she said. "You and I will get your stove going and Gus can put on the kettle at home. I know you're still Irish enough to need your cup of tea!"

Her kindness brought a lump into my throat. I kept my lips pressed together and nodded my thanks. In no time at all we had the stove going well and Sid also insisted on lighting fires in the back parlor and my bedroom. "We'll bank them up tonight and you'll be as warm as toast in the morning," she said.

I had just sat down at Sid and Gus's kitchen table with a cup of tea and a slice of gingerbread in front of me when the front door opened and Bridie's voice came down the hall. "Guess what, it's snowing," she called. "Do you think that means we might have a white Christmas after all? Do you think I'm too old to use Mrs. Sullivan's toboggan? Because there is a good hill at the back of her garden and . . ." She came through to the kitchen, her cheeks red with the cold, her light blonde hair windblown. She froze when she saw me.

"Molly," she exclaimed. "What's the matter? What are you doing back here? I thought Captain Sullivan was going to take me up to Mrs. Sullivan's to join you."

"We've had a change of plans," I said, keeping my voice even. "Mrs. Sullivan has gone to have Christmas with an old friend and we're going to have a grand time here. Just our family."

"Oh." I could see the disappointment in her eyes.

"Come and let me give you a hug," I said. "I swear you've grown an inch in a month."

"I have," she said. "I'm the second tallest in my class. I'm taller than most of the boys."

"And Miss Walcott says you're doing so well at school. I'm really proud of you."

Her smile faded and she nodded. "I'll be sorry to leave," she said. She turned away, staring out of the window, where snowflakes were now swirling. "Molly, I've had news from my father. He's alive and well, after all this time. We thought he must be dead, didn't we?"

I was determined to play my part. "Alive and well? Isn't that grand news?" I gave her a big smile. "And your brother? Is he well too?"

"He is. And they're on a ship, on their way to New York. I'm going to see them in the New Year."

"I'm so happy for you, my darling." I was still managing to smile, to sound excited. "You must be so pleased."

"No!" She blurted out. "I'm not pleased at all. I mean I'm glad my father and brother are alive but he's coming to take me away, Molly. He says he's made good money and he's taking us back to Ireland. And I don't want to go."

I was at a loss what to say now. Of course I didn't want her to go either. "He's your father, Bridie," I said. "He must have been missing you terribly."

"No, he hasn't. He didn't write to me for ages. He just went and left me here, and if you and Mrs. Sullivan hadn't taken me in, I'd be a servant by now." Her face was flushed with anger.

"He was a man left with two children to rear," I said. "He did his best by going down to work on that canal, and he knew he couldn't take you with him. But now you say he's made money. He'll buy you a fine house and send you to a good school."

She was shaking her head. "No, he won't. And I don't care about a fine house or a good school. I won't be with you, and with Miss Walcott and Miss Goldfarb. You're my family now. I don't want to leave you."

"I don't want to lose you either, my darling." I enfolded her in my arms as she sobbed on my shoulder. I was crying too now. Sid and Gus, sitting at the table, were also crying. Everyone but Liam, who had picked up his stuffed dog and held it up to Bridie. "Here, Bwidie. Dog," he said.

Sid and Gus tried to make it a jolly supper that night. Sid had been experimenting with some of the recipes from the Indian cookbook I had given her for Christmas the year before. She had made the curry a little too hot and each of us had to resort to the water glass while our eyes streamed.

"I suppose it must be easier to take this in a hot climate," Sid said as she swallowed a big gulp of water. "If you and I are really going to India next year, Gus, we must practice eating hot food so that we don't look like complete novices."

"You're really planning to go to India?" I asked.

"You know how long we've been talking about it," Gus said. "It's been our dream for ages. And with Bridie gone we'll be free to travel."

I felt as if I was on a slippery slope, plunging downward ever faster. No Bridie and now no Sid and no Gus. If they went to India, they'd be gone for months.

The conversation had moved on. Sid was telling Bridie how much she'd enjoy Dublin. And it was only a short trip across the sea to England and she'd be able to visit London and Oxford and Bath and Stonehenge. . . .

Bridie nodded as if Sid was telling her a fairy tale. Of

course she knew as well as I did that Seamus was not the type of man who'd appreciate culture. He was a kind man, I reminded myself. He wouldn't beat her like some fathers. But his idea of a good time would be several pints in his local pub—just like my own father, I thought. And it certainly wasn't generally accepted in Ireland that girls should be educated. The moment they married they started having babies—one after the other. All except me.

Gus got up to clear away our plates. "I've made a milk jelly for desert. I had a hunch we'd find that curry a little too hot." She grinned at Sid as she went out to the icebox.

She came back carrying a plate with the jelly turned out onto it, molded into the shape of a rabbit, which made Bridie smile. "It's a pity Liam's not still awake," she said. "This was always one of his favorite things."

She had just started to serve when there came a loud hammering on the front door.

"What in the name of goodness . . ." Sid demanded and went to open it.

We heard her say, "Captain Sullivan. What a surprise."

"What has been going on at my house?" Daniel's voice came loud and clear down the hallway to us. "I arrive home and find all the fires blazing away and nobody there. Has someone been living in our house, do you know?"

"Welcome home," Sid said evenly. "And if you'd like to come in, I think you'll find the explanation sitting at our kitchen table. Only watch your step. I'm sorry, you find us in the middle of packing."

I held my breath as I heard Daniel's progress down the hall and then he appeared in the kitchen doorway.

"Molly!" he exclaimed, and I watched the color drain from his face. "What are you doing here? Is something wrong? My mother? Has she taken a turn for the worse? She's not back in hospital, is she?"

"Your mother is absolutely fine, Daniel," I said. "In fact she's feeling so well that she's accepted an invitation to join a house party at a mansion on the Hudson. A very grand carriage came for her today. So we're back in the city for Christmas after all."

He still cast a worried look around the kitchen. "And Liam. Where's Liam? Where's my boy?"

"Will you calm down, Daniel?" I went over to him and put a hand on his shoulder. "Liam's quite well, but was rather tired after a day of traveling and then seeing his aunts and Bridie again, so we fed him a boiled egg and put him to bed. I was planning on staying here tonight as I thought our house was too cold to sleep in."

"It certainly isn't cold any longer," Daniel said. "It's like a Turkish steam bath in there now."

"All the same I think you should sleep over here tonight," Gus said. "Your sheets will need airing out."

Daniel went to say something, but I cut in first. "You're absolutely right. We don't want any of us coming down with a chill from sleeping on damp and cold sheets, do we?" I turned to give Daniel an encouraging smile.

"Have you eaten, Captain Sullivan?" Gus asked. "Sid has made a good curry and we've plenty left."

"Thank you. I ate on the train," Daniel said.

"Where were you coming from?" Sid asked. "Or is that confidential?"

"Not at all," Daniel said in that crisp and polite voice he used when addressing my friends. I think he always wanted to convey that he did not approve of their lifestyle choice. "I was only in our capital, discussing some matters of security with the president."

"With the president of the United States?" Bridie's eyes grew large. "You know the president?"

"I've had the honor of talking with him on occasion," Daniel said. "I wouldn't say that we're bosom friends. But as he's a Roosevelt, we do know some people in common. We grew up in the same part of the world after all."

"Your mother always refers to him as 'dear Teddy,'" I said with a grin, "even though she probably only knew him as a friend of a friend."

"Quite possibly." Daniel smiled now.

"Some jelly, Captain Sullivan?" Gus asked. "I was just about to serve and I can tell that Bridie is dying to have some."

"Uh, not for me, thank you," Daniel said. "But please don't let me interrupt your meal. I think I'll go across to our house and air out some sheets in front of the fire so that we can sleep in our own beds tonight."

He jerked a small bow to my friends. "Miss Walcott. Miss Goldfarb. I'll see you in a little while, Molly. I'll come and retrieve Liam when his bed is warm enough." With that he left.

I sat down again, feeling rather embarrassed and more than a little annoyed. I had expressed my wish to stay with Sid and Gus that night and he had overridden it. Hardly the happy reunion I had hoped for.

We finished our dinner, had coffee, and sat talking until Daniel returned to carry Liam across to our house. We hardly exchanged a word as Liam, still half-asleep, was tucked into his own bed. As we went into our bedroom I could contain myself no longer. "You know, it was rather rude of you to overrule me and decide that we were going to sleep here tonight," I said.

"It wasn't meant to be rude," he said. "But this is our house, after all. You should realize I'd want to sleep in my own bed if at all possible, after having endured lumpy hotel mattresses. And to sleep with my own wife after what seems like an eternity. I certainly couldn't do that in someone else's house."

He came over to me and slipped his arms around my waist. "I've missed you every moment I was away," he said. "It's been a strange year, hasn't it? So many worries. So many fears. And at last we're together in our own house. In our own bedroom." He was looking down at me tenderly. "I know it's been really hard on you, but I'm going to do my best to make it up to you. I'll make sure we have the best Christmas together, and we won't think about what has gone wrong this year or worry about what might come in our future."

His attempt to kiss me was thwarted when I burst into tears. He recoiled, looking stunned and mystified. "Now what have I said?" he asked.

"It's not you," I replied between sobs. "What you just said was lovely. Perfect. It's just that everything seems to be going wrong. I thought we'd have Christmas together in the country with your mother and now she's gone away.

And then I thought that Christmas here with Sid and Gus would be just as nice. But they are going away. And then I found out that we're going to be losing Bridie."

"Bridie? What do you mean?"

"She's just heard from her father, Daniel." I was still fighting back sobs. "He's alive and well and what's more he's made money. He's coming to claim her in the New Year and take her back to Ireland with him."

"But that's good news, surely." Daniel still looked perplexed.

"Not for me. I'm going to be losing a beloved child."

"But she's not your child, Molly. You've done a wonderful job of taking her under your wing. God knows what might have happened to her if you and my mother hadn't intervened. But her place is with her family. If you'd had to give up your child so that you could make enough money to guarantee her future, wouldn't you be longing to see her? Wouldn't you want her back again?"

"But he didn't write to her for ages," I said. "The poor mite didn't know whether he was alive or dead."

"We men are not always the best letter writers," Daniel said. "I've felt guilty several times while I've been in Washington that I should be writing to you more often. But frankly I never know what to say, except that I miss you. And you already know that."

"Oh, Daniel," I said, burying my head against his chest, smelling the familiar scent of his jacket. "I'm glad you're back. I've missed you so much."

"Now I'm home," he said. "And one way or another let's hope I won't have to go away again."

"You're not going to take up Mr. Wilkie's job offer? We won't have to move down to Washington?"

"Let's just see how things are with the new commissioner when he takes office in January, shall we?" he said. "And failing that, I hear there is to be an opening for chief of police in White Plains. We'd be able to live near my mother and keep an eye on her."

I couldn't very well say that this was the last thing in the world that I wanted. White Plains, where I knew nobody and where people cared about what family you were from and what social connections you had. But I forced myself to say, "You're right, Daniel. We'll just have to see what happens next."

"I think I can tell you what's going to happen next," Daniel said. "Come here." And then he kissed me.

Four

The next day Daniel went to report in to police headquarters. I was against this. "But what if they assign you to a case now and you're off and working over Christmas?" I demanded. "Surely you don't need to report back until after the holidays? They lent you to Mr. Wilkie for an indeterminate amount of time, didn't they? So they aren't expecting you back."

"All the same, I should let them know that my current assignment has ended and I am reinstating myself as police captain. That way I'm already on the books and in the hierarchy when the new commissioner takes office. And the old commissioner has already cleared out, so I've been told." He glanced toward the door, then back at me. "I think I'd be wise to test the direction of the wind, don't you? Let's see who welcomes me back and who doesn't."

I watched him go, my heart aching for him. He had been the best officer they could possibly have wanted: conscientious, brave, smart, and completely above corruption—which was something one couldn't say for many of New York's finest. However it was this refusal to bend, to overlook, to make deals, that had set him against the powers at Tammany Hall in the first place. And the last commissioner was Tammany's puppet, determined to find a way to get rid of Daniel. Who knew what the future would bring?

The uncertainty sent my stomach into knots. I started to clean the house furiously as if physical work might shut out everything going on inside my head. Liam sat on the rug, playing with his blocks and his toy dog, happy to be home, without a care in the world. I watched him with envy. How simple life was when you were that young. Somebody took care of you and fed you and all the grown-ups adored you. Life without a care. How long ago that seemed. I had been thrust into the role of mother to my own younger brothers at the age of fourteen, when my mother died. It seemed I had been taking care of other people ever since. I sighed and went back to sweeping the parlor carpet, my ferocious strokes churning up a cloud of dust.

The sky was becoming darker and I realized I should go and shop for provisions before it started to snow again. I had just bundled Liam into his winter coat and bonnet when there was a tap on my front door and Sid and Gus stood there. "Oh, you were going out. How lucky that we caught you," Sid said.

"Only to get in supplies. The cupboard is bare, so to speak."

"We came to say good-bye and merry Christmas," Gus said. "And to deliver your presents. It would have been much more fun to watch you open them, but you know they come with our love." And she handed me a sack, such as Santa Claus would have carried.

"Thank you," I said. "I feel terrible. I haven't even got presents for the two of you yet. I was planning to do my Christmas shopping up in White Plains and then to mail you a package."

"Don't worry about it," Sid said. "We'll have a second celebration when we return. And it's Bridie's last day of school, remember. She knows she's to come back to you after school this afternoon." She bent to Liam. "You be a good boy, Liam, and let's see what Santa Claus brings you."

"We have to go. The cab is here." Gus tugged at her sleeve.

I helped them carry their bags to the hansom cab and waved as they set off, managing my brightest smile. Then I put Liam into his buggy and pushed it over the snowy sidewalk to the stores on Greenwich Avenue.

Baking. I should start baking for the holidays, I told myself as I made a mental list. But I couldn't stir up any enthusiasm. Was it really worth the trouble of making mincemeat for just four people? And I hadn't even made a Christmas pudding. I knew it wasn't part of Daniel's tradition but it was certainly part of mine. Christmas pudding was one of the few luxuries we had all year at home. That and the chicken or goose once a year.

I went through the motions of shopping, making sure there would be a good meal for Daniel that night. I'd make Irish stew, his favorite. I reasoned I'd come back for the dried fruits and spices and flour for the Christmas baking once I'd settled in at home. No need to rush. There was almost a week until Christmas. *I'll wait until Bridie is here,* I told myself. *It will be fun for her, baking together. I want to make this a Christmas she'll always remember.* And then I think I cried again a little, turning away so that Liam wouldn't see me.

Bridie also looked a little tearful when she came home from school. "All the girls hugged me and said they were sorry I was going away," she said. "And my teacher gave me this." She held up a copy of the poems of Walt Whitman. Inside, her teacher had written: *I celebrate the me yet to come! We will both celebrate the bright young woman you will be, Bridie.*

"It's very nice," I said. "I don't know the poems of Walt Whitman. When I was growing up we didn't study American poets, just Tennyson and Keats and all those English fellows."

"He's very good," Bridie said. "He says lovely things."

"You'll have to read some of them to me while I'm doing the Christmas baking."

"All right." She smiled. "But I want to help with the baking too."

"Of course. You'll need to know how to bake." And immediately I wished I hadn't said that. Would she find herself as little mother to Seamus and her brother, the same way I was? Would they expect her to keep house for them and give up on her schooling? I made a resolution that whatever happened, I was going to have a word with Seamus to make sure he understood that he had an intelligent daughter and he needed to make sure she was properly educated.

Daniel returned that evening saying that he wasn't quite sure about his welcome at police headquarters. Some of the older officers were clearly glad to see him, but overall the reception wasn't exactly warm. He'd just have to see.

The next day I promised Bridie we'd start the baking and maybe go shopping for presents too. I thought perhaps she'd like to knit a scarf for Sid and Gus.

She nodded. "Something to remember me by," she said.

"I know," I said. "When Captain Sullivan is free let's do what we did last year. We'll take the trolley. Look at the decorated windows at Macy's department store and FAO Schwarz toy store, then play in the snow at Central Park and finish up with a hot chocolate at the Viennese coffeehouse on Fifth Avenue."

"All right. Liam would like that," she agreed, but without enthusiasm.

"Is there anything you'd like to do to make this Christmas special?" I asked.

"Stay here," she replied, turning away from me.

I think we might have both ended up hugging each other in tears again, but we were interrupted by the plop of a letter landing on the doormat.

"Someone has written to us," Bridie said as she ran down the hall. "It can't be Miss Walcott yet, because they only went away yesterday. Maybe it's my father to say he's changed his mind. . . ." She picked up the envelope. "It's from Mrs. Sullivan," she said, holding it up.

"That was quick," I replied. "Perhaps she wants to tell us how lovely it all is."

I saw that the letter was addressed to Captain and Mrs. Sullivan and wondered if I should wait for Daniel to open it, but then I reasoned it would just be a few lines, maybe thanking us for looking after her. Maybe even some money to spend for Christmas. I tore open the envelope and was slightly disappointed when no money or check fell out.

"What does it say?" Bridie asked.

I started to read. "'My dear ones,'" I read. "'Well, I arrived safely and was made extremely welcome by Florence and her niece Winnie, who seems to be a most sweet young woman. I had been expecting a large house party, and was surprised to find that I was the only guest, apart from family members. Aside from Mr. and Mrs. Van Aiken, the homeowners, it is just my friend, an elderly great-aunt of Mr. Van Aiken's, and Winnie's father, Mr. Carmichael. Rather a somber crowd, if you want my opinion. Florence obviously was feeling the same way because she brightened up immediately when I told her about you and Liam and Bridie, and immediately suggested that you come to join us. Obviously it is not her house and I was uncomfortable with this suggestion, but she put it to Winnie and that sweet girl was quite enthusiastic. She thought that more young people were just what was needed and urged me to write to you. So if you could bear to leave your friends in the city and come up to Greenbriars, it would make two old ladies extremely happy.

"'Winnie says you are to come as soon as you like. There is plenty of room. And if you send a telegram to say on which train you will be arriving at Scarborough station, the carriage will meet you. Do come. I miss little Liam already and I'm sure his bright little face will cheer the hearts of all present.'"

"Do we have to go?" Bridie looked at me with a worried little face.

"You don't want to? It would be an adventure going to a grand house for Christmas."

She shook her head. "I won't know how to behave and I'm sure I'll pick up the wrong fork or something."

I rather wished she hadn't brought that up. My first reaction had been the excitement of being part of a big, fancy gathering for the holiday. Now I was a trifle ambivalent myself. I was certainly disappointed about facing Christmas alone, without my friends. But the thought of that carriage made me feel the same way Bridie was feeling. Would I want to be the sole interlopers at a family gathering in a mansion? Would I know which fork to use?

The matter was decided for me as soon as Daniel read the letter. "How very kind of them," he said.

"Do you really want to go? Do you think we should? Wouldn't it be intruding?" I asked. I think I was hoping he'd agree with me and want to stay home.

"Of course we must go," he said. "I suspect that my mother is still feeling frail and would welcome having her dear ones there with her. Perhaps the distances one has to walk in a house like that are really too much for her, but she's too proud to ask for assistance. You know what she's like."

"She has taken Ivy with her for that very purpose," I said.

"Ivy?"

"You know—the girl she's taken in from the orphanage. You met her when you came to visit."

"So I did. Quiet little thing. How is she working out?"

"Well enough, I think. She seems bright and willing to please and your mother is quite taken with her. She'll probably wind up being another Bridie, being groomed for society." Of course the moment I said those words, expecting them to be a jest, I remembered. Bridie would be gone and Ivy could never take her place.

Daniel saw my expression falter. He patted my hand. "It will be good for all of us to have a carefree time. No cooking or baking for you. No worry for me. I'll send a telegram this afternoon. Do you think we can be ready to go tomorrow?"

"We can't go without presents," I said. "I haven't done any shopping yet. I have nothing for any of you, or for your mother."

"She won't really expect . . ." Daniel began in the way of men who find presents superfluous.

"Of course she'll expect," I said. "We have to get something for your mother, and for her friend Florence and presumably for the family."

"We're not millionaires," Daniel said. "Surely they realize that."

"Just little tokens," I said. "But we can't go empty-handed."

He sighed. "Very well. We'd better go shopping tomorrow then, and leave for this place the day after. What was the name of it again?"

"The house, or more accurately the mansion, is called Greenbriars," I said. "In a place called Scarborough. I think it's on the Hudson, isn't it?"

"Scarborough!" He chuckled. "No wonder Mother was excited about receiving an invitation there. Plenty of fine houses in that neck of the woods. Roosevelts, Astors. It will be an experience for all of us. What is the name of the family again?"

"Van Aiken," I said. "One of the old Dutch families, according to your mother."

"Van Aiken," Daniel said thoughtfully. "Now why does that name ring a bell?"

The next morning I bundled up Liam and we headed out into the city. It had snowed again during the night and Patchin Place lay pristine under a thin mantle of white, like a scene from a Christmas card. Having been stuck in the country for so long, I was unused to the hustle and bustle of the city and stared at the decorated shopwindows, the stalls of holly and mistletoe, and the bands of carol singers, as if I was a country bumpkin newly arrived from the back of beyond. We rode the trolley up Broadway, crammed in with excited shoppers and their packages. Even Bridie cheered up, tugging at my sleeve to look at mechanical figures of skaters in Macy's store windows. Liam was loving it all, carried high on Daniel's shoulders. We bought a shawl for Daniel's mother and embroidered handkerchiefs for her friend Florence, and then made our way across to Fifth Avenue and that spectacular toy store, FAO Schwarz. Approaching it and seeing the men dressed up as toy soldiers outside, I felt a jolt of excitement, and for a moment I was a child again. Daniel and Liam watched with enchantment the toy railway that ran around the whole store. Bridie eyed the dolls. Then, in a stroke of genius, I spotted the jigsaw puzzles. Now that would be the perfect present to take to the family we were staying with. It would be something to keep everyone occupied over the holiday. Then I spotted a dear little wooden horse and cart that would be perfect for Liam's present. He'd love to transport his blocks in it.

During the night I had thought long and hard about what I could buy for Bridie. I wanted to give her something to remember us by. In the end I sent Daniel off with the children into Central Park to throw snowballs while I went in search of Bridie's gift. I paused to gaze at the windows of Tiffany & Co., then reluctantly walked past and found a little jewelry store on a less prestigious side street. And inside that store I found the perfect gift. It was a little silver locket. I'd put our pictures inside it with a lock of Liam's hair, so that she wouldn't forget us. Then I doubled back to the toy store for Liam's horse and cart. That left Daniel. Men are always impossible to buy for. But I had been saving housekeeping money while I lived with Mrs. Sullivan and had come up with a brilliant idea. I would buy him a Brownie camera. He could record our son's progress. So I found a camera shop and came out with a Brownie II, the latest model, made in aluminum and costing all of $2.75, as well as a roll of film. Then, feeling satisfied with everything I'd accomplished, I went to find my dear ones having a rare old time in the park. By this time they were all liberally coated with snow and welcomed my suggestion of a hot chocolate before we returned home.

"Were you successful?" Daniel asked me.

I nodded. "Very." For once I was feeling pleased with myself.

"Then I'll take you and the children home and you can pack for us while I run a few errands of my own," Daniel said, giving me a mysterious smile.

I went through agonies debating what items of our clothing might be suitable for a smart Christmas gathering. Alas, there were not many. I had owned a couple of good dresses passed down from Gus, but they had gone up in flames when our house was bombed. I had then been given some lovely clothes by a kind friend, but they had been lost in the San Francisco earthquake and fire. It seemed whenever I had something I cared about it was taken from me again. Perhaps I was destined to remain simple and humble. It was probably my mother's doing, from her perch in heaven. She always did tell me I was getting above myself and would come to a bad end!

So I packed the best of what remained and by that night we had the suitcases ready in the front hall. It was a good thing I hadn't stocked up on too much food. My life seemed to be in constant motion these days. I wondered when we'd ever settle in one place and enjoy some tranquility. This was clearly a great change of heart from my younger days when I craved excitement, travel, and change. But I had been through so much of it recently, so much uncertainty and, yes, so much danger, that I wanted nothing more than a life of family routine. And a chance to feel safe again and to look forward to the future.

Five

The journey to Scarborough was delightful. More snow must have fallen out here in the countryside; a white wintery landscape greeted us as the train left the city behind. Ice had piled up in shining mounds at the edges of the Hudson, but it wasn't completely frozen over. I wondered if it ever did freeze completely during severe winters. I asked Daniel but he didn't seem to think so. Bridie wondered if they had toboggans and a hill at Greenbriars. Liam looked out of the train window, enjoying the speed.

"No," he said. I wondered what he was refusing until I realized he was saying, "Snow."

"Yes, darling. Lots of snow," I agreed.

We passed through one village after another and I was reminded of other trips I had taken up the Hudson, including one when I was carrying Liam. Of course that memory triggered the wrong sort of thoughts. Would I ever feel the joy of a child inside me again? I commanded myself to think positively. We were going to have a lovely Christmas and everything was going to be all right.

We alighted at Scarborough station. Unlike other country stations along the route it was an ornate little gingerbread house, indicating to me that the local inhabitants were not simple country folk and expected their station to live up to their standards. "Holy mother of God," I muttered to myself as the reality of spending Christmas with people who were far above my own social standing began to dawn on me. A porter arrived and whisked away our bags. He asked where we were headed and whether we needed a wagon. Daniel replied that we were going to Greenbriars and he thought a carriage would be waiting for us. And it was. Even finer than I remembered it. I have to confess a wee amount of satisfaction when I saw the porter's face as the coachman climbed down from his high seat to help me up into the carriage. He tucked rugs around us. "It's not a long ride," he said. "You'll soon be at Greenbriars."

We set off at a lively *clip-clop* along the bank of the river, which was almost as wide as a lake at this point. I peered out of the carriage window, which was already steaming up with our breath. There didn't seem to be much of a village. Just a few whitewashed wooden houses, a couple of shops, a post office, and a white church spire rising against a brilliant blue sky. Almost immediately we left houses behind as the road veered away from the riverbank and started to climb a hill. On either side of us were impressive gates and driveways, but any houses were hidden behind trees. In fact it felt as if we were right out in the country, in the middle of nowhere. We passed no other traffic and the road surface seemed almost pristine, as if not much traffic came this way. After barely a mile or so of passing trees and more trees the carriage turned in between tall brick gateposts. The driveway curved around and I caught my first glimpse of the house. You wouldn't have called it elegant. It was more like my impression of an Irish castle. It was large and square, built of plain gray stone, rising three or four stories high. Not exactly a welcoming sight.

Daniel must have been having similar thoughts because he muttered to me, "Not that different in appearance from the prison down at Ossining a couple of miles from here!"

I looked at him and we shared a grin, which made me feel quite reassured. Perhaps he wasn't entirely easy with this little jaunt either. Servants rushed out at the sound of the carriage, took Liam from my arms, and then helped me down. We were ushered into a high foyer with a staircase ascending on one side. Its banister was now swathed in greenery and tied with red bows. Beside the staircase stood an enormous Christmas tree. It had candles in place, but as yet no other form of decoration. Before I had time to take in any more I heard voices from the room to our right and a large and imposing elderly lady came into view, sweeping toward us like a ship in full sail.

"Welcome, welcome!" she said. "So the carriage made it all right up the hill? We were a little worried when more snow fell last night that the road would be too slippery, and they were going to get out the sleigh instead. But Winnie was concerned you'd be too cold in the sleigh so she begged them to give the carriage a try. She's such a thoughtful girl." She paused for breath and looked from one face to the next. "What a treat that you are here. I am Florence Lind, Mrs. Van Aiken's aunt. When the servants have divested you of your outer garments let me show you your rooms, and then you can come down to join us for a sherry before luncheon—unless you think you'd like a rest after your journey, in which case, we can have a tray sent up to you."

"We've only come from the city, not the North Pole," I replied, at which she burst into hearty laughter. "Oh, a woman of wit. Splendid. We shall get on well, I know. So you must be Mrs. Sullivan, and this handsome gent is Captain Sullivan."

"We are indeed," Daniel said, stepping forward to hold out his hand. "How do you do, Miss Lind?"

"And this little fellow is Master Sullivan?"

"Yes, this is our son, Liam. And may I present our young visitor, Bridie," Daniel said, reverting to his most formal.

"Splendid, splendid," she said again.

While we were talking two maids had slipped off our outer garments, except those of Liam, who objected to strange hands trying to take off his coat.

"Don't worry, I'll take care of him when we're in our room," I said before there could be an outburst.

"Would you like a tray sent up for him?" Miss Lind asked. "I'm afraid we've no proper nursery and no nanny in the house these days, but young Elsie here has a score of brothers and sisters and will be happy to take care of him." She indicated a young maid who smiled shyly and blushed at being singled out.

"I think a tray might be a good idea," Daniel replied before I could. "It certainly wouldn't be right to impose him on you at luncheon in the dining room."

I glanced at my husband. He was behaving as if this kind

of situation was quite normal to him. Then I reminded myself that he had once been engaged to a girl of this level of society, although he had not been born to it himself.

"Well, come on then," Miss Lind said, making for the staircase.

I had put down Liam when the maid took off my cape and hat. He let out a wail and lifted his arms. "Up," he complained. "Up."

Daniel picked him up again. "Come on, Son. We're going to see where we'll be sleeping."

Miss Lind set off at a great pace. As I followed it occurred to me that it was a little strange that the mistress of the house was not doing the welcoming herself. I hoped we really were welcome and that the aunt had not imposed her obviously strong will on her niece and nephew. At the top of the stairs, long hallways stretched in both directions. We set off to the right, continuing to the far end before Miss Lind opened a door.

"I thought I'd put you in here," she said. "It's the corner suite. You'll be quite private and undisturbed."

We stepped into an impressively large room with bay windows that looked out over snowy lawns to bare woodland with a glimpse of the river below. It had elegant striped wallpaper, heavy green velvet drapes tied back with gold tassels, and a high molded ceiling. The first thing I noticed was that there was no fireplace, but the room was surprisingly warm. Then I saw the radiators. They even had the luxury of central heating out here in the country. This really was going to be a most pleasant experience! An impressive four-poster bed stood against one wall, and the carved oak wardrobe would have taken up half the room in a tiny house like mine.

"It's very nice, thank you," I said. "But where is our son to sleep?" I knew that people of this level in society would probably stow their children away in a nursery on the top floor, but I wanted Liam near me.

"There's a little dressing room adjacent to this one." Miss Lind opened a door next to the wardrobe and I saw that a small bed had been put into the room. "Does he still need to sleep in a crib?"

"Oh, no. He's quite comfortable in a real bed," I said. "This will be most satisfactory. But what about Bridie?"

"We have a room ready for her, up one floor from here," Miss Lind said. "If you'd like to come with me, my dear?"

Bridie shot me a frightened look. I stepped forward. "If you don't mind, I'd rather she was closer to us. She's not used to a house this size."

Miss Lind frowned. "Mrs. Sullivan's young companion has a room up there. You'd be near someone your own age. Wouldn't that be nice?"

Daniel saved the day. "Would it be possible to have another small bed brought into this room so that Liam can sleep close to us, and then Bridie can take the little annex?"

"You want your child in a room with you?" Miss Lind's eyebrows went up. I could see her about to say that such things were unheard of in her world.

"That would be most kind," I said hurriedly. "He'll also feel more comfortable knowing his parents are nearby."

"I'll go and find one of the footmen to bring down another bed then," she said. "Your bags should be delivered momentarily and one of the maids will unpack for you."

As her footsteps died away down the hall I turned to Daniel. "Thank you for suggesting that. Poor Bridie was looking quite terrified."

"I didn't want to sleep all alone up there. I might never find my way back to you," Bridie said.

"I understand exactly, sweetheart." I put my arm around her shoulder. Daniel put Liam down and he ran around the room, exploring, then tried to climb up onto the impossibly tall bed.

"I think we've already blotted our copybooks, don't you?" I whispered to Daniel. "We've broken the code of the upper classes. They only see their children for ten minutes a day at tea time."

He grinned. "Perhaps Miss Lind will return saying, 'Never darken our door again.' She's definitely a force to be reckoned with, isn't she?"

"Isn't she," I agreed. "I wonder if she bossed your mother around when they were friends as girls?"

"She obviously rules the roost in this household," Daniel said. "Where are the couple who own the house? Surely it would be usual that they should be the ones to greet us."

He broke off suddenly as footsteps approached our door and Miss Lind entered, followed by a sweating footman carrying parts of a brass bed frame. Another footman followed him and in seconds they had the bed assembled, a mattress was brought in, and I was glad to see a rubber sheet. Liam did have the occasional accident still. Finally a maid made up the bed.

While the work was being done I went over to the window and looked out. I could glimpse an occasional rooftop, and smoke from hidden chimneys rose up among the trees, but the house was definitely remote, surrounded by its own parkland. Over to the right I could see one rooftop, taller than the rest, and hints of an old-style half-timbered building beneath it.

"That's certainly an impressive house," I commented, turning back to Miss Lind. "Who does it belong to?"

"Which house, my dear?" She came over to the window.

"That one. The Tudor design."

"Oh, that's not a house, it's the Briarcliff Lodge. A hotel. Awful great monstrosity, isn't it? Only just been built in the hopes of luring city folk out to stay in the country. One gathers it is full for Christmas, although why anybody would want to spend a holiday in a hotel, I can't imagine. Isn't that what family and friends are for?" She turned away from the window. "In my day the only people who went to hotels were salesmen or up to no good." She went over to examine the new bed. "Ah, there we are. All finished and ready. Elsie, go down and tell the cook that the young man would like a tray with something suitable for his luncheon. Rice pudding, maybe?"

Our bags arrived and were speedily unpacked for us, in spite of our protestations. Daniel was taken down to meet his mother, but Bridie elected to stay with me. The size and solemnity of the house had quite unnerved her. Then Liam's lunch tray appeared—a boiled egg followed by some kind of custard. He made short work of both, having a hearty appetite. Then I washed his face and hands and put him to bed. He was reluctant but clearly tired.

"I'll stay with him until he falls asleep," Bridie said.

"You don't have to."

"I want to. He will feel strange sleeping in a big room like this," she said.

"But you must come down in time for our luncheon," I said. "It would be rude not to come and meet our hosts."

"I thought that lady was our host."

"She's the aunt of the lady who owns this house," I said. "She is the one who is Mrs. Sullivan's friend. Now, it's time for your nap, Liam. Lie down like a good boy. Bridie will tell you a story."

He lay down, good as gold, and I left the room to the sound of Bridie's sweet little voice saying, "There were once three bears. . . ."

•

Six

I made my way down the stairs and followed the sound of Daniel's voice into the room on the far side of the foyer. It was more like a long gallery in a museum than a normal room in a home. Its walls were of carved oak wood, hung with paintings, and its tall windows were composed of tiny panes of leaded glass. In its center was a huge marble fireplace in which a fire was roaring away. And around this a group of people were grouped on sofas and armchairs. Daniel was standing beside his mother, who was working on a tapestry, while Ivy perched on a stool at her feet like an obedient pet. Closest to the fire was a frail-looking old lady, a rug over her knees, her sweet and innocent face surrounded by a halo of soft white curls. She shared a sofa with a fierce-looking older man, who was drinking what looked like a neat whiskey. With her back to me was a younger woman, her light brown hair rolled into a fashionable knot. Daniel looked up and spotted me before I had plucked up the courage to make an entrance.

"Ah. Here is my wife now," he said.

The older man had risen to his feet. "Mrs. Sullivan, you

are most welcome," he said in a booming voice that echoed with authority. He was a big fellow with bristling eyebrows and an upright stance, broad shouldered and powerful. *A colonel?* I wondered. *Used to ordering men?*

"Molly, my dear, come and join us and meet our hosts," Mrs. Sullivan said, holding out her hands to me. "This is Daniel's dear wife, Molly, who was so kind to me in my recent illness. She took such good care of me."

I crossed the broad expanse of floor toward them, feeling my cheeks burning with all those eyes on me.

"You are lucky to have such a caring daughter-in-law." The young woman looked up at me with a sweet smile. "Welcome to our house, Mrs. Sullivan. I am Winnie Van Aiken." She rose to her feet and I saw that she was not as petite as she'd seemed at first impression. Her height matched my own, but she was far slenderer than I. Her cheeks were hollow and I could see her collarbones at the neck of her dress. I took the fragile hand she extended to me, rather worrying that I might crush it if I shook it too hard.

"How do you do, Mrs. Van Aiken?" Her hand felt icy cold, even though the room was pleasantly warm. She patted the sofa beside her and still held my hand as I sat.

"And let me introduce my other family members," she went on. "My father, Mr. Carmichael, and my husband's great-aunt, Miss Van Aiken. They both live here at Greenbriars with us. You've met my aunt Florence, who is no doubt at this moment driving terror into the hearts of our servants. And I'm not sure where my husband is. I believe he had some business to attend to in his study. He will be with us shortly, I'm sure."

"Mr. Carmichael. Miss Van Aiken." I gave a polite nod to them. "I'm pleased to make your acquaintance. How lucky for Mrs. Van Aiken to have her family here with her."

"Yes, I'm extremely lucky." There was something in her voice I couldn't quite place. Was it sarcasm?

"Is this your long-lost sister we have never met come home at last?" the aged great-aunt asked, peering at me with interest.

"No, Aunt. This is Mrs. Sullivan. A guest come for Christmas," Winnie Van Aiken replied sharply.

"There is a resemblance to you so I thought that at last we would meet her," the elderly aunt went on, staring at me so intently that I gave her an embarrassed smile and then looked away.

"Winnie does not have a sister," Mr. Carmichael said, glaring at her.

"Oh, but I thought . . ." the elderly aunt said. "I must be getting confused again. I was sure that I heard someone say . . ."

"Let us change the subject," Mr. Carmichael said with firmness. "You are often confused these days, Aunt Clara." He turned to me. "I do apologize, Mrs. Sullivan."

There was an awkward pause.

"It is extremely kind of you to allow us to share in your Christmas festivities," I said, feeling it necessary to say something.

"On the contrary, it is we who are grateful. We live a quiet life. We need livening up."

"If my son is permitted to join in the festivities, I can assure you it will be lively enough," I said, laughing.

"Oh, yes. A lively young child is just what this place needs," Winnie said.

"You have a young child?" Aunt Clara asked, still regarding me with a puzzled frown. "How old is this child? Another little girl, is she?"

"No, a boy. Liam. And he's two."

"You should take good care of him then," Aunt Clara said. "Children can wander off so easily."

Again an awkward silence, then Winnie said brightly, "And you have a young ward with you too, don't you?"

"Yes, her name is Bridie and she is almost thirteen. She elected to stay with Liam so he wouldn't be anxious about falling asleep in a strange house."

"Please do let her know that she is most welcome to join us. And she'll be company for this young lady too, won't she?" She turned her smile to Ivy, who was looking at the ground, clearly mortified at being in such company. "What was your name again, my dear?"

"Her name is Ivy," Mrs. Sullivan said. "She has recently come to me from an orphanage in the city and is proving most satisfactory."

"Ivy. That's a pretty name," Winnie said.

"Not really." Ivy looked up shyly. "All the girls at the orphanage are given flower names. I think they must have run out of flowers when I came to them. Because ivy's not a flower, is it? It's plain and rather nasty and it strangles other plants."

"Then let's hope you don't live up to your name," Winnie said, laughing.

Mrs. Sullivan did not look amused. "Ivy, run up and fetch

my dark green yarn, would you? I seem to have left it on my bedside table."

"Yes, Mrs. Sullivan," Ivy said. She jumped up, turned, and promptly bumped into the wall with a clunk, making the pictures rattle.

"What is the matter with you, child?" Mrs. Sullivan said angrily.

"I'm so sorry," Ivy said, her face bright red. "I don't know what I was thinking. I must have forgotten where I was and thought I was at your house, where the door to the stairs is just behind your chair."

She gave us a frightened glance and fled from the room.

Mrs. Sullivan looked across at us. "I don't know what's gotten into the child. She has been so sweet and docile until now. Let's hope this is not her true nature coming out."

"People act out of character when they feel ill at ease," Winnie said.

"And I am sure it is easy to get two big houses confused when one is used to the confines of an orphanage," I said.

Winnie nodded. "I can imagine that a house like ours could be intimidating. I was quite intimidated when I first moved here, when I married Cedric."

"That may be true," Daniel's mother said. "But now I'm beginning to wish that I hadn't suggested she accompany me. I only brought her as my mobility is somewhat limited and I didn't want to inconvenience your servants."

"We're delighted to have her," Winnie said. "As I just told you, what this house needs is—" She broke off at the sound of footsteps.

At first I thought it would be Ivy returning and marveled at her speed. But instead it was a younger man, light haired with a Germanic look to him, dressed in what appeared to be the height of fashion, carrying himself with such a haughty air that I knew right away he had to be the master of the house.

"What does this house need, Winnie?" he asked. He spoke in a clipped way, as if English might not be his first language.

"Laughter," Winnie said. "A joyful holiday."

"And now we have guests, I see, and we shall certainly do our best to make the holiday joyful." He came across the room, moving with grace, and held out his hand to Daniel. "How do you do, sir? I am Cedric Van Aiken. You must be Captain Sullivan. We have enjoyed getting to know your mother."

"How do you do, Mr. Van Aiken? Thank you for including us in your celebration." Daniel shook his hand warmly. "It is most kind of you to invite strangers. May I present my wife, Molly. Our son and our young ward are both upstairs."

"Mrs. Sullivan, you are most welcome." Cedric Van Aiken came over to me, took my hand, and cradled it in his for a long moment. "Delightful," he said. "You've a handsome wife, Sullivan."

A shiver of alarm went through me. Was this a ladies' man? Would I have to watch that I didn't catch myself alone in a room with him? I had experienced some such in my life but it would be an added layer of awkwardness if he were the master of a household in which we were guests.

He looked across at Winnie as he still held my hand. "I hope you and Mrs. Sullivan become great friends, my dear," he said. "It's time you had more friends of your own." He turned back to me. "You live in the neighborhood, Mrs. Sullivan?"

"No, Cedric. I told you they live in New York City," Winnie said. "It is Captain Sullivan's mother who lives not far from us."

"I don't know how you can stand the city," he said. "Couldn't countenance it myself. I need my land around me and enough room to breathe."

"I'm afraid my profession demands that I live in the city. What kind of business are you in, Van Aiken?" Daniel asked.

"Me? I have no profession. A man of leisure. I was fortunate enough to have inherited this estate from my late father. I have made many improvements during my tenure here. I must give you a tour when you have settled in." He looked around with distaste. "But you haven't been offered anything to drink yet. A glass of sherry, Mrs. Sullivan? Or may I be so bold as to call you Molly, since we will be in close quarters for several days?"

"Oh, no, thank you. I am not used to drinking in the middle of the day," I said, stumbling over the words in my embarrassment. "But please feel free to call me by my Christian name."

"Oh, go on. You've had a long journey. You need to be fortified." Cedric went over to a sideboard where a decanter stood amid glasses and poured me a glass of amber liquid. He came back to me and thrust the glass into my hand. "And for you, Captain Sullivan?"

I noticed he hadn't wanted the same level of familiarity with Daniel.

"A whiskey like my father-in-law or a sherry?"

"A sherry would be most acceptable," Daniel said, casting a glance in my direction and clearly also ill at ease.

"You haven't asked me, Nephew," the great-aunt said in a petulant voice.

"You've already had one, Aunt Clara. I see a glass in your hand."

She looked down at her hand with surprise. "Oh, yes. Silly me. Of course. But I wouldn't say no to another."

"We can't have you dancing on the table at luncheon, can we?" Cedric said, with a chuckle.

"As if I ever danced on a table in my life," Great-Aunt Clara replied indignantly.

Ivy had crept back into the room and handed Daniel's mother her yarn. "Sorry I took so long," she whispered. "I get lost in this house. I was sure your room was to the left, but it was to the right."

"That's all right, child," Mrs. Sullivan said, patting her hand. "A house this size is quite confusing, even for me."

Ivy was going to sit on the stool again when I said, "Ivy, can I send you on another errand? Would you please go and fetch Bridie down? Tell her we are about to go in to eat and she should be introduced first. You turn right at the top of the stairs and go all the way to the end of that hallway. It's the last door on the right."

She looked puzzled. "Isn't that Mrs. Van Aiken's room?"

"No, dear. Ours is on the left," Winnie said. "Clearly you are at sixes and sevens today."

"I'm sorry. It's all too much to take in." She hung her head. "I'll go and find your Bridie for you, Mrs. Sullivan."

She had only just left when Aunt Florence appeared to say that luncheon was served. I put down my sherry glass, still almost full, glad that I didn't have to finish it. Winnie's father helped the frail Great-Aunt Clara to her feet. "Come along," he said. "It doesn't do to keep the dragon waiting, you know."

"Dragon?" she looked confused.

"She who wishes to rule the world," Mr. Carmichael said.

Aunt Florence turned back. "I heard that," she said. "And I have no wish to rule anything other than my own behavior." She went over to Daniel's mother. "Do you need help, Mary?"

"Thank you, Florence. How kind you are," Daniel's mother replied as Miss Lind helped her from her chair and then took her arm.

"We should wait for the girls or they will never find us," she said.

"Of course," Winnie agreed. "We just sent Ivy up to bring Bridie to join us."

"Do you want the young ladies to join us at the table or should we send them to eat in the kitchen, where they'd feel more comfortable?" Aunt Florence asked.

"Oh, that's a good thought," Winnie said. "What do you think, Molly?"

"I think both girls might welcome it today, since they are clearly overwhelmed by the house," I said.

As we reached the doorway leading to the foyer they were coming down the stairs, moving close together as if for protection. Bridie's light hair contrasted with the dark hair and eyes of the other girl and they made a handsome pair.

"Miss Lind has suggested that you might prefer to eat in the kitchen today, just until you feel comfortable in the house," I said. "Then you two can chat together."

"Yes, please," Bridie said. I saw the relief in her face as she looked at Ivy.

"Is Liam asleep?" I asked, feeling suddenly uneasy about leaving him alone in such a big house.

"Yes, he fell asleep right away."

I glanced at Daniel. "Perhaps I should go up to him? Or ask one of the maids to go up."

"Don't be silly, Molly. The door is shut, isn't it, Bridie? What harm can possibly happen to him if he wakes up?"

I told myself I was worrying about nothing. Liam was a good sleeper. He'd be out for a couple of hours. "Of course. He'll be fine," I said. "Off you go to your lunch then, girls."

I watched as they set off down a passage toward the back of the house.

We followed them but instead of going straight ahead and through a baize door to the servants' part of the house, we turned to our left, into a formidable dining room with a table long enough to seat thirty. Only one end of it had been set for us and we sat together, enjoying an excellent luncheon of a thick vegetable soup, meat pie and cauliflower in a cheese sauce, and finally a chocolate mousse and coffee. Afterward it was suggested that we go up to our rooms to rest, then maybe take a sleigh ride if the weather held.

There was no sign of Bridie. I presumed she and Ivy were chattering away somewhere, or even exploring the house together. As Daniel closed the door behind us he gave a long sigh.

"Not what I expected. How about you?"

"No. How strange that it's just elderly relatives and us. I wonder why they invited us."

"I think it was the formidable aunt who invited us," Daniel said. "And the others could hardly refuse. I have to confess I wish we hadn't come. I sense a tension in the air, don't you?"

I nodded. "There's definitely something strange."

"One thing is quite clear to me," Daniel said. "And that is Winnie Van Aiken seems to be afraid of her husband."

Seven

There was no question of a rest for us. I was not used to an afternoon rest in the first place and certainly not in such strange and grand surroundings as these. The matter was decided for us when Liam awoke from his nap and was ready to start exploring. We kept him amused until Daniel said that he'd heard voices going down the stairs. I took Liam to the bathroom, potted him, and washed his face before we took him downstairs to find the party, apart from the great-aunt, assembled around the fire in the gallery. Liam immediately went to his grandmother, of whom he was extremely fond.

"What a delightful little fellow," Winnie observed. "So full of joy."

"Yes, he is a happy little boy on the whole," I said. "Very active, but loving too."

"You are fortunate to have a son, Captain Sullivan." Cedric Van Aiken looked up from the newspaper he had been reading. "Although I don't suppose it is so important to carry on the name when there are many Sullivans in the world. I am the last of the Van Aikens in this country, unfortunately."

"You are both still young enough to have children, surely," Mrs. Sullivan said.

I didn't miss the look that passed between Winnie and Cedric. It wasn't one of sadness or regret. It was one of accusation. As the conversation continued I observed Winnie Van Aiken to see if I could pick up what Daniel had noticed. It was true that she shot her husband a nervous glance each time he addressed her, and her answers sounded short and defensive, even to the most innocent of questions. But Cedric seemed a harmless sort of chap—though rather full of his own importance, to be sure.

"Now how about that tour of the house?" Cedric said.

"Should we not take everyone for a sleigh ride while the weather holds up so fine?" Winnie asked.

I saw a frown cross Cedric's face. Then he said, "Of course. Good idea. Why not? Who feels like coming on a sleigh ride?"

"I, for one, would not wish to leave the comfort of the fire," Mrs. Sullivan said, "but where are the young girls? They will certainly enjoy it."

Bridie and Ivy were located in Ivy's room and needed no urging to come on a sleigh ride with us. We bundled into the sleigh pulled by a big draft horse and set off, sleigh bells jingling, across the estate. I had underestimated the size of the property. The snow crunched beneath the runners and the wind in our face was icy. A red sun was setting on the far shore of the lake, tingeing the snow pink. I expected the others had been on sleigh rides before, but it was my first and I found it quite magical. So did Liam, who gave little chirps of delight, and Bridie, who glanced at me from time to time. The worried look had vanished from her face and I was glad that we had come here, if only for her sake.

When we came to a wide meadow covered in pristine snow Cedric said, "We must come back here tomorrow, if the weather holds, and make the world's biggest snowman." He turned to Liam. "You'd like to make a snowman, wouldn't you, young man?"

"No-man?" I had to grab Liam as he was ready to scramble out of the sleigh at that moment.

I was surprised to see that Cedric looked enthusiastic. Maybe our coming had been a good thing after all. Maybe the reason for the tension and bitterness Daniel and I had noticed was that they couldn't have children. Obviously it was important to Cedric to have a son to inherit the property and carry on his name. I found myself wondering how Daniel and I would be getting along if we hadn't had Liam and knew there could be no child in our lives. Darkness was falling as we made our way back to the house, where servants greeted us with hot chocolate topped with whipped cream. All in all a satisfactory afternoon.

We took off our coats and hats and came into the gallery to find my mother-in-law and the two aunts deep in conversation. They looked up, smiling.

"You've had a good time, I can see," my mother-in-law said. "Rosy cheeks, and Liam has a mustache of cream from the hot chocolate." She patted the seat beside her. "Come over here and tell me about it, Bridie. And you too, Ivy. Was it your first sleigh ride?"

The two girls went over to her. Miss Lind came to me. "Do you have everything you need for the little boy, Mrs. Sullivan? I'm sure we can assign one of the maids to act as nanny so that you are not encumbered with him all the time. You should be enjoying your holiday too."

"He's really no trouble and I look after him all the time at home," I said.

"You have no servant?" She looked shocked.

"We have Bridie living with us and she is a great help when she is not in school." I realized as I said it that when Bridie left us, Daniel would insist I finally hire a servant to help with the chores. Maybe I'd find a girl from the same orphanage as Ivy. She seemed a nice enough little thing.

"Do you enjoy living in the city?" Miss Lind asked. "I must say I miss the noise and excitement in some ways. I don't miss the dirty, slushy sidewalks when it has snowed."

"Especially not when it freezes afterward," I agreed. "Walking is so treacherous."

"But apart from that?" she insisted.

"I have good friends nearby and Daniel is close to his work."

"His mother was saying that he is encountering problems and may well be looking for new employment. I understand he may be applying for the position of chief of police out here in White Plains. Wouldn't that be lovely? His mother would be so happy to have her family out here with her."

I glanced across at Mrs. Sullivan, who was chatting with the two girls. *Was this some kind of conspiracy to get Daniel out to Westchester County?* I wondered. I decided to change the subject. "I understand that you were actively involved in the suffrage movement?"

"I most certainly was, and still am," she said. "I am a passionate suffragist, Mrs. Sullivan. It makes no sense to me that half the population cannot have a say in the running of our country. Your mother-in-law disagrees with me. She liked her husband to make all the decisions. Having no husband I cannot understand that way of thought."

"I have a husband, but I agree with you," I said. "My close friends are also workers for the cause."

"You know you have come to a hotbed for the cause right here," she said. "One of our champions, Carrie Chapman Catt, has rented a house just up the road from here. Her husband had been ailing and died earlier this year so she decided to move out of New York for a while, to get over his death."

"I'm so sorry. I met her once at my friends' house," I said. "I was most impressed."

"Then you might want to accompany me tomorrow evening," she said. "Carrie is hosting a soiree for some friends and I plan to attend. Would you like to come?"

I glanced around, hesitating.

"That is, of course, if you think your husband will permit you to be among such dangerous women," she said with the hint of a laugh in her voice.

That did it. "I should be delighted to accompany you," I said. "I am sure Daniel can amuse himself and entertain his mother while we're away, and Bridie will be happy to watch over Liam."

She looked pleased. "Well, that's settled then. I think you

will find the assembly at Carrie's house most entertaining, and instructive too. She gives splendid parties."

As I had suspected Daniel wasn't at all keen on my going. "Surely it's not polite to walk out on one's hostess so soon after we have arrived," he said.

"You have observed Miss Lind," I said. "When she wants something she seems to get it, and she wants someone to accompany her to this gathering."

"I'm not sure that I want the word to get out that my wife is attending a meeting of suffragists," he said in the same sort of clipped voice that Cedric had used earlier.

"I don't know how you think the word is going to get out," I said. "Besides, it's a yuletide party, not a plotting session. And I've already accepted Miss Lind's kind invitation." Then I walked away from him.

I received a similar reaction from Winnie when I explained to her that I had been asked to accompany her aunt. "Are you sure that's wise, Molly?" she asked, her large blue eyes looking even larger. "I mean, you do know that Carrie Chapman Catt is the leader of the suffrage movement, don't you?"

"Of course. I have met her before at a friend's house. I was most impressed. A woman of substance."

"But what does your husband say? Surely he cannot be in favor."

"While I respect my husband I am not under his thumb," I said. "I am entitled to my own thoughts and opinions, and so should you be."

"You are lucky to be able to move freely in the city," she

said. "Out here I am told what to think by my husband and my father."

"You can't be happy with that arrangement," I burst out before I realized I should probably keep my opinion to myself.

"What choice do I have?" she said. "Cedric gives me a good life. I am well supplied with everything I need. I have a position in society. I have seen all too clearly what can happen if those things are taken away. I have come to the realization that it is the lot of a woman to be a beautiful adornment, rather like a bird in a cage."

I took her hand. "Then you and I will indeed become friends and you shall come to stay with me in the city, even though I live in a tiny house and have but two good dresses to my name. But we shall laugh and go to a theater and you shall meet my friends."

She looked at me, her eyes now wary but hopeful. "I'm not sure that Cedric would let me go," she said. "But it does sound wonderful."

I leaned closer, conspiratorially. "Then my task while I am here will be to convince your husband what a thoroughly good and reliable woman I am." Then impulsively I took her hand. "Come with us tomorrow," I said. "I'm sure you'd enjoy meeting a group of intelligent and witty women."

"Oh, no, I couldn't," she said, shaking her head so violently that a hairpin fell out and bounced across the marble floor. "If Cedric found out . . ." She paused. "Besides, not tomorrow. I couldn't go anywhere tomorrow."

Eight

The next day we awoke to find it snowing hard. White flakes whirled past our bedroom windows, blotting out the view of the lake and the hills. When we went down to breakfast we were informed that Winnie Van Aiken was not feeling well and was going to be resting quietly. She was of a delicate constitution, her husband told us. The excitement of guests was clearly overwhelming for her. As we were leaving the breakfast room I took Cedric Van Aiken aside.

"I'm so sorry," I said. "If we'd known our visit would have put a strain on your poor wife, we would never have come. We had no idea. Do you think we should leave?"

"Of course not," Cedric said. "I am still at your service and delighted to play host, and my wife's aunt could organize a battalion if necessary." He paused and a concerned frown crossed his face. "I'm afraid that my wife is rather frail. Sometimes she sinks into fits of the worst darkness for no apparent reason. She has been known to take to her bed for days. Almost as if she wants to shut herself off from life."

"I'm so sorry," I said. "How worrying it must be for you."

"Yes. I do worry about her all the time. I do everything I can to make her happy, but . . ." He let the rest of the sentence trail off.

"Has she seen a doctor, or maybe an alienist, a doctor of the mind?" I asked.

"She is well physically. As for her mind . . . she claims there is nothing wrong with her and refuses any kind of help. That's why I was in favor of your visit. I thought it might bring her out of her black mood."

Of course those words struck a key with me. I too had been battling my black mood for several months now. Had Daniel had to endure similar worry about me? "I would be happy to talk to her, if you like," I said. "It may just help to have someone to talk to."

"You are most kind," he said. "But let us leave her to herself for today." He moved closer to me although we were alone in the hallway. "Sometimes I wonder whether she does it to exert power. It is her way of turning the focus to herself, of obtaining pity and solicitation. She can be quite devious, you know."

"Oh, I don't think those suffering from depression deliberately choose to be the center of attention," I said hastily. "All they wish is that the black mood would go away. We must work together, Mr. Van Aiken, to make sure she has a really jolly Christmas."

"Yes," he said, giving me a big smile. "We will do our very best for her."

There was no question of an outside excursion that day but Aunt Florence sent the girls off to the kitchen to help the cook make gingerbread men. Liam was also set on a high stool at the kitchen table with some pie dough to cut with cookie cutters. Daniel's mother was content to sit by the fire with her tapestry and to chat with the elderly Great-Aunt Clara. The latter was in a reminiscing mood.

"When Cedric was a child we had such grand parties here—the ballroom filled with light and music. This house was known for its entertaining. And now, look at us. So quiet. So still. But now that Winnie's sister has returned, and we have a child in the house again, maybe we can start being gay once more."

"That's not Winnie's sister. It is Mrs. Sullivan, my daughter-in-law," Daniel's mother said.

Great-Aunt Clara touched the side of her nose. "It's all right. You don't have to pretend with me. I know the truth. I remember everything, you know. They say my memory has gone, but it hasn't." And she gave a wicked little grin. "And of course I recognize the gentleman too. I'm so glad he's come back after all this time. I did begin to worry. . . ."

I realized then that she was a bit touched, a bit senile. But I did wonder about Winnie's sister. Her father had said she had no sister. He had been quite angry when he said it. Had some kind of tragedy happened, long ago? Something that Great-Aunt Clara, with her addled mind, had now forgotten?

Aunt Clara turned to me. "Where is your child now? Not left alone, I hope."

"No, he's with Cook in the kitchen, making gingerbread."

"Cook? Yes, I think she can be trusted with him. Just as long as he doesn't go outside."

"My ward, Bridie, is with him too," I said, smiling at her.

She shook her head. "So many dangers in the world and so many people who cannot be trusted."

She broke off as Cedric came in and asked Daniel and me if we now would like our tour of the house. "I'd like to show you all the improvements I have made," he said. "You have to understand that this started off as a working farmhouse for my ancestors in the 1700s. Willem Van Aiken was given a land grant here and farmed several hundred acres. There was no lavish entertaining, so the rooms were small. My grandfather made some additions and improvements: it was he who added the wing at the back with the ballroom. I'll take you there in a minute, but let us start right here. This gallery was originally two smallish reception rooms with a passage behind them, leading to the foyer. I had the middle wall knocked out a few years ago, incorporated the passage into the rooms, and the fireplace moved to the center. It proved to be quite satisfactory, don't you think?"

"I do," Daniel said. "You have created a fine room."

Cedric looked quite pleased with himself. "Yes, I think I could have been an architect if I had had to choose a profession," he said. "But my father always insisted that a gentleman doesn't work."

"A gentleman has to earn enough money to support his family," I said. "But presumably you still have income from your farmlands?"

"No, those were sold off over the years, when other folk chose to leave the city and move out here. But we are blessed with family money, thank God."

He led us on then, to the other side of the foyer, where there was another reception room, this one more formal, a music room, a fine library, and at the rear of the house a ballroom. When I was a girl I had once seen a ballroom as grand as this, in the landowner's house in Ireland. But I didn't recall one since. Red velvet curtains hung over the windows and the room stretched away into darkness, but when Cedric flipped a switch the electric chandeliers blazed into light and the polished floor gleamed.

"It's quite magnificent," Daniel commented.

"But never used these days. Such a waste," Cedric said.

"Have you updated the bedrooms too?" I asked. "Ours is quite delightful. With a bathroom attached as well."

"You can thank my father for that," Cedric said. "He was the one who installed indoor plumbing. But that suite used to be ours. Until my wife decided she no longer wanted that view from her window and moved us to a room at the rear of the house."

We came back to the gallery to find that coffee had been served. The rest of the day passed quietly. It seemed strange to think it was only a few days before Christmas. If we'd still been at home, I would have been baking furiously, decorating the house, rushing out for last-minute gifts, and here I seemed to be trapped in a beautiful goldfish bowl.

I could tell that Daniel was still out of sorts as I dressed for the evening's soiree with Miss Lind.

"What if the snow worsens and you are stuck in a drift?" he demanded.

"I'm going to a house almost next door, not to the North Pole," I replied.

"What if Liam won't sleep without his mother near him?"

"You know very well that he likes Bridie to sing him to sleep or tell him a story," I replied. "And you need not come up with more reasons to make me feel guilty, because I'm going anyway." And I went on brushing my hair.

I joined Aunt Florence in the front hall at seven. A maid was standing by to help us into our outer garments.

"Make sure you bundle up warm," Aunt Florence said. Outside the sleigh was waiting for us.

"Well, this will be an adventure, won't it?" she said, giving me a satisfied smile. "A nighttime jaunt in a sleigh. Not something one does every day."

"Never before for me," I replied, pulling up the rugs around us as we were helped into our seat. "It hardly snows in my part of Ireland."

"Daniel's mother told me you are newly arrived in this country," Miss Lind said as the sleigh set off with bells jingling and two lights swinging above our heads. "You still have your charming accent."

"I've been here five years now, although it seems an age. It's hard even to imagine life before New York and before Daniel."

"His mother speaks highly of you," she said. "What a caring daughter-in-law you have been to her."

"I always felt she was disappointed in me," I confessed. "She wanted Daniel to make a better match with someone higher in society."

"That road doesn't always lead to happiness, as we have seen," she said. I thought of Winnie Van Aiken, keeping to her bed, and of Cedric's clipped comments.

Then I remembered something else. "Tell me," I said.

"The old aunt seemed to think that Winnie had a sister, but Mr. Carmichael denied it. Was there some kind of tragedy?"

"A tragedy to me," she said. "I was very fond of both the girls. I raised them after their mother died until their father disliked my influence on them and sent me packing. After that I devoted myself to my work for women's rights, and a most satisfying life it has been too."

"So what did happen to her sister?"

She gave a long sigh. "Her name was Lizzie. A lovely girl, full of sparkle. Her father was determined to make a good match for her and tried to marry her off to a man twice her age. I should point out that Mr. Carmichael was determined to rise to the highest levels of society, through his daughters and the right matches for them."

"Was he an army man? He seems to have a military bearing."

She laughed. "Oh, no, my dear. He was in commerce. He owned ships that carried freight up and down the Hudson. Mostly iron from Troy. He made a good deal of money, sold his business, and became a gentleman, but he started with nothing."

"So did Lizzie marry the older man as her father wanted?"

"Oh, no. She refused. Her father was furious. Then presumably to defy him she met up with a most unsuitable man. I wasn't there so I don't know exactly what happened but from what I've been told, she ran off with him. Anyway Mr. Carmichael disowned her. Said she was no longer his daughter. She has never been spoken of since."

"How sad," I said. "And does Winnie not know what happened to her sister? Were they not close?"

"Winnie was four years younger and was away at a ladies' seminary when all this drama happened. I'm sure she still misses her sister, but you have seen what their father is like. A real authoritarian. And I was far off in Boston and could do nothing." She paused and sighed. "Still I suppose we all make our own bed and have to lie in it."

"She may be very happy at this moment with her most unsuitable man," I said. "Not being of the right class does not imply that he was not a good person."

"That's true." She didn't sound convinced.

She said no more and we continued the journey in silence while the sleigh bells jingled on the horses' harness. While we had been in conversation, we had turned out of the driveway and onto the road. The horses strained to take us up a steep little hill but soon we saw lights ahead and turned into another gateway. This house was less grand but looked instantly more friendly, with lights shining out from all the windows over the snow. A line of sleighs and carriages was pulling up outside the front portico. Servants stood ready to help us out and aid us up the steps and into a warm front hall. There was music coming from a back room, but we had our outer garments removed and were ushered into a room at the front of the house. A large Christmas tree stood in the window, with presents piled at its base. A fire was blazing in the hearth and the room felt quite toasty. I looked around at the guests, who were already standing around in groups chatting away, and noticed they were all women.

Daniel would not approve, I thought with a smile.

From one of these groups the hostess spotted us, gave

a cry of joy, and came to greet us. "Florence, my dear. It's been an age. You can't imagine how happy I felt when I learned you were living close by. Welcome, welcome." Her gaze turned to me.

"And I have brought my friend Mrs. Sullivan," Miss Lind said.

Carrie Chapman Catt eyed me critically and for a second I thought she was about to say that there was no room for interlopers. But instead she said, "But we have met before, surely. Your face is quite familiar to me."

"That's right, Mrs. Catt," I said. "We met at my friends Sid and Gus's house in New York. In Greenwich Village."

"Ah, yes. Those dear girls. Of course. They'll be so pleased."

"I was sorry to hear about your husband, Mrs. Catt," I said because convention required it, although in truth she did not look as if she was in mourning, apart from the black silk dress.

"Thank you, my dear. It was hard to watch him suffer and I am glad he is finally at peace," she said. She paused, as if collecting herself, then went on. "Make yourself at home. We do not stand on ceremony here. Drinks on the table and the buffet will be in the dining room."

She turned back to the company and said in a booming voice. "More newcomers. My dear friend and tireless worker for the cause Miss Florence Lind, and Mrs. Sullivan."

Heads turned toward us and I felt myself blushing with all those eyes upon me. Suddenly a shriek rang out. "Molly! What in heaven's name are you doing here?"

And rushing toward me were Sid and Gus.

Nine

I stood staring at them in disbelief as they came toward me.

"What a lovely surprise," Gus said, her eyes shining as she enveloped me in a hug. "But what are you doing here? We thought you were spending Christmas in the city."

"We were," I said, my own smile reflecting the delight in their faces. "But then we received an invitation to join Daniel's mother at a house just down the hill called Greenbriars. So we packed hurriedly and came."

"Ah, we know Greenbriars, don't we?" Sid said. "Rather an austere, Gothic sort of castle, wouldn't you say? We can see it from our window, can't we, Gus?"

"It does look rather grim as one approaches it, but is a fine house inside," I said. "No expense spared. But where are you staying? I thought you were joining a group of your Vassar classmates."

"We are." Sid laughed. "We are staying at the Briarcliff Lodge—the rather fancy hotel that backs onto the Greenbriars estate. Our friends are all professional women and none of us wanted to have to be involved in domestic duties over the holiday, so we've treated ourselves to a week of pure indulgence at the lodge. Perhaps you can see us if your room faces in the right direction. It's the half-timbered monstrosity through the trees."

"I have seen it," I said, laughing with her. "To think we are so close to each other."

"We must set up a semaphore signaling system," Gus chimed in. "And communicate across the snow."

"And what brought you here tonight?" Sid asked.

"Miss Florence Lind is the aunt of the owner of Greenbriars," I said.

"Miss Lind?" Sid looked over to where Miss Lind was now deep in conversation with our hostess. "Why of course. You know she has been an absolute pillar of the suffrage movement," Sid said. "A tireless fighter for women's causes."

"I told her I had met Mrs. Catt and she insisted I come to the party with her." I moved a little closer. "And between you and me, the atmosphere at Greenbriars is rather strained so I welcomed the chance to escape for a while."

"Oh, dear," Gus said. "A strained atmosphere . . . and how many more days do you have there?"

"Obviously we can't leave until after the holiday," I said. "But I certainly don't want to stay through to the New Year. Our hostess seems to be of a delicate nature and has taken to her bed all day, which makes things rather awkward."

"Awkward indeed," Sid said. "Come on over and meet our friends."

I was led across the room to a group of women sitting in one corner. They were a motley group: some dressed in fashionable silks and velvets, others more unconventionally like Sid in trousers or gentlemen's smoking jackets, but all with bright, intelligent faces, now smiling at me. I was introduced by first names: Fran and Felicia, Edith, Annie and Josephine. I tried to match names with faces.

"Oh, so you are the famous neighbor," one of them (I think it was Edith) said when I was introduced. "We've been told about you and your detecting prowess."

"Oh, no," I protested, feeling myself blushing. "I used to have a small detective agency before I married, that's all."

"And presumably had to give it up the moment you said, 'I do,'" one of them commented. "How typical."

"Well, in my case it was a necessity," I said. "My husband is a senior detective with the New York police. It would not have been acceptable to have a wife in the same line of business. They would think I was interfering in his cases."

"Which I'm sure you were," one of the other women said, producing general laughter.

"On occasion," I agreed.

"So are you staying near here?" I was asked.

"She's staying at Greenbriars," Sid said. "You know, that estate we can see from our windows?"

Two of the women had moved over to make room for me on the sofa. I sat and was handed a cup of hot wine punch. The warmth of the punch, the warmth of the fire, and the warmth of the reception sent a glow through me. I felt the tensions in my body ease away.

"Greenbriars?" The tall, rather severe-looking one called Josephine said, frowning as she stared out past us across the room as if she was thinking. "Isn't that the Van Aiken place?"

"That's right," I said.

"And she's finding it rather gloomy and tense from what one gathers," Sid said.

"Just today because the hostess has been unwell," I said hastily. I glanced around uneasily to see if Miss Lind was within hearing distance. I didn't want her to think that I had been running down her family's hospitality.

"Well, no wonder it's gloomy and tense," Josephine went on.

"Why do you say that?" Gus asked.

"Well, that was where it happened, wasn't it?" Josephine said. "Greenbriars. Don't you remember? Everyone was talking about it. And it was at Christmas too."

"Oh, yes," the chubby one—Annie, I believe—agreed. "Of course. The Van Aiken child. I'd forgotten all about it."

"A child?" I asked. "The Van Aikens had a child?"

Josephine nodded and I noticed that the group of women had drawn closer together, as one does when sharing a secret. "A little girl." Josephine had lowered her voice. "She wandered out into the snow right before Christmas and was never seen again."

"How awful!" Gus exclaimed. "Yes, I remember reading about it now. She was never found, was she?"

"Never." Josephine shook her head.

"She wandered out into the snow from her own house?" I asked. "How old was she?"

"Two or three, wasn't she? A small child, anyway," one of the group chimed in.

"How could a small child be allowed to wander out into

the snow without supervision?" I asked. "Surely she had a nursemaid in a household like that."

"I know no details," Josephine said. "Perhaps there was a ransom note we knew nothing about."

"Do they think she was abducted then?" I asked. "It wasn't just a case of getting lost in the woods and freezing to death?"

"Her body was never found," one of them said.

"How long ago was this?" I asked.

"It must have been about ten years," Josephine said. "Yes, that's right. It would have been '96 because I was in my senior year at Vassar. I was home in Philadelphia for the holidays and my mother read it out from the newspaper. I remember being furious because the rest of my family treated it like any other item of news and brushed it aside for more important things like holiday parties. But it made a big impact on me, because it was in my neck of the woods. I could picture that estate."

"Ten years ago. Such a lot has happened in that time, hasn't it?" Annie said wistfully. "Look at all of us and how we have moved on with our lives. Teachers, writers, suffragists . . ."

"Did they never have more children?" The woman sitting beside me on the sofa turned to me.

I shook my head. "No more children."

"How sad."

There was a silence while we thought about this. The other women might have experienced the collective sadness of our sex for the loss of a child. To me it was overwhelming. It pierced me to the heart. I had lost a child, but it was a baby I never held in my arms, never saw smile at me, who never snuggled up to me, or ran to me on sturdy little legs. Winnie's child had done all these things. No wonder she seemed so sad and remote. No wonder she had taken to her bed on the anniversary of her child's disappearance. I couldn't imagine how she could bear the sadness.

Then, of course, I found myself wondering whether the child might still be alive. Had there been a ransom note? Had the police followed up on it? Who might have kidnapped her? I'm afraid one never stops being a detective.

The others had moved on, already laughing again at a comment one of them had made. I glanced across at Florence Lind. Maybe she knew more. I would have to work out how to ask questions carefully without opening old wounds. And something else struck me: Cedric Van Aiken had not appeared to be upset by the anniversary of the disappearance of his only child. Or perhaps he was only putting on a good show in front of the guests.

Ten

The party was a merry one. We ate, drank, and sang Christmas carols around the piano. It was late when Miss Lind came to me and said that she was ready to go home. Her poor old bones needed their bed, she explained. I was ready to go too. I had gone through the motions of the evening. I had attempted to join in the gaiety. I had sung lustily with the others—"We Wish You a Merry Christmas"; "tidings of comfort and joy"—but the image of that child in the snow swam before my eyes and wouldn't leave.

Sid and Gus hugged me. "You must come over and join us anytime you like," Sid said. "I don't think we'd better pay a call on you, given the circumstances. But if the gloom gets too depressing, then you know where we are. Send a message to us with one of the servants and we'll walk out to meet you."

"I'd like that," I said. "But I better not abandon Daniel. He wasn't exactly thrilled about my coming here tonight."

"Naturally. We're a bunch of rabble-rousing women. Quite dangerous," Sid said with a laugh.

"I'm afraid that's exactly what he did think. He's a good man in many ways, but still a typical man. He thinks a woman's place is in the home, not in the voting booth!"

"Well, you know where to find us," Gus said. "And we'd dearly love to see our darlings. Are they all right?"

"Oh, yes. Liam is having a grand old time exploring the house and Bridie has found a new friend in Ivy, Mrs. Sullivan's new maid or companion. She's fresh from the orphanage. She seems a bright little girl, but the poor thing is quite overwhelmed by the size of Greenbriars. I suppose it's understandable after a life in an orphanage."

"No doubt Daniel's mother will soon stop thinking of her as a servant and start educating her for society the way she did with Bridie," Sid commented dryly.

"No doubt." I laughed.

"Give Liam and Bridie our love then," they said. "Oh, and let us know what you find out about the child that disappeared. Knowing you, you won't rest until you get to the bottom of it."

Which showed how well they knew me!

We thanked our hostess, left with a basket of food and wine as a present from a neighbor to Greenbriars, and rode home in the sleigh. Miss Lind sighed with contentment as we left the music, still spilling from the house, behind. "That is what a Christmas should be like," she said. "It was splendid, wasn't it?"

"It was," I agreed. "I met so many interesting women."

"And it was good to—to see old friends," she added.

I took in the hesitancy and turned to look at her. "You

were about to say, 'It was good to get away,' weren't you?" I asked.

"As a matter of fact that's what I was thinking," she confessed. "It's my first Christmas at Greenbriars and I hoped I could instill some holiday spirit. Maybe it was a foolish whim of a sentimental old woman."

I had to laugh at this. "There is nothing sentimental about you," I said. "You were described to me as formidable and that fits you to a T."

"My problem is that I want to be the proverbial fairy godmother and make everything right for everybody."

I decided this was as good a moment as any to delve into the tragedy. I took a deep breath. "I heard tonight about the child who vanished," I said. "I hadn't known before. I was shocked. And I felt embarrassed that we had come to intrude upon their mourning."

"Of course, you weren't in the country when it happened," she said. "You couldn't have known. And I'm afraid it was I who insisted upon inviting you to join us. I supposed, maybe wrongly, that the presence of a young family would help to make the holiday season merry again. Clearly Winnie has not gotten over it yet—may never get over it."

We turned from the driveway onto the narrow road. The only lights were those that hung from our sleigh and we moved with just the swish of the runners and the muffled thud of the horses' hooves through a night of complete stillness.

"Poor Winnie. I can't imagine what anguish she has gone through all these years," I said. "And poor Cedric too."

"He seems to have weathered it better than his wife," she said dryly. "But then it wasn't a son."

"What an awful thing to say," I exclaimed. "Do you really think he didn't mind the loss of a daughter?"

"Obviously not as much. And presumably he thought they could have more children, which hasn't turned out to be the case."

Once I had opened this discussion I could not stop it. "I heard only the barest of facts about the child's disappearance," I said. "She vanished in the snow, they said. Is there more to it?"

"I was far away in Boston at the time," she said. "Winnie's father had made it clear he did not welcome my suffragist influence on his daughters. I was certainly not invited for Christmas."

"Did you ever see the little girl?" I asked.

"I did. I came to her christening when she was a baby and I paid a flying visit when I was passing through New York. I think the last time I saw her was that summer. She was an enchanting little thing. Big dark eyes and very advanced for her age. Chatted away with me and she was only two years old. I remember she told me the stories of all the tiles they had around the fireplace. That was before Cedric did all his rebuilding and tore down those rooms." She paused. "Yes. The last time I saw her. When I heard about the tragedy, I wrote, offering to come and be of assistance and solace, but I was turned down. And after that Winnie wrote to me from time to time, but she was never the best of letter writers and I was not in one place for long. And on the occasions I've seen her since then she has made a concerted effort to seem bright and gay to me, and has never brought up the subject once."

"I can understand that," I agreed. "It must be incredibly painful to stir up that memory. But it was true that the child simply vanished? How can that be?"

"This is what I heard," Miss Lind said, glancing up at the driver to make sure he couldn't overhear us. "There was a party for the servants that evening. They were all in the ballroom, helping to decorate it for a bigger party for the Van Aikens' friends the next evening. The child's nursemaid had put her to bed and then came down to join in the fun. It wasn't until the next morning that she discovered the girl was not in her bed. She thought at first that the girl had gone to her mother's bed, as she was allowed to do sometimes when she had a bad dream. So the nursemaid was horrified when Winnie appeared with no sign of her daughter.

"The house was searched and then they looked outside. Tiny footprints led across the grounds until they reached the brook that flows across the estate. You no doubt saw it yesterday when you went for your sleigh ride. In harsh winters it freezes over and that was the case that year. But it appeared the child had hesitated to cross the frozen stream. Her footsteps ended there, going neither to either side nor back to the house. As they said, she had simply vanished."

"Just a minute." I tried to make sense of what I was hearing. "You said her footprints—was she barefoot in the snow? How could she have walked so far? How could she not have frozen to death in that cold?"

"She was not barefoot. It appeared that she was wearing shoes, and her winter cape was missing."

"She got up from her bed and dressed herself in her outer garments?" I asked incredulously. "How could she do that? How old was she?"

"She had just turned three. A precocious little thing, but as to dressing herself—well, I've often wondered the same thing. But if someone came to take her away, wouldn't his or her footprints be beside the child's? And almost certainly he would have carried her."

"Was the nursemaid suspected?" I asked.

"She was. But she was in such a state of grief and torment that nobody could believe she might have had a part in a kidnapping."

"Was it true that no ransom note was ever received?"

"If one was sent, then I was not privy to it," she said.

My brain was working fast now. "Is it possible that she did step onto the frozen stream and her footprints did not show up on the ice? Or"—I took this thought one stage further—"she walked along the stream, the ice gave way, and she was swept downstream and drowned."

"But then her body would have been found, wouldn't it? They searched the grounds and the surrounding area most thoroughly. Volunteers from all over the area came to walk the woods, looking for her. Their first thought was that she had just wandered off and lost her way. They didn't notify the police for two days, hoping to find her."

"And the family had no suspicion of anyone who might have wanted to kidnap their daughter?"

We had reached the imposing gateway to Greenbriars and turned onto the drive.

"There was only one strange thing," Miss Lind said. "One

of the gardeners went missing around the same time. His body was found in a snowdrift close to the Hudson when the snow finally melted several weeks later. But he was a man known to like his drink and it was presumed that he had a little too much celebrating the holiday, lost his way home, and froze to death. It snowed heavily the night after the child went missing and the body would have been soon covered up. Anyway the verdict was given as death by misadventure."

"But it might be possible that he had a part in kidnapping the child and handing her over to someone—who then wanted him conveniently out of the way."

"It might," she agreed. "But we come back to the same thing, don't we? Why would someone take her and not send a ransom note?"

"I can think of several reasons," I said. "One would be for revenge, to get even. Or another that a deranged person wanted the child for his own reasons."

We were huddled close together in the sleigh for warmth. I felt her shudder beside me. "Don't," she said. "That thought has haunted my worst nightmares for years."

"And presumably Winnie's too," I said.

As we came to a halt at the front door I considered this idea. But there was a stumbling block to all of this: How could any stranger, with ill intent, have made the child walk, of her own volition, out of the house that night?

Eleven

The household was silent as we let ourselves in. As I closed the heavy front door behind us the thought struck me that no child of three could ever have let herself out of the house this way. Someone had opened the door for her and then she had walked across the snow quite alone and vanished. It made no sense at all.

No lights shone in the sitting rooms and we crept up the stairs like a pair of naughty schoolgirls. As I reached my bedroom I heard the grandfather clock in the foyer chiming midnight.

"Holy Mother of God!" I muttered to myself. I had no idea we had been out so late. It just shows that time really does fly when you are enjoying yourself without a care in the world. And then it struck me. I had enjoyed myself. For a little while I had been young Molly Murphy, without the worries of a husband and family to burden me. Maybe I was gradually emerging from my cocoon of depression. Life would go on and get better. I had a healthy son, and unlike Winnie Van Aiken, I would have more children one day.

The dim light from an electric bulb far down the hallway shone into my room as I opened the door cautiously. I half expected to see Daniel sitting up waiting for me and glaring. But he was already in bed and snoring gently. The light fell onto my son's face, looking so angelic with his tousled dark curls. He was clutching his favorite stuffed dog. I stood staring at him for a long moment, my heart overflowing with love for him. When I went to close the door I saw that I'd be in complete darkness. The heavy drapes had been drawn and the room felt almost too warm after the frigid sleigh ride. I left the door open a sliver so that I could see enough to undress without bumping into something and waking my family. I took the pins from my hair and shook it out over my shoulders, remembering how good it had felt when I was young and not required to put up my hair or wear a hat whenever I went out. I slipped into my nightgown and then eased myself into the bed beside Daniel. He grunted in his sleep as I snuggled up to him, and he wrapped an arm around me. I lay there, feeling the warmth of his closeness but still jittery from what I had been told. A child had disappeared from this house years ago and now I remembered that Aunt Clara had warned I should not leave Liam alone. "Just as long as he doesn't go outside," she had said. "Children can wander off so easily."

I knew she was an old lady whose mind was clearly failing, but did she know something about a danger that was still present?

"What time did you come home?" Daniel greeted me the next morning as he pulled back the drapes, letting in slanted sunlight. "I didn't come up to bed until after eleven and you still weren't back. I began to worry about you."

"So much that you were sound asleep when I crept in a little later," I teased. "And there was nothing to worry about. The house was practically next door."

I sat up and glanced over at Liam's bed. He was still sleeping peacefully.

"What on earth could a bunch of women find to talk about until after eleven?" Daniel asked, going over to the basin at the washstand to shave.

"Plenty," I said. "We were scheming and plotting all evening how to disrupt the workings of government in New York. We thought we might kidnap the mayor."

He turned back to me, a horrified look on his face. "You can't be serious!"

I burst out laughing. "Of course not. I'm joking. Actually we did more than talk. We ate a sumptuous buffet, we drank mulled wine, and we sang Christmas carols around the piano. It was most agreeable. And you'll never guess who was there."

When he shook his head I exclaimed, "Sid and Gus! What a lovely surprise, wasn't it? They are staying at the Briarcliff Lodge, which is that building we can see from the side window."

"Really?" He stared at me for a moment and I could read his thoughts, wondering if we had planned this between us.

"They were as astonished to see me as I was them," I replied. "I knew they were meeting a group of Vassar classmates, but they didn't say where."

"I don't think it would be wise to let them call upon you

here," Daniel said hastily. "Given the fragile state of our hostess."

"Of course not," I said.

"I wonder if she will make an appearance today? It will really be most embarrassing to be stuck here with the hostess up in her room. Cedric told me last night that sometimes she retires to her bed for days. Sinks into awful depressions. But she refuses to seek any medical help. He's clearly quite concerned about her."

"I take it Cedric did not expand on why she sinks into depression?"

"He did not."

"Daniel, I learned the reason last night. When I mentioned Greenbriars the other women at the party remembered what had happened here. The Van Aikens' little girl wandered out into the snow and disappeared, ten years ago at Christmas. She was never found. No wonder her poor mother is so distraught and melancholy."

Daniel frowned, thinking. "So that's why Greenbriars sounded familiar. Yes, of course. The Van Aiken child. I remember now. I was a fairly new officer at the time and we were given pamphlets with her likeness and asked to keep an eye out for her in the city. An almost impossible task given the holiday crowds swarming in the streets. But then on Christmas Eve there was a daring robbery at one of the department stores, the thieves shooting the manager dead as they made off with the Christmas takings, and we had more pressing things to think about. So the child was never found?"

I shook my head. "I tried to pump Miss Lind as to whether

there were any suspects, whether anyone might have wanted to get even with Cedric Van Aiken, but she lived far away at the time and knew no more than the papers told her. And Winnie has never wanted to talk about it. I wonder if . . ." I paused.

"Molly," Daniel said sternly. "I know you too well. You are already thinking that maybe you could look into this. You could find out what happened to the child after ten years. Stop it right now. You will only open up old wounds and bring them more grief."

"But they are out here in the country," I said. "Supposing an adequate investigation was never done? Supposing a vital clue was missed?"

Daniel was still frowning. "Molly, it has been ten years," he said. "The likelihood of her still being alive is very slim. And if she is still alive, what kind of unspeakable abuse may she have suffered? It would be better for her parents to never know."

"You're wrong." I drew myself up and stared him in the eye. "If she could be rescued now, and there is a chance for her redemption, wouldn't that be a good thing? And it is always better to know the truth, however bad it is."

"And what do you think you could do after ten years?" he asked. "The trail has gone rather cold, I'm afraid."

"Someone must have seen something," I said. "Unless she was murdered here in the vicinity and her body buried, she must have passed some kind of human habitation. And we know that the grounds and area were extensively searched. And we know that the ground was frozen. A killer could not have buried her body, only hidden it in the snow. So it would have come to light when the snow melted."

Daniel put a calming hand on my shoulder. I suppose I was becoming quite animated. "Molly, we are guests here at Greenbriars. We can't go out scouring the countryside for clues."

"You could pay a courtesy call on the local chief of police," I said. "Ask a few questions."

"For one thing we don't have a vehicle," Daniel pointed out. "I can hardly ask Van Aiken if I can borrow his carriage or sleigh to go poking around into the disappearance of his child."

"Perhaps he might want you to," I said. "Want us to. He might be suffering as much as his wife but putting on a brave face."

"Leave it, Molly," he said. We turned as Liam made a little moaning noise, then sat up and looked around him in surprise.

"It's all right." I swung myself down from the great bed and went over to him. "Mommy and Daddy are here."

He held out his arms. "Up," he said.

When we went down to breakfast a little later Winnie Van Aiken was sitting at the table, calmly buttering a slice of toast.

"Oh, there you are." She beamed at us. "Aunt Florence told me you had a splendid evening at Mrs. Catt's house. I'm so glad. And I must apologize. I get these bad headaches and the only remedy is to lie in a darkened room until they pass."

"I'm so sorry," I said. "And please don't apologize. We are happy to see you are feeling better."

"Yes." She nodded emphatically. "I'm feeling better today. I'm determined to enjoy Christmas this year." She gestured toward the sideboard. "Do help yourselves. Cook makes the most marvelous pancakes and there is ham and bacon."

"Your husband is already out and about?" Daniel asked as he returned to the table with a plate piled high.

"I don't know. I haven't seen him this morning," Winnie said. "Probably not. He likes to sleep late. Lucky man. I can rarely sleep more than a few hours a night unless I take one of the sleeping powders my doctor prescribes. And then I feel in such a fog when I awake that I try to avoid them."

I handed a plate to Bridie, who was too shy to help herself, or in too great a fear of spilling something. She grinned gratefully and went to sit down, well away from Winnie. I sat with Liam on my lap and fed him from my plate. His mouth opened like a little sparrow.

"And my mother is not up yet?" Daniel looked around. "That is unusual for her. She's normally up with the sun."

"She took breakfast in her room this morning," Winnie said. "I saw her little servant girl carrying up a tray. She's a pretty little thing, isn't she?"

I hadn't thought of Ivy as pretty. Maybe it was because she was at that gawky stage between child and woman, like Bridie. But I did have to concede she had interesting dark eyes.

"And you have a companion to play with, Bridie," Winnie addressed her, making her turn bright red. "Or are you now too old for play?"

"Yes, ma'am. I'm almost thirteen," Bridie said. "These days I like to read and knit."

"What do you like to read?"

Bridie's face was scarlet now. "Poetry. Novels. I love the books of Charles Dickens and Louisa May Alcott and Harriet Beecher Stowe . . . all kinds of books."

"Bridie has been staying with my neighbors who have a fine library," I said, smiling at her. "And her teacher at school has also been most inspiring."

"We have a good library here," Winnie said. "Do feel free to visit it and take out any book you choose. I want you to feel at ease here. Take Ivy with you. I don't suppose she has had much access to books at the orphanage."

"Thank you, ma'am," Bridie replied. "I'll tell Ivy."

Winnie turned back to us. "I thought I might take the carriage and go into Briarcliff Manor today," she said. "There is a big farm—Briarcliff Farms, it's called—that has dairy cattle and poultry and wonderful greenhouses. We have ordered a goose and some chickens from them and I want to pick out the goose myself. Cedric is always so particular. Also I like to visit the greenhouses and see what flowers they may be growing at this time of year. Flowers for the table would be a good idea, don't you think?"

"A lovely idea," I agreed. "Would you like company? Daniel and I would be happy to come with you."

"Would you really? That would be splendid." She looked pleased.

"We don't often get the chance to ride in a carriage," I admitted. "Especially not such a fine one as yours." I caught Daniel's eye. He gave me a warning look, trying to work out where my scheming thoughts were going. "I'm sure you don't mind looking after Liam, do you, Bridie?" I said.

"Of course not. We'll find Ivy and go exploring."

"You must ask Mrs. Van Aiken's permission before you do any exploring," I said.

She flushed. "Oh, only going up and down the staircases and things. Not prying."

Winnie smiled at her. "You are welcome to look around. A big house like this must be fascinating to you and even more to Ivy."

"Oh, yes, ma'am. Ivy is completely overcome with the size of it. She says it's like being a princess in a castle."

"Sometimes it feels like that," Winnie agreed.

"Well, you two go and find Ivy then," I said. "When do you want to leave, Winnie?"

"As soon as we're finished with breakfast," Winnie said. "I'll send for the carriage." She got up and went over to the window. "I think the snow is starting to melt. Easier to get into town, but it would be a shame if we don't have a white Christmas, wouldn't it?"

I looked out of the window where she was standing. Indeed the sun was shining and I could see small patches of green on the lawn. There was a big expanse of grass before the trees around the edge of the estate, and yet a small child had walked across it, alone and in the dark. *What child would do that willingly?* I wondered. And it occurred to me that she would only do it if she were running toward someone she knew and wanted to see.

Twelve

After a most satisfying breakfast Daniel and I put on our coats and hats while Bridie took Liam off to find Ivy and explore upstairs. He went with her without a backward glance, holding her hand and looking up at her. I pictured the Van Aikens' daughter holding someone's hand as she crossed that lawn, secure in the knowledge that she was with a grown-up she trusted. Only there were no footprints beside her tiny ones. Would Liam walk alone in complete darkness across a snowy lawn? I thought not. It made no sense. I wondered if I'd have a chance to ask any questions today.

I went over to Daniel, who was tucking in a scarf around his throat. "It wouldn't hurt to pay your respects to the local police and find out what you can about the Van Aiken girl," I said.

He shook his head. "Molly, I think we have to let this lie. I know it has upset you and I know how you always want to make everything right, but it was ten years ago. If they found any vital clues, do you think they wouldn't have acted on them then?"

"They might not have realized they had vital clues in their possession," I said.

"Anyway, we are going into Briarcliff Manor, not Scarborough," Daniel pointed out. "I doubt there is even a police station in such a small community."

We found Winnie waiting for us in the front hall. She was dressed in a red cape and hood trimmed with white fur, looking most jolly and festive. She gave us a pleased and excited smile. "All set then? I asked Aunt Florence if she wanted to join us, but she said she'd stay home with Captain Sullivan's mother, since you two were keeping me company."

We were assisted into the carriage and off we went. The sun shone down and the snow was indeed melting on the road so that the horses' hooves splashed up mud. Luckily we were safely inside the carriage, but it occurred to me that it would need a good cleaning when we came home. Winnie seemed quite cheerful today.

"You'll be amazed by Briarcliff Farms," she said. "This Mr. Walter Law has bought up thousands of acres of land and has a huge dairy herd, chickens, and pigs, as well as vegetables and flowers. He has built houses for his workers and now quite a little township has sprung up. They are even building a community hall and a library."

"It's amazing what one person can do if he has vision," Daniel said.

"And money," I added.

Winnie smiled. "Yes, the money does help. I've been fortunate. My father made a fortune. I've never had to think of money all my life."

"That is indeed fortunate," I said. I opened my mouth to say more, that money doesn't buy happiness, but shut it again before I could blurt out the words. Was Winnie happy? I didn't think so. Cedric did not appear to be a doting husband and there were no more children. How could someone be happy cut off from the world on a remote estate with no purpose in life? But perhaps I had misjudged them. I have been known to jump to conclusions.

"Do you also have a house in the city?" I asked. "Or do you spend the whole year out here?"

She shook her head. "Cedric is so attached to his family home that he will live nowhere else," she said. "We have plenty of acquaintances in the neighborhood and I have to confess I find the city rather frightening and overwhelming." She paused. "Now that Aunt Florence has come to live with us, I shall have someone to accompany me, so perhaps it will be different. If she decides to stay, that is. . . ."

"You think she might choose to go away again?" I asked.

"I hope not," she said, "but my father has always been against her. He sent Aunt Florence away when we were growing up, claiming her influence was bad for us. Now he can't banish her as it is my home, not his, but he can still be unpleasant to her."

"Your aunt seems a strong person to me," I said. "I would think that criticism and harsh words would slide off her like water off a duck's back."

This made her laugh. "I hope so," she said. "I do love having her here again. I don't remember my own mother. I was only three when she died. So Aunt Florence was the only mother I ever had. I was so happy when she wrote to me and asked to come and live with us for a while. She hadn't been well, I gather, and between ourselves, I think that she might be running low on funds. She has a small private income, but things are so expensive these days."

"Perhaps she just wanted the company of her family as she got older," I said.

"That may be true. I'm the only family she has left, now that . . ." She broke off, leaving the rest of the sentence unsaid. But she had meant now that she had no sister.

Melting snow dripped from the overhanging trees onto the roof of the carriage as the narrow road went up the hill. Then we came to a small village. It was little more than a couple of shops and a few newly built homes.

"So this is Briarcliff Manor," I said, peeking out of the window. "I don't suppose they have a police station here, do they? Daniel always feels it's his duty to pay his respects to the local police chief."

Winnie chuckled. "Police chief? You won't find one of those closer than White Plains. And I don't think they even have a constable in Briarcliff. There's a small police station in Scarborough and a bigger one in Tarrytown. But why the need to pay respects to the police?"

"Did you not know that Daniel is a detective captain with the New York police?" I asked. "Did his mother not tell you?"

"She did not! I had no idea. When I heard you addressed as Captain Sullivan I naturally thought former army or navy captain. " She gave a nervous little laugh. "Do forgive me."

"Nothing to forgive," Daniel said. "And as it is up in the air whether I shall resume my duties with the police department or take another position, I don't think it's important at the moment."

"Oh, dear. You are considering changing your place of employment? Are you not happy?"

"The police department has gone through a difficult time of upheaval," I said for him. "The last commissioner did not make things easy, especially for officers like Daniel who were not under the thumb of Tammany Hall."

"Goodness," Winnie said. "One hears about such things, but has never experienced them personally. Poor Captain Sullivan. So what will you do next, do you think?"

"We'll have to see if the wind changes with the new commissioner," Daniel said. "Otherwise I have other options, including applying for that position of chief of police in White Plains that my mother is so keen on for me. I thought it might be a good idea to get a feel for local law enforcement from the officers around here."

I shot him a quick glance. He was going to help me after all. Amazing!

As we were finishing this conversation the carriage turned between wrought-iron gates with the words *Briarcliff Farms* fashioned into them. On either side fields stretched away, divided by neat picket fences and each stocked with cream-colored Jersey cows. There was a barn or shelter in each field, all of them looking spanking new. In front of us was the main farm building and around it henhouses, and behind it long greenhouses stretched away. A laborer came running out at the sound of the carriage, wiping his hands on his trousers before assisting us down from the carriage. He then invited us to follow him into the farm building.

"Ah, Mrs. Van Aiken. Such an honor." A wiry little man wearing a leather apron over his suit came toward her. "Come to select your poultry, so I understand."

"That's right, Mr. Dexter. My husband wants to make sure we choose a nice plump goose this year. Last year's was something of a disappointment. And I'd like to see what you have in the hothouses in the way of blooms for the dining table."

"Have we blooms at the moment? Madam, let me escort you to our greenhouse. Your eyes will be dazzled."

We followed him across a muddy forecourt and he opened a greenhouse door for us. The heat that greeted us was palpable. We stepped inside and he closed the door rapidly. Along the whole length of the building oil heaters were spaced at intervals, giving off a pleasant warmth, which, mingled with the rich dampness of soil and growing things, made one think one was in a much more southerly clime. The beds on either side were filled with color. White narcissi, blue hyacinths, multicolored freesias.

"All bulbs in this area," he said. "All forced, of course, ready for Christmas. They go to market in the city early tomorrow morning so you can take your pick today."

Winnie was attracted to the freesias, as I was. They gave off a beautiful sweet scent.

"Oh, I can just see these along the dinner table, can't you?" she said, as our worker gathered up some for us.

"And you can't leave without poinsettias," Mr. Dexter said. "We've a whole greenhouse full of them. This way, please."

We followed him out of one greenhouse to the next, this time full of splashes of various reds and pinks. Winnie chose six big red plants to add to her horde and then, at our host's suggestion, some white chrysanthemums for contrast.

"Oh, this will be so lovely," she said, clapping her hands like a small child. "Should we have them around the sitting room fireplace, do you think? Or in the windows? Or the front hall?"

"Let's see where they look best when we get them home," I said.

"Do you want me to load them behind the carriage or deliver them to you, Mrs. Van Aiken?" Mr. Dexter asked.

"Oh, I think we'd like to take them now, if you can secure them in boxes."

"No problem at all, Mrs. Van Aiken. Delighted to oblige."

The way he bowed made me think that Winnie was a good customer. "And now for those birds."

We picked our way cautiously across another muddy yard to an enclosure where hundreds of chickens, ducks, and geese were pecking at the dirt. They rushed toward us, hoping to be fed. One of the geese was of an aggressive nature, pecking at lesser birds and then hissing at us.

"He looks about the right size," I said to Winnie.

"Oh, I wouldn't be sorry to see that one go," Mr. Dexter said. "Goes straight for our shins the moment we step inside the pen. Some of my boys won't even go in there."

"Then we'll save the world from aggressive geese," Winnie said. "And two nice chickens as well." She turned back to Daniel and me. "Cedric insists on his goose for Christmas because that was his family's tradition, but I have to say that I prefer my ham and chicken. So we'll have all three this year." As we walked back to the front of the property

Winnie added to her order a prime rib of beef and a pail of cream to be delivered as well on the next day, which would be Christmas Eve, of course. It was funny how living out here had made me forget that Christmas was almost upon us.

Winnie looked quite triumphant as we returned to Greenbriars. "I think we made good purchases, don't you?" she said.

"I do. I'm overwhelmed. Do you think we'll eat all this meat?"

"Of course. The beef should keep for a few days, maybe until New Year's. You are staying for New Year's, aren't you?"

"I'm not sure," I said. "Bridie's father is coming to take her home, so we must be back in New York in good time to get her ready."

"Take her home?"

"To Ireland," I said. "We're all very sad about it. Bridie has been like my daughter for so long now."

She reached across and touched my hand. "I do feel for you, my dear Molly. I know what it's like to lose a beloved daughter. It is an ache in the heart that never goes away."

I knew I was treading on very delicate ground, but it was a chance I couldn't ignore. "I am so sorry," I said. "I only just found out about your tragic loss. My heart goes out to you."

A frown crossed her face. "I thought the whole world knew of our suffering," she said. "That is one of the reasons we have stayed so much out of society since it happened. It is hard to bear constant pity."

"I'm sure it is. But not as hard as constantly wondering what happened to your child." There was a silence and I dared to ask, "What do you think happened to her?"

"I think she was taken away by somebody and I only hope that she's being treated kindly."

"You think she's still alive?"

She turned to look out of the window. "I have to, don't I? Otherwise I'd lose all hope."

"Winnie," I said softly, "I may be saying the wrong thing here. I'm rather noted for putting my foot in it."

Daniel put a warning hand over mine and said, "Molly, don't go on," in a low voice.

I ignored him, as I have done on other such occasions, not all leading to successful outcomes. "I was going to say that my husband is a noted detective. I have detective skills of my own. If there is anything you think we might do, any way we could be of help, we are offering our services."

"To find Charlotte, you mean?" For a second I saw a flash of hope cross her face, then the blank look returned. "But it was ten years ago. The trail is long cold."

"What was done at the time?"

"Everything possible," she said. "All the local people were kind enough to volunteer to search every inch of woodland in the area. But other than her little footprints there was no trace of anything, not even a piece of clothing she might have been wearing."

"And nobody reported seeing the child when her picture was published in the newspapers?"

"Nobody." Her expression was bleak. "That has to mean she has been taken far, far away if she is still alive. If she is still alive," she repeated.

"Do you believe in your heart of hearts that she is?" I asked gently.

"Sometimes I really do. Then I dream of her grave, deep in the woods."

My rational self was telling me to stop now, but I went on. "You don't know of anybody who might have taken her?"

"Know of anybody? What kind of person?"

"Someone who was connected to your family? Who might have taken the child out of spite or revenge?"

"And never returned her? What kind of cruel monster would that be?"

"Winnie, I understand that your sister fled from the family, or was banished and never spoken of again. . . ."

"And you think that Lizzie might have come for my child? To spite the family?" she demanded. Her voice was shrill now. "Lizzie and I were close. We loved each other. She would never have tried to hurt me. Never."

"I'm sorry," I said. "I should never have spoken my thoughts out loud. A bad habit of mine, as my husband will tell you."

"I can vouch for that," Daniel said. "She means well, but she leaps before she looks too often. And she has this burning desire for justice, to make everything right."

Winnie smiled now. "Just like my aunt Florence," she said. "You two have a lot in common."

I let the subject drop then. I saw nowhere to go that would not cause more grief. Winnie had not leapt at the offer of help and she was clearly at a loss as to what had happened to her child. It was highly possible that her dream had been the true answer—that a monster snatched the little girl and that her remains now lay in a wooded glade.

Thirteen

As the carriage pulled up outside the house, we were met by Cedric, striding out to meet us with a look of extreme displeasure on his face.

"There you are at last," he called, his voice echoing in the still air. "And where have you been?"

"I went to Briarcliff Farms to make the final arrangements for the poultry, and to choose some flowers for the table," Winnie said as the coachman helped her down from the carriage.

Cedric came up to her, standing over her. "You went without Aunt Florence? You went alone?"

"Of course not," she said. "Mr. and Mrs. Sullivan were kind enough to accompany me."

"I see." He paused, looking up at us now being helped from the carriage. "Did it not occur to you to ask if I might need the carriage first?"

"You were asleep when we left, Cedric."

"Not asleep. I was in my study writing letters," he said.

"I had no idea you needed the carriage. You did not say so."

"I had a package arriving for me on the train this morning. From my tailor in New York." He sounded quite put out.

"If you had mentioned it, I would have been happy to have gone into Scarborough and picked it up for you," she said.

"I'm sure I did mention it to you. Really, Winnie, you are becoming quite forgetful these days."

She stared at him, stony-faced. "If you wish the carriage now, it's all yours." Then she turned to the coachman. "Put the flowers in the front hall, Johnson."

"Very good, ma'am," he said.

Then she flounced ahead of us into the house. Cedric turned to us, slightly embarrassed that we had witnessed this scene. "I must apologize," he said. "I don't know what has gotten into my wife. It is not in her nature to go running off without telling anyone. And she is becoming so forgetful too." He came closer to us. "Frankly I am worried about her. These bouts of depression are becoming more frequent. . . ."

"Maybe she needs to get out into society more," I said. "Have you thought about taking an apartment in the city for a while? I and my friends would be happy to keep her amused."

"You are most kind, but I cannot abide the noise and dirt of the city," he said. "I have tried to keep abreast of the social calendar out here in Westchester County, but Winnie shows little interest in making friends or even attending social gatherings."

"Have you considered an alienist for your wife?" Daniel asked. "I understand that they have made great strides in treating the mind these days."

"Of course I have suggested it, many times, but she flatly

refused." Cedric gave a long sigh. "I would gladly have brought in the best man from Europe if it could make her well and happy again."

"I don't think there is anything wrong with her mind," I said. "She is clearly still in mourning for her lost child. The worst thing in the world is not knowing."

"Ah, so you have been told about the child," he said. "I wondered if you knew. Yes, that is the cause of her depression, but one would think, after ten years, that she would be able to put it behind her. I have done so. It requires strength of character, which maybe she doesn't possess."

I thought of Winnie's dominant father, of her sister who cut off all ties with the family. Maybe Winnie did not have her sister's strength. She was sent off to school quite young when Aunt Florence was banished. So essentially she grew up with no one to love or support her. And from what I had observed of Cedric, he was hardly the doting husband.

I glanced at the carriage and had an idea. "If it would be any help, we are already dressed for travel. We would be happy to go into Scarborough and retrieve your package for you. As I said to your wife, we have no carriage of our own and a carriage ride is a novelty for us."

"Would you really? That is most kind of you," he said. "And I do have some letters that need to be mailed, if I could possibly ask you to take on that task as well? Then when you return I have promised the children that we will build a snowman, if the snow cooperates and stays long enough."

As he went into the house Daniel turned to me. "What are you up to now?" he asked.

"I thought it couldn't do any harm to ask some questions

in Scarborough. And they do have a resident constable you could visit."

He turned to face me. "Molly, you heard what she said. Nobody knows anything. It was ten years ago and there were no clues."

"You're wrong, Daniel," I said. "Somebody must know something. If someone did abduct the child and then murdered her, then that person knows where her body is buried. And if someone took her away in a vehicle or on the train, then somebody, somewhere, saw them."

"So what do you plan to do now? Ride the rails up and down the Hudson until you find someone?" He gave me a disparaging smile.

"I'm going to do what I can, within reason," I said. "You see that poor woman. She has given up on life. If I can do anything to make her feel better, I will."

"Did it not occur to you that she might have a real disease of the mind that is above your skill to cure?"

I couldn't answer that, but the thought nagged at the back of my mind as Cedric handed us his letters. I noticed that one of them was to a Dr. Heggenburger. *Was this possibly an alienist?* I wondered. And then a worrying thought came to me. Cedric seemed genuinely concerned about his wife's sickness, but he wouldn't be the first man who got rid of an inconvenient wife by having her committed to an asylum. In the state of New York all it took was a signature from a doctor and a husband to have a wife locked away for life. And perhaps Cedric Van Aiken would like to be rid of a wife who could give him no more children and for whom he had lost all affection. Again I realized I was jumping to conclusions. Cedric's upbringing might just have produced a man who fought to keep his emotions under control and not express his feelings in public.

"Drive Captain and Mrs. Sullivan into town now, Johnson," Cedric said.

"Very good, sir." The coachman remained stony-faced as he assisted us back into the carriage. As we set off again Daniel shook his head. "This is becoming more unpleasant by the minute, is it not?" he said.

I had been staring out of the window, observing the stream that crossed the front lawns. The stream, which had been frozen at the time and at which the small footprints stopped. The weather wasn't so cold this year and the stream was still unfrozen, bouncing and splashing over rocks as it continued downhill to join the Hudson. But it wasn't deep. I tried to picture the child stepping tentatively onto the ice, the ice giving way. . . . She could have fallen in and even drowned, but her body would not have been swept far away. It would have been found quickly. I turned back to my husband.

"I don't like it, Daniel," I said. "First, one could see that there was little affection expressed between husband and wife, and you observed that she was afraid of him. That was just borne out when he suspected she had been out alone, but now I'm worried that he is trying to prove her mentally unstable."

"Why would he try to do that?"

"So that he could have her committed to a mental asylum and be free of her," I said. "Her father made a fortune, so I presume he is now enjoying her money."

"That's an awful accusation to make, Molly. And I think you do him an injustice. The poor fellow is clearly genuinely concerned for her," Daniel said. "If he is seeking a doctor for her, it is surely with the best of intentions and hoping for her cure. After all, she has demonstrated signs of mental instability."

"Staying in her room on the anniversary of the day her child vanished?" I demanded. "I might very well do the same thing. Would you have me put away because I've been mourning the loss of a baby I never saw or held?"

"Of course not," he said.

"We must do what we can to help her, Daniel. And if only we could find something that would put her mind at ease, some clue that could lead to her missing daughter. . . ." I reached across and touched his hand. "Promise me that you will at least speak with the local constable."

He sighed. "Very well. I will speak with him, but I can't see what good it could do."

We came to the bottom of the hill and into the few houses that constituted the village. A train had just arrived from New York and we watched people rushing forward to greet friends and loved ones arriving for the holiday celebration. The few shops were doing a lively trade and a young boy passed us, dragging a fir tree on a sled. From the church came the sound of an organ, practicing Christmas carols. I was reminded that the day was drawing near. I wondered if it could possibly be a merry one.

As we left the carriage I sent Daniel off to find the police constable while I went into the station. I asked the stationmaster about Cedric's package and he sent the porter to find it for me. While I was waiting I mentioned that we were staying at Greenbriars for the holidays and commented that I thought the Van Aikens were brave to host a party when Christmas was such a tragic time for them.

"You're right there, ma'am," he said. "This whole community was thrown into shock when it happened. Everybody was suspicious of everyone else. People started muttering that Old Dan had been acting strangely or that this person was later coming home than he should have been. And of course we all joined in the search, scouring every inch of those woods, but she was never found."

"Were you working at the station that evening?" I asked. "Do you recall anything unusual? Anybody who asked directions to Greenbriars? Anybody you hadn't seen before?"

He shook his head. "Can't recall anybody asking directions to Greenbriars, but then there are always traps outside waiting to transport people. And as for people I didn't know, well, you see what it's like today. It's always a bit chaotic around Christmas, you know, plenty of visitors coming to join family. And I went off work at six. So I would have been home by the time the child disappeared."

"And nobody reported seeing the little girl at the station that evening?"

"Well, young Jeff, who was porter here at the time, did say he'd seen a man and a child getting onto the upriver train together round about nine o'clock, but he always was a bit fanciful. He once saw mermaids out in the Hudson."

"A man and a child, going away from the city?"

"That's right."

"Was the child a girl?"

"He couldn't tell. The kid was wrapped in a big blanket and seemed to be sleeping so he couldn't tell how old it was or whether it was a boy or girl."

"I see. So it could possibly have been the Van Aikens' daughter and she could have been knocked out with chloroform or a sleeping draft."

His eyes widened at this suggestion. "I suppose so. From what he said it sounded more like a baby than a girl of three. Carried like a baby, that's what Jeff said. And I believe the police did follow up on it at stations up the line, but nothing ever came of it."

"He didn't happen to give a description of the man?" I asked hopefully.

"Didn't really see much. It's dark on the platform. Big chap," he said. "Not high society. Workman's boots."

At this moment the current porter, a pimply lad with a perpetual inane grin on his face, returned with the package. "For Mr. Van Aiken, you said, right?"

"That's correct." I took the package from him and thanked him, handing over a small tip and making him flush with embarrassment.

I left the station and wandered into the street, amusing myself by looking in the shops until Daniel reappeared. I was eyeing a smart fountain pen in the stationer's window when the shop door opened with the jangle of a bell and Sid and Gus came out.

"Molly, you are constantly taking us by surprise these days," Gus said. "We are doing some last-minute Christmas shopping. Our first directive was no presents. But then one of our friends announced that it would be fun to have a bran tub with gifts so we are looking for small knickknacks."

"This little shop was surprisingly well stocked," Sid said. She held several neatly wrapped packages in her arms. "We bought some of those little glass-fronted puzzles—you know, the kind where you have to roll balls through a maze. We thought they'd be fun."

"Oh, yes, they would be," I said. "Maybe Bridie and Mrs. Sullivan's girl, Ivy, would like one of those. I'll go in and see."

"And they have snow globes," Sid went on. "Gus can never resist a snow globe, can you, my sweet?"

Gus grinned. "I like anything magical. As a girl I had a snow globe with a little girl dressed like Little Red Riding Hood in the middle of a forest. I used to picture myself as that little girl and wonder if the wolf was hiding. And they have an almost identical snow globe in this store."

This, of course, reminded me of the Van Aiken child. "Daniel and I are trying to see if there is anything we can do to further the case of the missing Van Aikens' daughter," I said.

This made them laugh. "You and Daniel?" Sid said. "My guess is that you are at best forcing Daniel to be a co-conspirator."

"Probably true," I agreed, "but I did make some headway just now in the station. The porter at the time saw a man carrying a child bundled up in a blanket get on the train going upriver. The man was described as being not of the upper ranks of society. Wearing workman's boots."

"So you think he might have been kidnapping the child?"

"It's possible."

"In which case, why was no ransom note sent?"

"Perhaps something went wrong," I suggested. "Perhaps he killed her by mistake. She cried out. He put his hand over her mouth to silence her and . . ." I paused. "I know of one case where this really did happen."

"Poor child," Gus said. "But then he must have disposed of the body."

"Weighted it down and threw it into the Hudson?" I suggested.

"All too probable," Sid agreed. "What a sad case. No wonder the poor mother still grieves."

A brilliant thought had just occurred to me. "Perhaps I could enlist you as my assistants," I suggested. "There was one thing said that might be relevant to this case."

"You know we always love to help," Gus said, giving Sid an excited glance.

"Well, one of the gardeners who worked at Greenbriars went missing around the same time that the child vanished," I said.

"So he was the one in workman's boots who took her on the train?"

I shook my head. "No. His body was found much later, in a snowdrift by the river nearby. He was known to like his tipple and it was thought that he was drunk, lost his way in a blizzard, and froze to death. His body was soon covered in snow and not found until the snowmelt in spring."

"And no child's body was found, I take it?" Sid asked.

"No."

"He could have been part of the scheme," Sid continued. "His job was to remove her from the estate, deliver her to the station. He was then paid handsomely and spent his money on drink, after which he found that the wages of sin are death!"

"How terribly biblical of you," Gus exclaimed, laughing. "But we can certainly look into this man. Do you happen to know his name?"

"Just that he was a gardener at Greenbriars. I imagine his story is well known around here."

"Then we shall do our sleuthing and report our findings," Gus said. "And perhaps enlist our friends to ask questions around the neighborhood."

"Oh, please, no," I said, holding up a hand. "I think the Van Aikens would not take it kindly to hear that strangers had been poking their noses into their history. Discreet inquiries from the two of you is one thing, but from strange women all over Scarborough is something else."

"Point taken," Sid said. "Oh, look. Here comes your beloved. We'd better make ourselves scarce. He will probably not be pleased that we are close by and extending our bad influence over you."

She grinned.

"Daniel doesn't feel that way," I said.

"Oh, but he does," Sid said. "Has he ever called one of us by our first names? Has he ever looked pleased to see us?"

"He does appreciate what you do for me," I said. "He's just not very good at expressing it." We looked up at the crunch of Daniel's approaching footsteps on the snow. "Well, good morning, Captain Sullivan," Sid called, maybe a little too heartily. "A lovely day, isn't it?"

The look on Daniel's face almost made me laugh out loud.

Fourteen

"Did you know that your neighbors were going to be in this neighborhood?" Daniel had waited until we were back in the carriage before putting this question to me. He had exchanged pleasantries with Sid and Gus in a most civilized manner. He had accompanied me into the little shop and waited while I purchased snow globes for Bridie and Ivy.

"Isn't Ivy meant to be a maid?" he did ask as I was paying for the globes. "Does one normally shower the servants with gifts?"

"One snow globe is hardly showering her with gifts," I said, feeling definitely testy now. "And besides, she is at your mother's side as a companion here. She'll watch Bridie open her gifts. It's not fair to give her nothing. And besides that"—I added—"the poor little girl won't have had many presents in the orphanage. Just hand-me-down clothes and a Bible, I expect. And besides this—"

Daniel held up his hand. "Please, no more besides . . . I can't take another one."

"You were the one who started this," I said. "I was

going to say that I like the child and I want to give her a present."

Then I stalked ahead of him, back to the carriage. We waited in silence until it took off, bouncing us over packed ridges of snow.

"So did you?" Daniel asked.

"What?"

"Know our neighbors were going to be in the neighborhood? It just occurred to me now that maybe that was why you were so keen to accept my mother's invitation. Or were you the one to suggest that my mother secure an invitation for us?"

I felt the blood rising in my cheeks. "In answer to your first question," I said frostily, "I knew nothing of my friends' whereabouts until I bumped into them at the party last night. We were both extremely surprised and delighted. In answer to your second question, it was you, I remember, who was so keen to accept your mother's invitation when I would have preferred to stay home. If I remember correctly, your words were something along the lines of 'Of course we must go. My mother is still feeling frail and would welcome us there.' Am I correct?"

There was a chilly silence in the carriage to match the weather outside.

"Well?" I said again.

"Yes, I have to admit you are correct. I did say those things."

"Then an apology would be nice," I said. "Although why I would have to be chastised for wanting to meet my dearest friends I don't know."

Another long and frosty pause. Then he cleared his throat. "No, you are right and I am wrong. I know how dear these women are to you and I do appreciate how much they have helped you through difficult times. But I sincerely hope we will not be conveniently running into them every few minutes of our stay here. I did mention to you earlier that it would be a bad idea for them to come and visit at Greenbriars."

"Of course they understand that," I said. "And I'm sure they would have no wish to come visiting. They are here because they want to share Christmas with dear old friends. They'll be enjoying themselves far too much to think of us stuck in that gloomy palace."

We continued on in silence until I asked, "So did you pay your respects to the local policeman?"

"I did. Nice sort of fellow. Not too sharp, I would say."

"Was he here at the time of the girl's disappearance?"

"He was. I told him I'd been a young officer in New York and we'd been asked to keep an eye out for her, but we'd never heard any more and all these years I'd wondered what had happened."

"Well put," I said. "What did he say?"

"Not very much. He said he wished he could give me a happy ending but he couldn't. They'd never found a trace of the girl. Posters had been put on stations up and down the line but no one reported seeing her. No child's body had been recovered and God knew they'd been over the woods around Greenbriars enough times."

"Did he mention the gardener who vanished around the same time?"

"He did. Harris was the name, but he said it wouldn't have been the first time the guy passed out drunk, and he couldn't see how a man fallen into a snowdrift near the riverbank could have anything to do with a missing child."

"So we're none the wiser," I said.

"Molly, they've had people working on this for ten years. If no clues have emerged by now, they are not going to. Something tragic happened to the child and we'll never know what."

"I think there's something we're not being told," I said.

"By whom?"

"I don't know. I just feel there is one piece of the puzzle that is missing. Why wait two days to report her missing?"

"Because they assumed she had wandered out into the grounds and simply lost her way," Daniel said.

"A three-year-old girl puts on her own cloak and shoes and goes off into the dark? Can you picture Liam doing that? He's going to be three this year. Someone helped her, Daniel. Someone at that house knows something."

We came back into the warmth of the house to hear raised voices coming from a distant room.

"She doesn't need your help!" a man's voice was booming. "You tried to meddle before and now you think you can come back and do the same thing."

"She's not happy. She should be taken away before something bad happens."

"Nonsense. She was quite content before you showed up here."

"Not content, Jacob, resigned. She has given up on life, can't you see that?"

Daniel and I stood in the front hall feeling awkward as one does when overhearing strangers arguing. We glanced at each other, deposited Cedric's package on the front table, then started to tiptoe up the stairs. We were halfway up, at the bend, when we heard the tap of footsteps and Aunt Florence emerged from the drawing room on the right.

"Insufferable man," she muttered to herself then stalked on through to the gallery without noticing us.

"It seems that the aunt's arrival has stirred up a hornets' nest," Daniel said once we were safely in our own bedroom. "I thought she might be a troublemaker."

"I have to say I agree with her," I said. "Winnie does give the impression of one who has given up on life. She can't be any more than thirty, Daniel. Scarcely older than I. And yet she has no friends; she can't go out apparently without her husband's permission. She's a prisoner. No wonder she's depressed."

"I think you are exaggerating a little," Daniel said. "Maybe it is she who doesn't want to go out and make friends. Maybe the shock of losing her child has plunged her into a deep depression from which she can't emerge. And perhaps her husband does not want to let her out alone because of proven erratic behavior. She could have tried to kill herself or do herself harm, you know." He paused, looking at me while I digested this. "I do think an alienist may be able to help her if they find the right one."

This conversation was interrupted by the sound of

running feet and the appearance of Bridie and Liam. Liam's little face was lit up with excitement. "Horsey," he said. "Go fast."

"We were exploring and we found an old nursery," Bridie exclaimed.

"I don't think you should have been prying behind closed doors," I said. "Did Mrs. Van Aiken give you permission to go in there?"

"She said we could explore so we looked in the rooms up near where Ivy is sleeping. Not the grand rooms like on this floor. Just old bedrooms and things covered in spooky dust sheets." Bridie's face was pink with excitement and embarrassment. "We made ourselves quite scared by daring each other to pull dust sheets off things. And then we found the nursery. It's in the corner above this room. And guess what—it has a huge rocking horse, almost big enough for Ivy and me to ride. But we didn't because we're grown-up now. But we put Liam on it and he loved it."

"Horsey," Liam agreed, still beaming. "Giddy-up."

"It wasn't on rockers like most of them are," Bridie went on, more animated than she usually was. "It was on gliders and it looked as if it was flying. Ivy was so funny. She said since it was a flying horse we'd have to call it Pegadus. I told her she meant Pegasus. 'Are you sure?' she asked. Wasn't that funny?"

"You shouldn't make fun of her," I said as Daniel scooped Liam up into his arms. "In an orphanage she wouldn't have the same access to books that you have. Would you have known about Pegasus if you'd continued to live with your aunt Nuala in the Lower East Side?"

"I wouldn't have known about anything except bad words and getting drunk if I'd lived with her. I think I would have run away." She stopped and the smile vanished from her face. "If you hadn't taken me in, I don't know what would have happened to me, Molly. You saved my life."

I put my arm around her. "I think you'd have turned out just grand wherever you were," I whispered. "But I'm glad I got the chance to watch you grow into such a lovely girl."

"Don't say that." She looked away. "I don't want to think about it."

"Then don't. We're going to put all worrying thoughts aside and have a marvelous Christmas."

"Horsey? More?" Liam asked, reaching out from Daniel to be put down.

The clock in the foyer chimed twelve.

"We should probably go down and see about feeding this young man. If he doesn't get a nap soon he's going to be overtired." Daniel hoisted up Liam, holding on to him tightly.

"Good idea. Maybe we can feed him in the kitchen, where you had your lunch yesterday, Bridie," I said. "I don't want to bother one of the servants with having to bring up trays for him all the time."

"I'll show you the way," Bridie said, going ahead of us.

As we came down the stairs we saw Winnie coming from the back of the house. "How was your excursion into town?" she asked.

"Uneventful," I said. "We picked up your husband's package and did a little shopping. The shops look quite festive, don't they?"

"Yes, I suppose they do," she said. "In their own small way."

"You should see the decorations in New York," I said. "We made a point of going to look in Macy's windows and then visited the FAO Schwarz toy store. They were impressive, weren't they, Bridie?"

Bridie nodded. "Macy's had skaters in the windows and they really skated over the ice although they were only dolls."

"And Liam went mad for the train set at Schwarz," Daniel added. "The train goes all around the store."

"You should come down to the city for a couple of days next year," I said, still attempting to sound bright. "You'd love it. You could go to a show and do some shopping."

"Yes, it does sound like fun," Winnie said wistfully, almost as if I'd been describing a lovely dream to her.

"I'll take you around, if you like," I went on. I almost added "I'll be your chaperone" but then I stopped short. Why should she need a chaperone? She was a married woman, with her own money. Or it should have been her own money. Perhaps she had become too accustomed to having her father and husband control everything for her.

Before she could answer this, Cedric appeared from the other side of the hall. "Ah, you found my package for me." He picked it up from the hall table. "Excellent. My new waistcoat. I shall wear it for Christmas."

He beamed at us, all affability now. "Did you have a good time in our little township?"

"My wife did find a couple of gifts at one of the shops," Daniel said.

"And I ran into some friends who are staying at the Briarcliff Lodge," I said. "So all in all a most pleasant morning."

"Splendid. Splendid." Cedric beamed at us again. "And this afternoon I had promised to take the children to build a snowman, but the way the snow looks now, it will have to be a very small one. Perhaps a snow-dwarf!" And he chuckled at his own joke. He glanced up at the clock. "Time for a sherry before luncheon, I think. Shall we go through?"

I turned to Winnie. "I thought I might feed Liam in the kitchen, where the girls had their meal yesterday. Then I can put him down for his nap."

"If you wish, although I can easily have one of the maids bring up a tray for him."

"I don't want to be any trouble," I said. "Bridie can show me the way and maybe the cook can find him some more of that delicious soup."

At that moment Liam squirmed to get down again. "Horsey?" he asked. "Go horsey?"

"We found a rocking horse," Bridie said.

"A rocking horse?" Winnie had gone quite white.

"You said we could explore," Bridie said hastily. "And we found an old nursery. And Liam rode the rocking horse. I hope that was all right?"

Winnie gave a weak smile. "Why, yes. Yes, of course it was all right. There is no reason at all why Liam should not enjoy the rocking horse. It has been sitting there doing nothing for so long now."

Her voice sounded light and breezy, but I could see from her face that she was making a supreme effort.

Fifteen

I sent Bridie to find Ivy and then followed them to the rear of the house. The kitchen was big and warm, hung with copper pots, and permeated with many good smells. The elderly cook looked up, red-faced from stirring something over a giant cast-iron stove, but she smiled when she saw us.

"So the young'uns have come for their food again, have they?" she asked. She turned to the young girl who was chopping vegetables at the scrubbed pine table. "Rose, leave that and serve some of that stew to the young folk. They look like they need fattening up." Rose shot us a shy little smile. "This way," she said and took us through to what was clearly a servants' dining room. She laid places at one end, returning with bowls of hot stew. Bridie took Liam on her lap and held him while Ivy fed him, the two girls giggling as he leaned forward and opened his mouth eagerly. I left them to it and went to rejoin the grown-ups.

The mood around the table at luncheon was a festive one.

"Christmas Eve tomorrow," Cedric said, looking around at us with a pleased expression on his face. "This takes me back to old times. Although my grandfather kept the Dutch tradition, you know. Our big day was Saint Nicholas. He came on December 5. You put out your shoes and if you'd been a good child, they were filled with candy and little presents by morning. Then on Christmas Eve it was the Christ child who came. So tomorrow night we'll finish decorating the tree and we'll sing carols and have hot grog. The young ones will love it. Actually I'll enjoy it myself."

"We look forward to it," I said because I felt that someone should say something.

A bowl of butternut squash soup was served—thick and creamy, and just what was needed on a cold December day.

Winnie looked out of the window. "I think it might snow again. We may have our white Christmas after all."

Indeed the day had now clouded over and heavy yellowish clouds hung in the sky. "I can't tell you how delighted I am that our friends have finally returned to us," the aged Great-Aunt Cara said, beaming at us. "So many years with no company and now look at us. And I'm especially glad to see you again." She was sitting next to Daniel and patted his hand. "Where have you been all this time? I'm sure we've all missed you. I know Winnie has missed you."

There was a silence, then Daniel laughed and said, "I'm afraid you're mixing me up with someone else. I haven't visited this house before."

"I never forget a face," Aunt Clara said indignantly. "It might be years, but I still remember you."

"You're confused again, Aunt Clara," Cedric said. "This man is Captain Sullivan." He turned to Daniel. "And I meant to ask, are you a sea captain? Nobody ever explained to me."

Daniel shook his head. "I'm afraid nothing so glamorous. And I'm surprised my mother hasn't told you. She usually recounts every one of my exploits since the day I learned to walk. I'm a captain with the New York Police Department."

"Police?" Cedric registered a moment's shock, then gave a carefree laugh. "Then we'd all better be on our best behavior, hadn't we?"

The main course was served: ham with a parsley sauce, parsnips, and baked potatoes, followed by an apple tart. Simple country fare but good. Cedric was clearly making an effort to remain jolly but Winnie was tense. I saw her glancing at Great-Aunt Clara and then at Daniel a few times. *Who did Daniel resemble?* I wondered.

When lunch was over I went to retrieve the children from their meal. I found Liam sitting on the floor, eating a gingerbread man, while the girls were at the table helping to cut dough for little tarts.

"You've got good little helpers here," Cook said.

I picked up Liam. "Time for your nap, young man."

He protested, trying to wiggle out of my arms. He was becoming so strong and heavy that I had to fight to hold him. *No longer a baby,* I thought. *A little boy with a mind of his own.* And I tried to picture the Van Aikens' daughter putting on her boots or shoes. There was no way that Liam could dress himself. Someone in this house had dressed that child and led her to the door. Then sent her out into the night, to what?

I looked across at the cook. "You must have been with this family for a long time," I said.

"Oh, indeed. I came here as kitchen maid over forty years ago. I served Mr. Cedric's father and his grandfather. I remember when he was born. So happy they were. They'd been married for years and no child. And this was a boy to carry on the name."

"Then it is sad that Mr. and Mrs. Van Aiken have no son," I said. "There will be no one to inherit this lovely house."

She moved closer to me, wiping her hands on her apron. "You know they did have a child. A little girl. Vanished ten years ago."

"I did hear that," I said. "What a terrible thing. And she was never found. I've only heard the gist of the story. None of the details. But I was told she went out of the house on her own in the dark. How could that be?"

"I've no idea, ma'am," she said. "We asked ourselves that at the time. But we were all in the ballroom, you see. Having our own holiday party while we decorated the ballroom to be ready for the big party the next night. And the nursemaid was with us. She thought the little girl was asleep or she'd never have left her."

"What did the servants think? Was there anyone they suspected?"

"None of us, ma'am. There wasn't one of the servants who would have done such a cruel thing. Least of all the girl's nursemaid. Adored little Charlotte, she did. Worshipped her. And after she was gone she couldn't stop crying. 'If only I'd stayed with her,' she kept on saying. And then the police were here and they kept questioning her, hinting that she must have been in the pay of kidnappers. It was too much for the poor soul to bear. We heard she'd died soon afterward. Took her own life." She had lowered her voice. "But it couldn't have been kidnappers, could it? They never got a ransom note or Mr. Cedric would willingly have paid it to get his daughter back."

"Did he dote on his daughter?"

"I'm back here in the kitchen, ma'am," she said. "But from what I heard he was clearly disappointed she wasn't a son. He wasn't cruel to her or anything, but I don't think he ever really took to her. Unlike her mother, who doted on the child. But that's the way of things, isn't it? Men are not made for nurturing children."

"I heard there was a gardener who might have been involved," I said.

"Harris, you mean? Yes, that's what they were saying. Of course the gardeners don't have much to do when the snow's lying deep on the ground, so it was only discovered he wasn't in his quarters when the gardeners were called out to search the grounds. And who knew how long he'd been gone. One of the stable boys claimed they saw him here, on the estate, the evening after the child vanished, and the word was that he was not missing but just getting out of work, which would have been like him. We indoor staff never mixed with them much but the rumor was that he liked his drink a little too much. And anyway what could he have to do with the kidnapping of a child from the house? Outdoor staff never set foot anywhere but the kitchen and it was plain enough that the child went out through the front door."

The clock in the hall chimed two. She roused herself, as if suddenly aware that she'd been gossiping with me. "This will never do," she said. "I need to get those pies in the oven."

"And I need to put this young man to bed," I said, brushing his hair with a kiss.

"It doesn't do no good rehashing it, does it?" she said, heading back to the table. "All the talking in the world won't bring her back."

By the time I had finally got Liam off to sleep and came to join the others in the gallery, it was snowing hard—great white flakes swirling about the windows and blocking the view across the grounds.

"Lucky we went to see about the poultry this morning," I said as I came to perch beside Daniel's mother, who was busy with her tapestry again. "I hope they'll be able to deliver them all right."

"It's not far," Winnie said. "At worst they can send a boy out on skis or snowshoes. People out here use them to get around all the time."

My mind was still on my conversation with the cook. *Skis or snowshoes,* I thought. *Had the person who took Charlotte come for her on skis, thus leaving no footprints? But then skis leave tracks too, don't they?* I pushed worrying thoughts to the back of my mind. As the cook said, no amount of talking or thinking or worrying could bring the child back. But I glanced across at Daniel, who was deep in conversation with Cedric, and thought about the old aunt at the table, mixing him up with another man. I hadn't asked whether there had been guests in the house for Christmas and whether one of them might have had a hand in taking Charlotte. I certainly couldn't ask Winnie or Cedric. It was lucky that Liam was taking his meals in the servants' quarters. I'd have to have another chat with the cook.

"We need some Christmas music," Great-Aunt Clara said, quite animated now. "Why don't you play the piano for us, Henry? You play so beautifully. I still remember."

Daniel looked uncomfortable. "I'm afraid my name is Daniel and I do not play the piano," he said.

"Are you sure? You're not trying to fool an old lady whose eyesight is failing?"

"Whose mind is failing too," Cedric said abruptly. "This is nobody you know or remember, Aunt."

"And he doesn't play the piano?"

"I'm afraid not," Daniel said.

"Oh, what a pity." Great-Aunt Clara frowned. "Why is everything so jumbled suddenly?"

"I will play the piano later, Aunt," Cedric said, going over to her and putting a comforting hand on her shoulder. "And tomorrow we will sing Christmas carols when the tree is decorated."

Great-Aunt Clara stood up with difficulty. "I think I will go up to my room."

"Good idea. Take a little nap. There will be a lot of feasting and fun in the coming days," Aunt Florence said. "We all need to keep up our strength."

"Oh, no. I try not to nap in the daytime," Great-Aunt Clara said. "Such a weakness. I shall sit at my window and see which of our old friends is coming to visit next to surprise us."

She went from the room with great dignity.

Cedric shook his head. "Really, her confusion gets worse by the day."

"Poor old thing," Aunt Florence said, giving Daniel's mother an understanding smile. "I suppose it will come to all of us in the end, but one doesn't like to think about it."

"You will remain sharp until your dying day, Florence," Daniel's mother said.

"Sometimes too sharp for her own good," Winnie's father muttered in a low voice.

"I heard that," Florence said, making us all laugh and breaking the tension.

It was still snowing hard as night fell. We heard the *clip-clop* of hooves and jingle of sleigh bells. Bridie and Ivy had been in the kitchen and came running through to tell us that the goose and chickens had been delivered, and boxes of other good things. It was good to see Bridie's face alight with joy for a change. I vowed to make this a Christmas she would never forget.

Sixteen

When Daniel and I were finally alone in our bedroom and the children were asleep I sat at the dressing table, brushing out my hair. Daniel came up behind me and stood looking at my reflection in the mirror.

"You're still a handsome woman, Molly Murphy Sullivan," he said. He ran his hands over my shoulders and caressed my neck. A shiver went through me. I glanced up at him and smiled.

"That's more like the girl I married," he said. "Recently you've been looking as if you've the weight of the world on your shoulders. So coming here was the right thing to do after all?"

"Maybe it was," I said. "I think I've been wounded in too many ways recently. I just needed time to heal."

"And now you think you are finally healed?"

"I'm on that path," I said. "My thoughts are no longer all turned inward. I have that missing child to think about."

"I wouldn't get any hopes up about finding her after all this time." Daniel's hands still massaged my shoulders.

"I don't know. Something that was brought up today made me realize there were aspects we haven't looked into yet." I swiveled to look at him. "This Henry person that the old lady mistook you for. He obviously used to be a guest here, but doesn't come anymore? We know the servants were all in the ballroom, having their own party when the child disappeared. But we don't know if there were guests in the house, just like we are, for Christmas. Why has nobody mentioned them?"

"You are suggesting that one of their guests went off with the child? Rather far-fetched, don't you think? For one thing they'd be able to give names and addresses to the police and track the person down rapidly, and for another, why would someone who was a guest in their house want to steal their child?"

"I don't know. Madness? Revenge? The desire for a child of their own?"

Daniel wagged a finger at me. "Molly, if this was suspected, every policeman in New York State would be hunting for the person. They would have been found."

I thought he was probably right, but I didn't want to give up so quickly. "Remember that case you were investigating where I was able to help you? The young girl who was having those dreams?" Daniel grunted. I don't think he liked to admit that I had actually solved something the police had been working on for months. "Remember that unbalanced young man was trying to take the girl with him on a ship? Who knows whether something like that happened to the Van Aikens' child and she was taken to South America or God knows where?"

"Do you not think that every port would have been notified? Every passenger list checked?"

"They would have traveled under an assumed name."

"And you do not find it odd that Cedric and Winnie have not mentioned this? Have kept quiet about it all these years? If your friend Augusta ran off with Liam would you have sat quietly and done nothing for ten years? No, you would have pursued her to the ends of the earth."

"Unless Gus thought that I was a bad parent and was taking the child away for his own safety," I said, toying with the words.

Daniel went across the room and pulled back the velvet drapes. "I think you should leave it, Molly. A good detective relies on facts, not flights of fancy and not besmirching characters without any modicum of proof."

I got up from the stool and came over to stand with him at the window. "Maybe you are right," I said. "It's just that I want . . ."

"You want to make things right. You always have," Daniel said gently. "Come to bed, do, or you'll get cold."

I let him lead me across to our bed and lay content in the warmth of his arms.

Christmas Eve dawned bright and clear. I got up to see a slit of sunlight streaming between the drapes, went over to the window, and pulled them back. The new snow sparkled from bare tree branches and from the expanse of lawn. A true Christmas scene. I glanced at Liam's bed and saw that it was empty. A jolt of fear shot through me.

"Liam?" I could hardly get the word out. "Liam?"

Daniel roused himself and sat up, rubbing his eyes. "What's the matter?"

"Liam's not in his bed." My heart was pounding now. "Children can wander off so easily," the old woman had said.

"Calm down, Molly," Daniel said. "I expect he's just . . ." As he was pulling back the covers we heard a distinct giggle from the next room. I ran to the door and there was my son, bouncing on Bridie's bed while she pretended to sleep.

"Wait-up," he was saying.

And then she turned suddenly and said in a ferocious voice, "Who is waking me up?" And he burst into giggles again.

A normal, happy morning scene. One that had been played out dozens of times at our house. And yet for a moment I had experienced the fear that must have shot through Winnie Van Aiken when she realized that her child had gone. How could I not want to make things right?

I dressed, then bathed and dressed my son and took him down to a hearty breakfast in the warmth of the servants' dining room, off the kitchen. I watched with satisfaction as he worked his way through a bowl of oatmeal, insisting on holding the spoon himself, and then dipped fingers of bread into a boiled egg. From next door in the kitchen came sounds of frenzied activity, the clatter of pots and pans, shouted instructions, and plenty of admonitions. "Don't drop that bird, Rose. Mind what you're doing!"

"I am minding, Mrs. Edwards."

"And don't answer back." As she said these words the cook came through to us. "That girl will be the death of me," she said, but she said it with a smile. "Always got a glib tongue and a ready excuse for anything that goes wrong. She'll come to a bad end, you mark my words."

She leaned forward to pick up Liam's plate. "All finished? Now that's what I call a good eater. That's what I like to see. Not finicky like some of them."

"He certainly enjoys his food," I said, wiping egg from Liam's face before I picked him up. "And before you go, there was one thing I wanted to ask you. A friend called Henry was mentioned yesterday. . . ."

"That would be Mr. Wheaton," she said. "His name hasn't been mentioned here for years now. He used to be a constant visitor but not anymore."

"He was a good friend of the family, was he?"

"Mr. Cedric's best friend when they were young men at Princeton together. Such a pleasant young man too. We were all very fond of him."

"You say he hasn't visited for years—was there a falling out?"

She shook her head. "Not that I ever heard. Of course we don't know so much what goes on in their part of the house when we're stuck in the kitchen. We have to rely on the maids to report back to us. But no. I never heard there was any kind of falling out between the master and Mr. Henry. At least not here."

I waited for her to go on, and at last she said, "That's the way of it, isn't it? Young men go their separate ways, get jobs in far-flung places. Marry. Settle down and lose touch."

"Was he staying at the house that Christmas—when the little girl disappeared?" I asked.

She frowned, then shook her head. "He wasn't. Not that year."

"And were there other guests in the house?"

"The night when the child . . ." She couldn't say the rest of the words. "Not houseguests like yourselves. No. They were planning a big party for the next evening. That was why we servants had our party on that night, because we'd have no time to celebrate over the actual holiday. But people were just invited to dine and dance, mind you. Nobody was going to stay overnight."

"So it really was just family and servants in the house when Charlotte vanished?"

She paused and smiled. "Charlotte. Little Lottie. Yes, that was her name. I had almost forgotten. It hasn't been spoken in years."

"And I was wondering. You said all the servants were at the party. Could anyone have left the ballroom for a short time and not been noticed?"

She frowned. "I suppose so. We were all having a good time, laughing and eating and drinking and putting the finishing touches to the decorations. I don't think we'd have noticed if anyone slipped away for a few minutes. But I told you, ma'am, those servants were all good people. Most of them I'd known all my life. Not one of them would have harmed Miss Charlotte." She gave me a sort of sideways glance. "If I were you, ma'am, I'd leave well alone. No good can come of bringing up the past. It won't bring her back."

She shook her head and I saw tears in her eyes.

"I'm sorry," I said. "But my husband is a police officer. I

just wondered if there was any stone that had been left unturned, you know."

"I understand. We all wished we could make it right for Mrs. Van Aiken." A thoughtful look came over her face. "That's funny, now you come to mention it. The only person I did see leave the party that night was Mrs. Van Aiken herself. I heard her telling the master she had a headache and needed to take one of her powders."

I left her then and went to my own breakfast. Cedric was at his most amiable. "What did I tell you?" he said to Bridie, who was trying to be invisible as she worked her way through a big plate of eggs and ham. "I promised we'd build a snowman and now look. The perfect day for it. Everyone get bundled up and we'll go out at eleven."

Bridie was almost as excited as Liam. He was saying "Noman?" at regular intervals as she buttoned him into his winter coat and hood. The older ladies turned down the invitation to join us and Winnie was nowhere to be seen. I hoped she had not taken to her bed again on the eve of Christmas. That would make the holiday celebration extremely awkward. So it was Daniel and I, Bridie, Ivy, and Liam who set out across the untouched expanse of whiteness.

"We'll go toward the back of the property," Cedric said. "There's a bit of a slope there where we can roll balls down the hill and make our task easier. It's where I always used to make snowmen when I was a child."

"Is the hill big enough for sledding?" Ivy asked.

Cedric looked at her with surprise. "Have you ever been sledding?"

"No, but I've read about it. It sounds like fun, going so fast."

"Yes, it's fun," he said. "I think there are still the old sleds in the attic, but they haven't been used for years. I'll have one of the staff see if they can locate them for you. I might even have a go myself, if I'm not too heavy now."

He grinned and she responded. I stared at her with surprise. She had seemed such a timid little thing and here she was, exchanging grins with the master of this big estate. Maybe she was just realizing the possibilities of her life now that she was no longer in the orphanage. I found myself wondering if Daniel's mother would be able to keep her a maid rather than a companion after this exposure to the finer things of life.

We stomped together through the snow. Liam insisted on walking to start with but found it such heavy going that Daniel had to pick him up, much to his annoyance. We came to where the stream crossed the property. Snow covered the rocks, but the water still splashed and gurgled unhindered.

"You'd think it would have frozen over, wouldn't you?" Ivy whispered to Bridie.

"Perhaps it's not cold enough yet," Bridie answered.

At last we came to the gentle slope that led up to the trees at the back of the property. Daniel put Liam down. Cedric started to form the first ball and to roll it down. Liam was enchanted as it grew, gathering speed. Then we all pitched in and pushed it over and over until it was an impressive start for a snowman. We had just gone up to the top of the slope to repeat the process when we heard a bloodcurdling scream coming from among the trees.

Seventeen

Daniel plunged ahead. I turned back to Bridie. "Hang on to Liam," I shouted and struggled through the snow in pursuit of Daniel. But he could move so much more quickly with his trousers tucked into his boots than I could with all those layers of petticoats and skirts, already weighted down with wet snow. Bushes snatched at me and held me back. I fought myself free, following Daniel's fleeting figure. We had just reached the boundary of the estate where a low wall divided Greenbriars from the adjacent property when the screams came again. My heart was pounding now. I came, gasping, up to the wall. Daniel was scrambling over. It was a little above waist high and I was in no position to join him without displaying more of my undergarments than would have been considered proper. Normally propriety wouldn't bother me, but I reminded myself that Cedric was right behind me and I had to set a standard for those girls. So I had to wait.

It didn't take more than a few seconds, however, before one of the screamers came into view. It was a young woman, dressed in a dark green cape, running toward us through the trees on the other side of the wall. Something came whizzing past my head. I heard it thud into a tree just to my right. My first thought was that someone was shooting at her and a bullet had just missed me. It wouldn't have been the first time I'd been shot at. Then in hot pursuit were other young women, their hoods thrown back, their hair flying loose and shouting with laughter as they threw snowballs.

Daniel had come to a halt and turned to me with a look of disgust. "Snowball fight," he said. "And to think that I . . ." He didn't need to finish. I had had similar thoughts. And now as they were closing in on us I recognized the women. Sid and Gus's group staying at the Briarcliff Lodge. Sure enough Sid and Gus were among them.

Sid spotted me and waved. "Look, Gus, there is Molly. And Bridie and Liam. How splendid. They can come over and join in."

"We thought something was seriously amiss," Daniel said, frowning as the women came toward us. "We heard screams."

"Yes, that was me, I'm afraid," admitted the young woman who was being pursued. "I didn't want a snowball down my neck. I'm sorry if I alarmed you."

"We were re-creating our favorite game from our Vassar years," Gus explained. "The snowball war between dorms. We had a ceremonial snowball fight every year, and our dorm always won. We were merciless."

"They still are," the woman who had been chased agreed, while attempting to brush snow off her back. "I have been pounded and hounded."

"We should get back to the others and our snowman," Daniel said impatiently.

"Oh, don't Bridie and Liam want to come and join us?" Gus asked.

"Not now. They were having fun building the snowman," Daniel replied before I could speak. Actually I thought the snowball fight might have been a lot of fun.

"Then maybe we can come over and help build too," Gus suggested.

"I think it might be better if . . ." Daniel began, but Cedric had joined us now.

"Of course. Why not? Delighted. If you can scale the wall, of course. A tad tricky with skirts on."

"These are our neighbors in New York and their friends from their Vassar days," I said.

"So I heard. Come on then, let me give you a hand." He helped them gallantly to scramble over the wall. The women threw themselves with enthusiasm into snowman building and I watched them with amazement and a tinge of envy. These were women of my own age or a little older who had no responsibilities of husband and family, who had enough money for a comfortable life, and thus they still knew how to play. They still thought that having fun was important. And I realized how bleak my last few months had been. Would I ever learn to enjoy myself like that again?

As we worked at our snowman Sid came up to me. "So this is the husband, eh, Molly? He seems jolly enough. But we were told in the village that he seems something of a recluse, that the family has shut themselves off from most social contact."

"What else did they tell you in the village?" I whispered back.

"Nothing too revealing. They hardly ever saw the child and probably wouldn't have recognized her if she had been taken to the station. But they confirmed that the gardener, Harris, was a reputed bad lot. His wife had left him or he had left her, I'm not sure which. He liked his drink and he was involved in some shady deals. Also"—she paused, glancing around at where Cedric was now sticking two pieces of coal onto the snowman's face—"apparently Harris was seen by the carter who delivers beer barrels the night after the child disappeared. He was already quite drunk but had not been to the bar in town. He said he wouldn't need the carter anymore as it was going to be whiskey every night from now on. And he wouldn't stop to talk. He said he had to see a man about a dog."

"About a dog?" I was puzzled.

"It's a saying, isn't it? 'I'm going to see a man about a dog' means I'm off for a secret meeting with someone important. But he was walking away from town, not toward it."

"Interesting," I said, "and chilling too. If he was on his way to deliver a ransom note, for example, and fell down drunk in the snow first, then that note was never delivered."

"But the kidnapper would surely have sent a second note," Sid suggested. "He would have been stuck with the child."

"And might have killed her in desperation," I pointed out.

We walked back to join the others, a somber couple amid riots of laughter.

We parted ways soon, my friends having received an invitation from Cedric to stop by for a cup of cheer tomorrow. Our luncheon was awaiting us, a splendid affair with oyster soup, roast leg of pork, and then apple dumplings. Winnie was present and quite cheerful. She pointed out that we were having such a heavy midday meal because it would be a simple supper, so that we could decorate the tree and sing carols.

After our meal we went upstairs for a rest. I lay on the bed, my thoughts still a jumble of worry. There was nothing I could do, I told myself. I suspected that Harris the gardener held the key, that he was somehow involved in the kidnapping of the little girl, and I could only imagine the worst about what happened to her afterward. Maybe Winnie also had the same thoughts and that's why she was so depressed.

We had an early supper—a simple beef stew and a bread pudding with vanilla sauce, then Cedric ushered us all into the front hall to decorate the tree. He handed delicate glass-blown ornaments to the two girls to hang on the lower branches, then invited us to join in. There were birds with real feathers in their tails, tiny trumpets that really blew a note, violins, angels, and animals. We attached them carefully to the branches, taking care not to disturb the candles. Then Cedric climbed a stepladder and fixed a star to the top.

"Come on, Liam, we can touch the star for good luck," Ivy said, leading my son up the stairs.

"Don't lift him over the railing," I said rapidly.

"Oh, no. You can touch the star if you reach through," Ivy said and showed him. The star was just the right height for him.

"Now we light the candles," Cedric said. He was handed a taper by one of the watching servants and one by one the candles were lit, filling the foyer with soft flickering light. Liam was entranced. I moved unobtrusively up the stairs to rescue him from Ivy. I didn't think he could slip between the railings, but I didn't want to give him the chance to try. I took his hand and we walked down the stairs, one by one. We had just reached the bottom step when there was a knock at the front door.

"Now who could that be?" Aunt Florence asked. "You didn't invite anybody to join us, did you, Cedric?"

"Of course not," he said, frowning.

"And not a tradesman at this late hour."

"Let one of the maids answer it," Cedric called, putting out a restraining hand to Aunt Florence. One of the maids, who had been watching the proceedings from the passageway that led back to the kitchen, smoothed down her apron and straightened her cap as she hurried across the foyer. She opened the front door. We heard her say, "Can I help you, miss?"

And a small voice outside said, "Is this Greenbriars?"

"Yes, miss," the maid responded.

Then the voice said, "Then I've come home."

"Home, miss?"

"Yes. Would you tell them that I'm Charlotte?"

Eighteen

Nobody moved. Then a girl, her face still hidden beneath the hood of her cloak, stepped into the front hall. She was covered in a dusting of snow. She took off her mittens and her frozen fingers trembled as she tried to undo the clasp at her throat. She was tall and thin for her age, with mid-brown curls and a delicate, pointed little face like a china doll. She looked around from one face to the next, then her eyes lit up. "Oh, the Christmas tree. You have the Christmas tree in its usual place. How lovely." She started to walk toward it.

"How did you get here?" Cedric's voice was harsh. He ran to the front door, opened it, and stared out into the snowy darkness. Then he took in the one set of footprints leading up to the front door, shook his head in disbelief, and came back to the girl.

"I walked up from the train." She turned to look up at him. "It's a long way in the snow. I hadn't realized how far it was. I was scared I wasn't going to make it." She let her cape fall and then swayed as if she was going to fall herself.

Winnie gave a sobbing cry and burst forward. "My child.

My little Charlotte has come home to us. It's a Christmas miracle, Cedric. A miracle."

She took the girl's face in her hands and peered at it, trying to picture the three-year-old in those features.

"Mother?" the girl said tentatively. "Are you my mother?" She was staring at the face with wonder in her eye. "Yes, I do remember you. You haven't changed at all. And look at me. I'm almost grown-up."

"Yes, you are. Quite a young woman." Winnie was stammering, finding it hard to get the words out. "Isn't she, Cedric? Our daughter is almost grown-up."

"Hold on, Winnie." Cedric came forward now and put a hand on his wife's shoulder. "How do we know this girl is our daughter? This could well be a cruel Christmas prank, or the girl could have been set up to do this by someone wanting to make money from us."

"Papa?" The girl turned to him. "Don't you remember me at all? I remember you, but you didn't have a mustache, did you?"

"Quite right. I grew it after—"

"After I went away," she said. She swayed again. "I need to sit down," she said. "I've had nothing to eat all day."

"Of course, my darling," Winnie said. She turned to the maid who had picked up the cape. "Elsie, bring a bowl of soup for Miss Charlotte." She took the girl's hand tentatively as if she was afraid she'd break, or vanish again. "Come through to the fire in the gallery."

"Where is the gallery?" Charlotte looked around as Winnie led her away from the rest of us and into the large room. The electric lights had been switched off so that we could appreciate the glow of the Christmas tree, and Winnie flicked the switch to flood the room with light.

Charlotte hesitated in the doorway. "I don't know this room. It's different. Where's the little cozy room with the fireplace? And the fireplace had pictures on it?"

"Yes, it did. Delft tiles," Cedric said. "We took down some walls and made one big room with a bigger fireplace."

"You used to love those tiles," Winnie said. "You liked the ladies dancing."

"And the wolf," Charlotte said. "Wasn't there a wolf peeking around a cottage?"

"There was." Winnie looked up at Cedric, her eyes shining. "She's come home. Now surely you can't doubt any longer."

Cedric was still frowning. "My dear child, where were you all these years? What happened to you?"

Winnie sat on the sofa by the fire and eased Charlotte down beside her.

"I came from Boston just now," Charlotte said. "We lived lots of other places before that, but the last few years we were in Boston."

"Who are 'we'? Who were you with?" Cedric's voice was still harsh.

"My mother," Charlotte said.

There was a gasp from Winnie and the rest of us. "Your mother?"

Charlotte went red. "Well, I know now that she wasn't my mother." She stammered to bring the words out. "But that's what I'd always called her. I thought she was my mother until she told me the truth."

"Was she the one who took you from us?" Winnie was holding both the girl's hands in hers, staring at her face as if she wanted to imprint it on her mind forever.

"I don't remember," Charlotte said. "I don't remember much except the rooms where we lived. It was really cold in Canada. I remember that."

"Canada!" Winnie exclaimed. Her eyes lit up. "Did you hear that, Cedric? Canada. I knew she must have been taken out of the country or we would have found her."

"You don't remember who took you away from here?" Cedric asked, standing, arms folded, and staring down at her. He was frowning.

The girl shook her head. "I remember it was something bad. I think they put something over my face. A man put something over my face and I couldn't breathe. And when I woke up I was far, far away."

"In Canada?" Cedric asked.

"I don't know. In a room. We didn't go out. I only knew rooms."

Of course they would have kept her hidden, I thought. *And of course a three-year-old would have no way of knowing where she was.*

"And who was with you in the room?" Cedric asked.

"My mother. She said she was my mother."

"Did she have a name?"

"I don't know. Yes, but I called her Mother. I'm sorry," Charlotte said. She put a hand up to her face. "But the room is spinning around. I don't think . . ." And then she fainted.

Winnie turned to Cedric, her eyes blazing as she dropped to the floor beside her daughter. "Now look what you've done. You've terrified her. My own darling daughter has come back and you don't want to admit it. Well, I'm having her taken straight to bed tonight and I'll feed her the soup from lunch and if you want to ask her more questions, then you'll have to wait until the morning."

Cedric was looking absolutely white and stunned. He put his hands on Winnie's shoulders. "Winnie, I know it seems like a miracle, but we can't be sure. I don't recognize her."

"Of course she's changed since she was three," Winnie snapped, cradling the girl's head. "But she knew about your mustache. She knew we'd made the gallery and taken away the delft tiles. She has to be Charlotte. She has to be."

"We'll talk about it more in the morning," Cedric said. He turned to Aunt Florence. "Aunt Florence, can you arrange for a bed to be made up for Charlotte? Her old room? Maybe that would help bring back memories."

"We are using the bed from her old room for young Bridie at the moment," Aunt Florence said. "Why don't we put her in one of the guest bedrooms tonight? The poor thing will no doubt sleep until morning wherever she is."

"No, I want her in my room, with me," Winnie said emphatically. "Have James and Frederick carry her up to my room, and we'll bring her up some soup and milk and brandy."

"No, Winnie." Cedric turned to Aunt Florence. "The guest room is a better idea. We don't want Winnie becoming too attached to her too soon. Just in case."

"You are cruel!" Winnie said as the girl stirred and tried to sit up.

"No, my dear, I'm cautious. Arriving home on Christmas Eve, alone in the snow. We need to find out a good deal more before I'll accept her as my long-lost daughter. By all means feed her her soup, but we will let her sleep alone tonight. I insist."

"All right, Cedric," Winnie said in a small voice. "If that's what you want."

"I'm doing this for you, Winnie," he said. "For your good."

"I'll go and make sure her bed is nice and warm for her," Winnie said.

Aunt Florence put a hand on Winnie's shoulder. "You stay where you are. You look as if you could do with a glass of brandy yourself. You're as white as a sheet. Pour her one, Cedric. I'll take care of Charlotte for you."

She bustled out of the room and in no time at all had returned with two footmen. As they tried to lift her, Charlotte woke up and cried out in alarm at seeing strange men's faces.

"It's all right, my dear," Aunt Florence said calmly. "These men are just going to carry you up to your room. And I'm going to stay with you and feed you some good soup. And then you can sleep."

"Thank you," the girl replied weakly and allowed herself to be carried out.

Winnie sat on the sofa as if turned to stone. Cedric went over to the side table and poured his wife a brandy. Then he looked at us. "I think we all need one, don't you?" he asked. "We've all had a shock."

"You don't believe she is your daughter, Cedric?" Mr. Carmichael asked.

"She's not how I remember her," Cedric said. "She was darker, wasn't she?"

"Her hair was a little darker, but those things change with time, don't they?" Winnie said. "And her eyes—there's something about her eyes that I recognized immediately."

I had been watching the scene unfold rather like an intriguing play. And I had noticed the immediate resemblance between Charlotte and Winnie. Surely Cedric could see it too, or perhaps he was afraid to see it, because he didn't want to raise false hopes. He was busy pouring glasses of brandy and handing them to each of us.

"So the child came home," Great-Aunt Clara said as she accepted her glass of brandy. "Well, that's a turn-up for the books, isn't it? I bet she has a story to tell. I wonder how much she remembers, or what memories will come back to her now that she is among us again?"

"I don't think one remembers much from when one is three," I said.

"But an event like a kidnapping would be imprinted upon the memory, surely?" Daniel's mother said. "And if the memory is jolted by returning to the scene, then I wouldn't be surprised if she couldn't tell us exactly what happened."

"And her kidnappers would be brought to justice," Daniel said with satisfaction.

I was watching Winnie's face. There was something in it that I couldn't quite read. Was it fear?

Cedric handed me my glass of brandy. "No more carol singing tonight, I think," he said. "And we'd better blow out the candles on the tree in case there is a fire. So perhaps it's early to bed and a good night's sleep so that we can all enjoy Christmas day."

We sat around the fire, sipping our drinks, each of us wrapped up in our own thoughts. I was thinking how lovely it was for Winnie and Cedric that their daughter had returned. Was this case now solved? Presumably in the morning we'd find out the truth about who kidnapped her and why. I supposed I could understand Cedric's reluctance to admit his child had come home. It did seem almost too good to be true, and of course I was also dying to find out where she had been and how she had now been allowed to return to her family.

Daniel and I stayed awake for a long time, waiting until Bridie was asleep before we put stockings with gifts at the bottoms of the children's beds. I smiled, picturing Liam's face when he saw his stocking. And Bridie too. She might be almost thirteen but she was still a little girl at heart.

"Well, that was a rum do, wasn't it?" Daniel said to me as I snuggled up to him in bed. "Did you ever imagine in a million years that the girl would come home?"

"No, I don't think I did," I confessed. "I had given her up for dead, if you want to know."

"Me too."

"In all your years with the police did you ever come across a kidnapper who released his victim years later?"

"I can't say that I did. Of course she might not have been released. She might have found a chance to escape and taken it."

"That would indeed be a bold move, given that she was

only three when she was taken and knew no other life," I said.

"No point in speculating about it now," Daniel said. "I've no doubt we'll find out more in the morning." He leaned across and kissed my forehead. "Merry Christmas in advance."

"And you too, my darling," I said. "We are so lucky that we have each other and Liam. Such a blessing."

I was just drifting off to sleep when a terrible thought struck me. Cedric's insistence that the girl did not sleep in a room with her mother. His profound desire to protect Winnie. And Winnie's mental instability . . . And the cook had said that Winnie was the only one who left the party that night. Could it be that he was afraid Winnie might try to harm her daughter again?

Nineteen

I was woken by a cry or a shout. I sat up, heart beating fast, only to see that Liam was awake and had discovered his stocking. Or rather he had discovered the wooden horse and cart that was too big to fit into his stocking and was now pushing it over the carpet, saying, "Horsey. Giddy-up."

I woke Daniel and we sat on the floor beside him while he explored the contents of the stocking. He had to be refrained from eating the sugar pig before breakfast and from throwing the ball across the room, but then contented himself with giving them both rides in his new cart. I could see that the toy would be a huge success.

While Daniel was watching him play I handed him his gift. "Merry Christmas," I said. His eyes grew large, like a small child's when he saw what the gift was. "A camera? Molly—do we have the money for a camera?"

"I was frugal with the housekeeping," I said. "I didn't spend much money when we looked after your mother."

"I've always wanted one." He turned it over in his hand. "Does it have a roll of film with it?"

"It does. Look inside the box."

"Then I can take pictures today. I can immortalize our Christmas and our time with Bridie and Liam at two. Oh, this is a wonderful idea."

He wrapped me in his arms and kissed me.

"I have something for you," he said. "Nothing so exciting, I'm afraid." He handed me a big package. I opened it and found a lovely dark blue velvet fabric.

"I know you lost all your things in the fire and then had to leave everything in San Francisco after the earthquake," he said. "So I thought you should have a least one expensive dress. My mother knows a good dressmaker and she has promised to take you to her."

"Daniel, that is so thoughtful." I returned the kiss.

Liam's rolling the cart over the bare boards around the carpet had woken Bridie. We watched her as she picked up her own Christmas stocking and tipped out the orange in silver foil, a new hair ribbon, a skein of knitting yarn, a little bag of chocolates, and then the red leather box. She opened it and took out the locket, staring at it in wonder.

"Open it," I said gently.

She did so. "Liam's hair," she said. "And your pictures. It's wonderful. I won't ever take it off. All my life I'll remember . . ." And she burst into tears.

We sat together on her bed, hugging each other. I think I cried too.

Then I dressed Liam in his smartest sailor suit and we put on our finest array before going down to breakfast. There was no sign of Charlotte, but Daniel's mother and Ivy were there.

"Look. I have a present!" Ivy sprang up when we came in. "I have a new dress. It's the first time I've ever had a new dress made just for me. It was always hand-me-downs before." Her dark eyes were glowing and her little pixie face looked quite different when she smiled. The dress was a simple one, as befits someone who is a servant or companion, in a soft cambric, light blue with a navy blue bow at her neck. She looked absurdly young in it. Daniel's mother was smiling at her, as if she enjoyed the giving as much as Ivy did the receiving.

I went over and kissed her. "Merry Christmas, Mother Sullivan," I said.

"And you too, my dear." She reached up and patted my cheek.

As Daniel bent to embrace his mother, Bridie sidled over to me. "I wish I had a present for Ivy," she whispered to me.

"We have one for her. I bought it yesterday. We'll give it to her when gifts are exchanged later," I whispered back. "She'll love it."

Bridie gave me a conspiratorial smile. Then her face clouded again. "But we've nothing for Charlotte, have we? I didn't know she'd been lost all these years. I knew there was a nursery so I thought there might have been a child once, but I thought she had died. And now it's wonderful that she's come home, but there are no gifts for her."

I had been so wrapped up in watching my family unwrap their gifts that I had momentarily forgotten about last night's drama and the return of the lost child. It did seem too miraculous to be true, but I hoped it was, for Winnie's sake. I could tell it was going to take a lot more to convince Cedric.

"No, I'm afraid we have nothing for Charlotte," I said. "But I'm sure her parents will quickly make it up to her. In fact I'm sure her mother will spoil her."

Bridie nodded. "They did before she went away. Have you seen the nursery yet? There is a whole shelf of dolls. A whole shelf. And a doll's buggy and a cradle, and the rocking horse."

"I expect she'll have a good time reconnecting with them," I said. I looked up as Cedric came in. He was wearing a bright-red silk vest under his jacket, embroidered with gold thread—the new one we had collected at the station, I surmised.

"Well, here you all are," he said. "Winnie is taking her breakfast upstairs with the young lady, but I wanted to come down and wish my guests a merry Christmas."

"And a particularly merry one for you, I should imagine," Mrs. Sullivan said. "Your prayers finally answered."

"If she really is our daughter," he said. "I am not convinced myself."

"But she resembles your wife," I said. "And she knew about your mustache and the tiles on the old fireplace."

"Anyone could have told her those things."

"For what purpose?" I asked.

Cedric frowned. "We are a wealthy family. It is not beyond the realm of possibility that someone should scheme to put the girl in our care—a girl who would one day inherit everything."

He turned to Daniel. "Captain Sullivan, you are a detective. How would one go about verifying that she is our daughter? Or who she really is?"

"It wouldn't be easy," Daniel said. "The key would be the woman who looked after her all these years. Who called herself her mother. If we knew her identity, we could easily check if she had any criminal connections. We could visit old addresses and get reports on who visited her there."

"Would you do that for me?" Cedric asked. "I will pay you well for your time. But I have to know the truth. It's most important to me."

"Even if the truth is painful?" Daniel said. "You saw your wife's face last night. She wants to believe her daughter has come home to her. Do you want to take her away again?"

"Rather than admit a little cuckoo into our nest," he said. Then he forced himself into a brighter demeanor. "I hope the cook has laid on a splendid breakfast," he said. "But don't eat too much. There will be a feast later."

We went over to the sideboard and helped ourselves to eggs and bacon and apple fritters with hot maple syrup. Indeed a splendid breakfast.

"Has Santa Claus already been?" Cedric asked Liam, who was eating heartily again.

"He has," I said for my son. "There were stockings beside the beds this morning."

"He may well have left more things under the tree," Cedric said. "We'll have to see after breakfast. We have to wait for the others to come down. I haven't seen either aunt or my father-in-law this morning. Of course they have probably already eaten theirs hours ago. These New Englanders are early risers, even on Christmas Day. Up with the dawn to chop wood and milk the cows, uh?" And he laughed.

At that moment Mr. Carmichael came in. "It's a fine morning," he said. "I've already been out for a walk." And he wondered why we all laughed this time.

We finished our breakfast and I carried Liam through to the gallery, which was warm and inviting with a big fire blazing in the hearth. I set him down, and immediately he remembered the horse and cart. "Horsey?" he said, heading straight for the stairs.

"You stay here with Bridie. I'll go and get horsey," I said. I turned to Bridie. "Watch that he doesn't try to follow me up the stairs."

I went up and retrieved the horse and cart, as well as the two snow globes and the gifts for Daniel's mother, Aunt Florence, and the Van Aikens. I was carrying down this tottering pile when Winnie rushed up to me. "Let me help, Molly," she said. "That looks quite precarious and we don't want you to trip on the stairs on such a momentous day."

I stood while she relieved me of some of the packages. Her newly arrived daughter, Charlotte, stood behind her, smiling shyly at me.

"Won't this be fun," Winnie said, turning to beam at her daughter. "I only wish you'd arrived a few days earlier, Charlotte, darling. Then I could have bought a big pile of gifts for you. As it is I can only give you one or two things that were special to me, but after the holiday we'll have such a splendid time. We'll go into New York and order you lots of new outfits. You'll be the smartest young lady in Westchester County. And we'll have to think about schooling. . . . A tutor at the house or a school nearby? I'm not sending you away to a seminary like I was. Not so soon after I have you back again."

Her face was radiant and I was ashamed of my suspicion last night that somehow Winnie was not to be trusted with her daughter. I found myself wishing that Cedric would leave things alone. How could he not see that Charlotte was his daughter? To me she looked just like a younger version of Winnie, even down to the way she smiled. But if Daniel could prove that the girl was not their daughter, how would fragile Winnie handle a loss for a second time?

I took the packages from Winnie and placed them under the tree in the foyer, where there was already an impressive pile of packages, then I went through to the gallery and handed Liam his horse and cart. A bowl of nuts lay on one of the side tables and I gave him some to transport around. Aunt Florence had now joined us, sitting beside Daniel's mother. Conversation stopped as Winnie and Charlotte entered.

"Well, here they are," Aunt Florence said. "And don't you look well, my dear. A good night's sleep works wonders, doesn't it? And we'll soon have you fattened up."

As I examined Charlotte I decided that she didn't need to be fattened up. She was a healthy-looking girl, already with the hint of a woman's breasts curving the dress that she wore. I glanced across at Bridie and Ivy. Charlotte was about the same age as them, but she had blossomed into womanhood whereas they were both still little girls.

"We'll wait for Papa before we open gifts," Winnie said,

perching herself on the arm of the sofa next to Aunt Florence. "Where can he have gotten to?"

"He was with us in the breakfast room a few moments ago," I said.

"I think he went into his study." Aunt Florence looked up at the doorway.

"He spends too much time in that gloomy place," Winnie said. "Perhaps he won't be so willing to hide himself away now that his daughter has come home."

"Go and fetch him, Winnie," Aunt Florence said. "I'd do it but he sees me as a meddlesome old woman and would likely not come."

Winnie stood up. I could see her hesitating. Then she said. "Yes. Why not? He should be with his family on Christmas Day. And we're all dying to open our gifts."

"Why don't you girls go and sit on that sofa and get to know each other?" Aunt Florence suggested. "I'm so glad you have some companions of your own age, Charlotte dear. You won't remember me, but I am your mother's aunt."

"I think I do remember you," Charlotte said and she gave the older woman a warm smile.

"Is Great-Aunt Clara not down yet?" Aunt Florence asked. "Was she not at breakfast?"

"Perhaps she had a tray sent up," Mr. Carmichael said. "You know it takes her longer and longer to get ready in the mornings these days and she likes to look well turned out."

"Of course," Aunt Florence said. "But she'll want to join in the festivities and watch the opening of gifts. I'll go up and bring her down."

The three girls sat together, and I could hear them whispering shyly to each other.

"Show Grandmamma your horse and cart, Liam," Daniel's mother said, and we smiled as he galloped it over to her. We looked up as Winnie returned alone. "Cedric will be with us in a moment," she said. "He is putting the finishing touches to . . ."

Before she could finish the sentence we heard a loud "Ho ho ho." And in came Cedric, now wearing a white beard and red Santa Claus costume.

"Who has been good this year?" he asked. Liam scuttled over to me, alarmed by this strange new figure. "Up," he said.

"It's Santa Claus. The man who brings us presents," I said, taking him onto my knee.

"Let me see who I have gifts for in my sack outside the door," Cedric said. He disappeared into the foyer, then returned with a stack of packages. "Who do we have here? This one says Mrs. Sullivan. And this one Aunt Florence." He paused and looked around. "Where is Aunt Florence?"

"She was here a moment ago," Winnie said.

"She went up to fetch your great-aunt," Daniel's mother said.

"Well then, we'd better wait until they join us." Cedric put the packages down on the nearest table.

We looked up as we heard the brisk tap of Aunt Florence's shoes coming toward the gallery. The moment she came in we knew something was wrong.

"I'm sorry to tell you that Great-Aunt Clara passed away during the night," she said in a low voice.

Twenty

Oh, no. Poor Auntie." Winnie stood up. "How very sad. Should I go up to her? Is there anything we can do?"

"She's dead, Winnie," Cedric said. He threw back the red hood and pulled off the beard. "There's nothing anyone can do."

"You should call a doctor," Aunt Florence suggested. "A death certificate will need to be signed."

"We can't call him out on Christmas Day, Aunt," Cedric said. "That wouldn't be fair. Leave it until tomorrow, then I'll go into town and summon both doctor and undertaker. She'll be buried in the family plot of course."

There was a silence. It seemed only fitting.

"She led a long, happy life, didn't she?" Winnie's father said at last. "Almost ninety. In the bosom of her family. Surrounded by those she loved. You can't ask for more than that."

"Quite," Cedric said. He looked upset.

"But it's still sad that she had to depart this life on Christmas morning," Winnie said. "Now it seems wrong to celebrate at all. We should be in mourning. Should I go and change into black, do you think?"

"Absolutely not," Cedric said. "She would not want us to be sad on her behalf. She is liberated from an old and tired body. And she was beginning to lose her grip on reality, wasn't she?"

"She was," I agreed. "She thought I was Winnie's sister and Daniel was a college friend of Cedric's."

"I have to admit that I feel a trifle guilty," Cedric said, pacing the room and walking over to the window. We looked up at him. "I gave her that brandy last night. It might have been too much for her poor old heart."

"She did like her tipple, didn't she?" Mr. Carmichael agreed.

That phrase sent a jolt through me. Those were the words used about Harris the gardener, who had wound up dead in a snowbank. Was it possible that Aunt Clara's death was not an accident, but that someone in the house was worried that her seemingly harmless ramblings might stray to a forbidden topic? I looked around the room—pale and delicate Winnie, handsome Cedric, stout Aunt Florence, and the rather forbidding Mr. Carmichael. Did one of them have something that was better lying hidden? Or even the new arrival, whom Cedric was not willing to admit was his long-lost daughter? Perhaps I should take a look at the body, although I wasn't sure what I could find out. If she had been poisoned, I'd never know. Then I shook my head. That was the problem with having been a detective for so long. One sees crimes, murder, and intrigue where there are none.

But something else that had been said had struck a chord. The old lady had thought I was Winnie's sister and Daniel was Henry Wheaton, Cedric's college friend. Was there a connection between those two, a family scandal that she had reawoken? Could he have been the unsuitable young man with whom Winnie's sister ran off? Was that why he had not been seen for years? Because he was now persona non grata with the family?

I took this one step further: Could there also be a connection to Charlotte's disappearance? Had they indeed kidnapped the child as a sort of revenge? It seemed outlandish, but could that have been why Winnie's face had shown fear when it was suggested that Charlotte's memory would return to her? She didn't want her sister punished, however much she had made Winnie and Cedric suffer.

Oh, dear, I thought. *I do wish we had stayed home this Christmas and had never gotten ourselves mixed up in this mess.*

I forced myself to return to the present and to the conversation that was going on. "So who was the aunt who died?" Charlotte asked Winnie. "Was she your aunt, like Aunt Florence?"

"No, she was Papa's great-aunt," Winnie said. "She had lived in this house all her life, first with Cedric's grandfather, then his father, and then with us. Don't you remember her at all? She was very fond of you."

"I don't think so," Charlotte said.

"She was a frail-looking little old lady with wisps of white hair and a very sweet face. You used to sit at her feet on the bearskin rug and she would tell you stories—the goblins who lived in the forest, remember? You were scared of that one. And the princess who turned into a swan?"

Charlotte shook her head. "I wish I did remember, but I don't. "

"Don't worry about it, my darling. You are back and that's all that matters." Winnie took her hand and brought it to her lips.

"Presents!" Cedric exclaimed. "We were going to open presents when we were interrupted. Nothing is going to spoil our Christmas Day. So let's get on with it." He started handing around packages. I went to get ours.

"Youngest to oldest," Cedric said.

"That's you, Liam." Daniel held out a package to him and we all watched, laughing, as Liam ripped open the paper. It was from Daniel's mother, a knitted coat, hood, and leggings. Of course he didn't think much of it, but we thanked her profusely.

"Whose is next? Bridie, Ivy, or Charlotte?" I said, looking at the three girls, who now sat, faces bright with anticipation.

"I'm still twelve," Bridie said.

"I'm already thirteen," Charlotte said.

"So am I." Ivy hardly dared to say the words, looking down shyly. "But I'm not expecting any presents."

"Bridie it is, then," Cedric said and handed her a big package.

"That's also from me, my dear," Daniel's mother said.

She opened it, delicately and trying not to rip the paper. It was a new winter cape, the hood trimmed with white fur, and a white fur muff. "Oh, my." Bridie was at a loss for words. She looked up at Mrs. Sullivan. "It's beautiful," she said. "I never had anything so lovely in my life."

"Put it on," Winnie said.

Blushing bright red with so many eyes on her, Bridie put on the cape. She put the muff chain around her neck, tucked her hands into the fur, then twirled around to show us how the cape swirled out.

"Lovely. Just lovely," Daniel's mother said. "I want you to be the best-dressed young lady in New York." I realized immediately that we had not told her the news about Bridie's father and her return to Ireland. I was trying to think what to say to smooth over the moment when Bridie herself said, "Thank you very much. I shall treasure this forever."

I could have hugged her.

Aunt Florence was pleased with her handkerchiefs; Winnie and Cedric also seemed to be pleased with the chocolates and jigsaw puzzle.

"I didn't know how many people would be present, or what ages," I said, half apologizing, "so I wanted something we could all enjoy."

"And so we shall," Cedric said. "The weather outside does not look kind today. We shall clear off one of these tables and start on the puzzle as soon as the present giving is over."

He handed out gifts from them. A book of poetry for Bridie, a stuffed bear for Liam, and a silver condiment dish and spoon for Daniel and me. I suspected they had all come from the house, as Winnie would not have found them in the little township and would not have had time to order them from farther away. The dish was very beautiful and far grander than anything I had ever owned. Liam approved of the bear, immediately seating it in the cart and giving it a ride. I wondered if it had once belonged to Charlotte and if she now recognized it. She showed no signs of doing so.

The rest of the presents were a success. Daniel's mother loved the soft shawl we had given her. All very satisfactory. Winnie and Cedric had obviously exchanged gifts in private and there was no mention of those.

"And my darling, Little Lottie," Winnie said. "If only I'd known, I'd have showered you with gifts."

"Don't worry about it, Mama," Charlotte said. "Being here is the greatest gift I could ever have."

"We will make it up to you, I promise, but in the meantime here is a gift from my heart. It is something my mother gave to me and that I have treasured since her death." Charlotte took off the tissue paper and it was a tiny golden birdcage.

"Wind it up," Winnie said. Charlotte did and the bird inside began to sing and his head moved to and fro.

"Oh, it's lovely," Charlotte said. "I shall treasure it."

I glanced at Ivy. She was staring at it with such longing in her eyes. *Poor little thing*, I thought. *She has probably never seen such a lovely object.* "Oh," she said, and held out her hand as if she wanted to touch it. Charlotte picked it up rapidly.

I jumped to my feet. "But I have something for you other lovely young ladies," I said. I retrieved the snow globes and watched with satisfaction as the girls unwrapped them. They were both entranced. They looked down at the snow globes, then up at each other for confirmation that these were the best things in the universe.

"So now everyone is content," Cedric said. "That is how it should be."

I could not put aside the tension that gripped at my stomach, however much I wanted to enjoy the moment with my family. Bridie had taken off her cape and put it back in its box. She and Ivy were now kneeling together with their snow globes, telling each other stories about the girl in the red cape, lost in the woods.

"And there are wolves and goblins in the woods," Bridie said, warming to the topic. "And the goblins come and take her away."

Ivy pushed the snow globe away from her. "Don't say that," she said. "It's too frightening."

"All right." Bridie nodded amiably. "There was a woodcutter in a cottage and he came and rescued her and took her home with him."

"And his wife took her in as their own little girl, because they didn't have one." Ivy liked this ending. She looked across at Charlotte, who was sitting with her bird on her lap. "Would you like a turn with the snow globe, Charlotte?" I suspected this was because she was dying to have a turn with the bird in the cage.

"No, thank you," Charlotte said. "I'd rather just sit here and watch everything. It's so new, being among a lot of people. And in a big house like this."

"Of course it is, my darling," Winnie said. "You must be feeling quite overwhelmed."

"Charlotte, there are so many questions I'd like to ask you," Cedric said. "Can we go somewhere quiet, like my study?"

"Oh, not today, surely," Winnie interrupted. "Let the child enjoy Christmas with her family, for heaven's sake."

"I was not intending to interrogate her." Cedric frowned. "But I would dearly like to know more so that we can track down this mysterious woman who looked after her all these years."

"But you can't track her down," Charlotte burst out with more emotion than we had seen from her. "She's dead."

"What?" Cedric strode over to face the girl, then pulled up a chair opposite her. "She's dead, you say?"

"That's why I'm here," Charlotte said patiently. "She's already dead or she will be dead soon. She never told me who I was, you see. I don't think she knew for a long time. But a short while ago she sat me down and told me she had a confession to make. She said that she had figured out who I must be but she couldn't go to the authorities because then she might be put in prison or even hanged for kidnapping me. Then she said that the doctor had told her she didn't have long to live and she wanted to do the right thing for once. So she gave me money, took me to the train station, and told me how to find you."

"Remarkable," Cedric said. I couldn't tell from his voice whether he believed her or not. "So did you wait until she died before you came here?"

She shook her head. "She didn't want me to be there when she died. She told me I should go back to my family at Christmas, because it was important." She looked up suddenly and her eyes were full of tears. "You have to understand that I loved her. She was the only mother I ever knew. She was always kind to me. We had very little money but she made sure I was happy."

"What was her name, did you say?" Cedric was determined to press on.

"I think her name was Ada. Ada Smith—at least that's what she went by."

"Smith. How convenient," Cedric said. "Look, I'm glad this woman was good to you but you have to realize that she was a criminal, or at least connected with the criminal classes."

"Not necessarily, Cedric," Winnie said. "She might have just been a woman who needed a little extra money and who answered an advertisement to look after a child. She could have been told any kind of story—that the parents were sick, or she was an orphan."

"Highly unlikely." Cedric snapped out the words. "Whoever took the child could not risk that a random woman would put two and two together and realize who the child was and go to the police, or even resort to blackmail. No, whoever did this had to have some kind of hold over the woman to force her into the arrangement. Ada Smith."

"What did she look like, this lady?" Winnie asked. "Was she young? Was she pretty?"

Charlotte grinned. "No. She looked like any lady you'd see on the street. Not young. Not at all pretty like you. But nice. Kind."

"And what did she tell you your name was? What name did she call you?"

"She called me Amy," the girl said softly. "Amy Smith."

"How did she sound?" Cedric's tone was still aggressive. "Like an educated woman?"

Charlotte looked puzzled. "I don't know what an educated woman sounds like. She spoke to me kindly, gently. She held me at night when I had one of my nightmares. That's all I know."

"Why are you attacking the child like this?" Aunt Florence demanded. "One might think you weren't glad that your own daughter had come home to you, against all odds."

"Of course I'm glad," Cedric said. I could tell he was about to add "If she really is my daughter." But instead he said, "I just want to be sure. It's such a big surprise. A big shock. Overwhelming. It will take a while."

"I don't need to take a while," Winnie said. "I am thrilled and grateful she is here and I'm looking forward to our new life together. You should be too."

She gave Cedric a disparaging glance.

"Charlotte," Cedric addressed her directly. "You understand that I am not attacking you when I ask questions. Somebody stole you from our house when you were a little girl. Whoever did this was wrong. I don't know why they did it—presumably for money. But your mother has lived in grief all these years and these people have to be caught and punished. You say this Ada Smith has died. She sounds like a decent enough person, but I'd still like to go after the one who brought you to her. You understand that, don't you?"

She nodded. "Yes, Papa," she said quietly.

"Wouldn't you also like justice, Charlotte? Wouldn't you

like to see the man punished who took you away from this life, from your mother who loved you?"

"I suppose so," she admitted.

"Good. Then I'll need the addresses of the places where you lived," Cedric said, "so that we can start checking."

Charlotte shook her head. "I don't know addresses. We didn't often go out—at least my mother—I mean Ada Smith—went out, but I had to stay indoors."

"Did you never go to school?"

She shook her head. "No. I wanted to, but Mother—I mean Ada—taught me at home."

"So she was an educated woman?"

"Yes. She could read and write. And Uncle brought books for me."

"Uncle? A man came to visit you?"

She nodded. "Yes. He was very nice."

"What was his name? Uncle what?" Cedric demanded.

"I just called him Uncle," she said.

"Didn't Ada Smith call him by any name?"

Charlotte frowned, trying to remember. Then she shook her head. "I don't think so. Sometimes they talked together quietly, away from me."

"What did this uncle look like?" Winnie asked, her voice sharp now.

"He was an older man. Maybe forty or even fifty. His hair was gray at the sides."

"Was he tall or short? How did he look?" Winnie asked.

"Oh, very tall. Very handsome. And he wore such smart clothes. And he spoke kindly to me. Gently. He brought me presents sometimes and he gave us money."

"An older man." Cedric looked across at Winnie. "That's a turn-up for the books. I wonder who he could be and how he was involved in this?" He turned back to Charlotte. "So you never heard his name? Or where he lived?"

"In a big house. That's all I knew. Mother said he lived in a fine house," she said. "Anyway he stopped coming. Mother said he died, a couple of years ago. And then things were bad for us because there wasn't any money. And then she got very sick. . . ."

She looked as if she was about to burst into tears. Winnie rushed over to her side. "That's enough, Cedric. You can see you're upsetting her. She was obviously fond of these people and now they are dead."

"We only want to get to the truth, don't we, Winnie?" he said, looking directly at her. "However painful it may be."

Winnie returned his stare. "If you really want the whole truth, Cedric, then I suppose the answer is yes. However painful it may be."

Twenty-one

Aunt Florence rose from her seat on the sofa. "It's Christmas Day," she said. "A day of great joy to the world. Let us put this aside for a more appropriate occasion, shall we? Games. We must have games." She saw the jigsaw puzzle. "Nothing too rowdy, because we have a death in the family and poor Great-Aunt Clara is still lying upstairs." She picked up the box. "This is what we need to take our minds off unpleasant topics at this moment. Something we can all enjoy." She tipped the puzzle pieces out onto a table and started to turn them over. The girls came over to help her. The adults clustered around. Cedric motioned to Daniel to follow him. I was certainly not going to be left out of this. I stood up too and started to follow them. Cedric crossed the foyer, into the sitting room on the other side. When he saw that I had joined Daniel he raised an eyebrow, glanced at Daniel, went to say something but didn't. He closed the door behind us.

"What do you make of that, Sullivan?" he asked. "Have you ever come across a case like that before?"

"I can't say I have," Daniel said. "Her kidnappers sound like civilized people. A well-dressed older gentleman?"

"She's never been out into society," Cedric responded. "She told you herself that her life has been confined to a series of rooms. So how does she know what a well-dressed gentleman looks like? He might have been a criminal with a flashy kind of style that appealed to a young girl."

Daniel nodded. "Quite possibly. But the whole thing comes down to motive. Why did this gentleman pay some-one to keep her all these years? For what reason? Not money, because a ransom note was never delivered. Other than that, why would anyone take a child?"

"They were childless and wanted a child of their own?" I suggested.

"Surely that would be a deranged person," Daniel said, turning back to frown at me. "A normal childless couple ac-cepts their fate and gets on with life. A woman may volunteer to work with poor children and orphans. She may keep cats. But her thoughts don't turn to stealing another woman's child. No, I was thinking more along the lines of payback, revenge."

"Revenge?" Cedric sounded uncertain.

"Have you ever made an enemy who could possibly have done this to you?" Daniel asked.

"One does not always get along with everyone one meets," Cedric said. "But it would take more than a usual slight to make someone do something so heinous and final."

"Perhaps it didn't start out to be final," I said. "Perhaps on the spur of the moment someone took your child to pay you back for something. Then he saw notices in the news-papers, a reward offered, and realized the terrible consequences. If he confessed to taking the child, he might well be put into prison for life or even executed. And so he paid someone to keep the child safe and hidden away."

Cedric brushed back his hair as if it was annoying him. "Plausible, except that I cannot think of any person who might have hated me so thoroughly that he would have done such a deed. Our only hope is to find out more about this Ada Smith. Does what the girl said give you anything to go on?"

I noticed that he had called her "the girl" and not "Charlotte" or "my daughter." He still believed her to be an impostor. That was possible, I had to admit. Some cunning person could train a young actress and plant her on the grieving couple's doorstep on Christmas Eve, and there was a good chance she'd be accepted as their long-lost child. She'd live a good life and in time inherit and pass along some of the spoils to her trainers. Except that she looked like a younger version of Winnie. And she remembered the tiles on the fireplace, and that the rooms were different. She had definitely been in the house before.

"I could start by doing a search on the name. We can see if Ada Smith comes up in any criminal records. But I doubt it will. I suspect it is an assumed name. Smith, isn't that what anyone would call herself if she wished to remain anonymous?"

Daniel looked at Cedric and me for confirmation and we nodded.

"Apart from that there isn't much. If we could only have an address to go on," Daniel continued. "The name of a street. Then I could send men to ask questions of neighbors. There is usually someone nosy enough to have noticed a thing or two. The girl must have seen landmarks, even if they were small ones—the name of a tailor opposite, a church spire. She must have heard sounds—the bell of a trolley, the toot of a tugboat on a river, or the chiming of a particular clock. Maybe Molly or even Winnie could draw those facts out of her in a nonthreatening way."

"Good point," Cedric said.

A thought had just struck me. "You invited my friends to stop by for a Christmas toast sometime today," I said. "Miss Walcott is from Boston and well familiar with various neighborhoods. Perhaps she could begin to reminisce with Charlotte and see if she can pinpoint the location where they used to live."

"Excellent." Cedric nodded. "That would be most helpful. I wonder why Boston—was there perhaps a connection between the cities she lived in, or were cities chosen at random?"

"We must see if she can give us chronological names of places," Daniel said. "So far we only have Canada and then Boston. Were there others in between?"

"This is part of my problem in believing her," Cedric said. "Is it possible to live somewhere and not know where you are? Did she really never go out? Not to church? Not to the market? A whole life locked in a room?"

"It's possible," Daniel said. "If her captors were always in fear that she could be recognized."

"But she doesn't resemble the little girl of my memory," Cedric said. "I would not have picked her out from a crowd."

"The resemblance to your wife is quite striking to me," I said.

"Perhaps. I don't see it myself," he said. "I must admit I am keen to press ahead with this as soon as possible,

Sullivan. I don't want Winnie to become too fond of the girl only to find out she is an impostor. Frankly I don't know whether her heart can stand to be broken for a second time." He slammed one fist into the other. "No, by God, it must be nipped in the bud before too much damage is done."

Cedric glanced at me. "If we could have a word in private, Sullivan?" he said. "In my study?"

Obviously I was not wanted or needed. I knew that Daniel would share any information with me later so I said graciously, "I think I left my handkerchief upstairs. I'd better go and find it." And I made my exit.

The upstairs hallway was dark and silent. No servants in sight. I decided this was the perfect moment to go and look at Great-Aunt Clara. I wasn't sure what I hoped or expected to see, but I felt it had to be done. I had often prided myself on my Celtic sixth sense when something was wrong. It had been nagging at me ever since I arrived in this house that something was not as it seemed, that something was being concealed or distorted. This was a house of secrets.

I wasn't sure which room was Aunt Clara's. I had been told that Winnie and Cedric now had rooms at the far end of the other hallway. I tried to remember if I had passed a maid carrying a tray up to the great-aunt? There was nothing for it but a process of elimination. If I were spotted, I'd simply say that my mother-in-law had asked me to fetch something for her and I'd forgotten which one was her room. Perfectly safe. I moved from door to door, opening each carefully. The rooms beside ours were shrouded in dust sheets for the whole length of our hallway until I came to the one closest to the stairs, and that obviously belonged to Winnie's father. It was in all ways a masculine room and a plaid woolen dressing gown lay neatly across the bottom of the bed, along with large leather slippers beneath it. A faint smell of pipe tobacco hung in the air.

At the central landing I paused, glancing upward. Was it possible her room was up a second flight of stairs where the old nursery had been and where Ivy now slept? Surely they would not expect an aged woman to climb too many stairs?

I crossed the central landing as silently as I could and started on the other side. The room closest to me was clearly my mother-in-law's. I recognized the robe and slippers. The room next to hers had to belong to Aunt Florence. I should have guessed this neat and rather Spartan room belonged to her, even before I saw the book she had been reading on the bedside table.

Another empty room after that. Then I opened the next door. The heavy curtains were drawn and the room shrouded in darkness. Through the gloom I could make out the bed with the sheet covering what had to be the corpse. I tiptoed into the room, wondering what I would say if I was seen at this moment. I crossed the room and opened the curtains a fraction to give me a little light. Then, holding my breath, I pulled back the shroud. The old lady lay, eyes closed, and looking so peaceful that one could have sworn she was sleeping. *What was I doing here?* I asked myself. Of course she had died of natural causes. She was almost ninety and her heart had simply stopped. That's all there was to it. Her skin was so white it almost had a bluish tinge to it. I was about to re-cover her when on impulse I lifted one of her eyelids. I closed it instantly, and hastily pulled the sheet over her again. So my hunch had been right. I had noticed the small pink spots on her eyes. And I knew from past experience what those pink spots meant. It seemed that Great-Aunt Clara might have been suffocated.

I stood in the silence of the room, considering this. Aunt Clara's mind was wandering and she was starting to remember things that nobody else wanted talked about. And someone in the house had decided she had to be silenced before she said anything even more incriminating. But which of them: the forceful father? Cedric, whose family ancestry and name meant a lot to him? Aunt Florence, who might want to go to any lengths to protect Winnie, whom she had raised? Or Winnie herself? And then there was the newly arrived girl who claimed to be Charlotte, but who might be much older than she claimed. It was hard to believe it of any of them, but I thought I was experienced enough by now to recognize the signs of suffocation.

I looked around the room, noting the small armchair placed in the window. The table beside it. And a pen and inkwell on the table, but no notepaper, no diary. Great-Aunt Clara had sat in her window a lot and observed the world outside. I went over to the window and realized that the angle of the chair would not have given her a view of the driveway and the front of the house, but the side, where the outbuildings and the stables were situated, and obviously where there was more activity. But she would also have had a view across the lawns where the black line of the stream cut across the whiteness. Was it possible that she had witnessed the child being taken and someone in the house had been afraid she would blurt out the truth?

Twenty-two

I came downstairs without anyone having seen me. Back in the gallery the girls and Winnie were still working at the jigsaw puzzle. Aunt Florence stood behind them, offering suggestions. My mother-in-law was amusing Liam, helping him to prop his new bear into the horse and wagon. Mr. Carmichael sat in an armchair by the fire, watching the proceedings. It was hard to tell from his expression what he was feeling or what his true thoughts were on the girl who now claimed to be his granddaughter. I noticed he had hardly said a word all morning. *What was his place in this family home?* I wondered. A man of action, a businessman who had made a fortune. He still looked hale and hearty, in peak form, and yet he now had adopted the role of elderly relative in the home of his daughter and son-in-law. Was this the price he had been prepared to pay for moving into a higher level of society?

The girls had become frustrated and decided to leave the puzzle for a while. There was still no sign of Daniel or Cedric. I was dying of curiosity. I wanted to know what secrets Cedric might be sharing with Daniel in his study, and I was equally dying to share what I had discovered about Great-Aunt Clara. Coffee was wheeled in and an assortment of cookies with it. The younger members needed no urging to go and help themselves. Liam abandoned his horse and cart and sat chewing on a gingerbread man. It was all so ordinary, so civilized. I felt I was being stretched to the snapping point. I wanted to shout out, "Somebody tell me the truth, for God's sake!" Instead I took a seat beside Aunt Florence and forced myself to make small talk.

Daniel joined us and perched on the arm of my sofa as he drank a cup of coffee. I looked up at him and he smiled.

"Did you and Cedric have a nice chat?" I asked.

He shrugged. "We chatted. I wasn't able to be much help."

"But did you learn anything?"

"Not particularly."

I wondered if he was holding back from me, if Cedric had asked him to keep a piece of information to himself. I tried to wonder what that would be, but couldn't come up with anything. I was glad when Liam finally became whiny and frustrated when the bear fell out of the cart at the edge of the carpet. I swept him up and suggested that I should feed him his lunch and then put him down for a nap before we had our big meal.

"You can help me, Daniel," I added.

"What?" Mr. Carmichael roused himself. "You can't expect a man to help with child-rearing, surely?"

"My son is clearly overexcited in a strange house and his father always has a calming effect on him," I said.

Daniel shot me an interested look but didn't argue. He put down his coffee cup and followed me out of the room.

"What's this about?" he asked. "Calming effect, indeed."

"I wanted to get you out of the room," I said. "There's something I want you to see for yourself before it's too late."

I moved closer to him. "I want you to go up and take a look at Great-Aunt Clara. I just did and I think she might have been suffocated. There are pink spots on her eyes."

Daniel looked at me in horror. "Are you sure?"

"I'd like you to confirm it. Go and see for yourself."

Daniel shifted uncomfortably, looking around before he spoke. "This is a very serious charge, Molly. We are guests in someone's house. Why would anyone want to kill a harmless old woman? Not for her money, since she was living as a guest in the house of rich relatives. She was a spinster great-aunt. Of no value to anybody."

"I think it was because her mind was wandering. She was saying things out loud that the family had agreed to keep hidden, or at least one person wanted hidden. Or she may have seen something from her chair in the window. Either way she had become a threat."

Daniel glanced up the stairs now. "But I can't just barge into her room. What if I am seen?"

"Then you say that you were sent up by your mother to fetch something from her room and couldn't remember which one it was."

"You are devious, you know that?" He actually smiled. "But I'm glad to see the old Molly coming to the surface again."

"Oh, and there's one more thing you can do while you

are there," I said. "Close the drapes again. I think I left one half-open."

"All right," he said. "I'll do it while they are all occupied."

I went on with Liam through to the kitchen, where he enjoyed a good meal of mashed vegetables and gravy followed by stewed apples and custard. Then I carried him upstairs, and put him to bed. He was overstimulated and clingy, tossing around and saying, "No. No sleeping."

So I was more than glad when Bridie appeared. "I thought you might have trouble making him lie down," she said. "I wanted to put away my cape anyway. Isn't it beautiful?"

"It is," I agreed. "I'd have loved one like that when I was your age."

"I wonder if they wear such fancy things in Ireland." Her voice was wistful.

"No doubt in the cities they would. Perhaps your father will decide to settle you in Belfast or Dublin and you can show off your cape in church every Sunday."

"What if he buys a farm and we're out in the countryside?"

"There are still dances and socials even in the countryside," I said. Then I remembered. "Don't say anything about it to Mrs. Sullivan at the moment. Don't spoil her Christmas. She'll be so sad to lose you."

She nodded. "She does have Ivy now," she said.

"Ivy was supposed to be trained as a maid," I pointed out.

She had to smile at this. "Not for long," she said. "I was supposed to be a maid too and look how she took to me and made me into a proper family member. I bet she'll do the same for Ivy. And I'm glad. Ivy shouldn't be a servant. She's so nice and funny, she should have the chance to go to school like I have."

"That's not up to us to decide," I said. "At least she has been rescued from an orphanage and she has the prospect of a good life now. Captain Sullivan's mother will do her best for her, I'm sure."

Bridie nodded. She went to retrieve Liam, who had taken advantage of the conversation by getting off his bed and rolling his new ball around the floor. Bridie picked him up. He squirmed until she said, "What story are we going to have today? The three bears?"

"Free bears," he agreed.

I left them, Bridie's sweet voice making Liam lie peacefully, his eyes closing. As I came out I saw Daniel coming from the opposite hallway. He had a grim look on his face.

"You were right," he said to me.

I motioned him to one side, safely away from the staircase, where we couldn't be overheard.

"So what are we going to do?" I whispered.

"At the moment nothing. It would hardly be right to open a murder investigation on a frail old woman when we have nothing to go on. Cedric has asked me to go into town tomorrow and send a telegraph to my colleagues. I'm not even sure what I can ask them if more details of Charlotte's life do not emerge. They can try and identify Ada Smith, but I haven't much hope the name will lead us anywhere."

"You can ask about Henry Wheaton," I said.

Now he did look surprised. "Henry Wheaton?"

"The man for whom Aunt Clara mistook you. He was Cedric's best friend in his college days."

"But what could he have to do with any of this?"

"He used to visit often and then he stopped coming. Why? Was there a falling out? The cook didn't know of one."

"There are plenty of reasons college friends drift apart," Daniel said. "He could have taken a job in another part of the country."

"He could," I agreed. "But I have a strange sense about this whole business. I almost get the feeling that they don't want us to get to the truth. Or they know the truth and are keeping silent about it. Which could be a good motive for killing Great-Aunt Clara."

Daniel smiled at me. "All right, oh brilliant one. What is your deduction?"

"Winnie's sister," I said. "We know that she was cut off from the family when she ran off with an unsuitable man, right? So what if Henry Wheaton was that unsuitable man?"

"Hardly unsuitable if he went to college with Cedric," Daniel remarked.

"He could have been penniless, or liked his drink, or even come from a humble family. You can see what Winnie's father is like. Very ambitious. And I heard that he wanted her to marry an older man and she refused. Mr. Carmichael does not like to be crossed, that is obvious."

"So Winnie's sister ran off with Henry Wheaton. Now what?"

"Winnie's sister was angry when she saw Winnie happily married and rich, when she herself was struggling and poor. And perhaps she couldn't have a child and Winnie had a lovely little girl. So she came and snatched the child."

"And then gave it to Ada Smith to look after? Why would that be?"

I frowned. "Ada Smith was possibly Winnie's sister?"

Daniel shook his head. "She has been described as older and like any of the women you see on the street. And what about the man who came to visit and brought presents? He was a middle-aged man, therefore not Henry Wheaton."

I sighed. "I know it's complicated, but I sense that he is somehow involved in this. So you can ask about him when you telegraph to the police, can't you? And don't tell the Van Aikens that you are doing so. Let them just think you are checking into Ada Smith."

He nodded. "All right. If it makes you happy." He took my face into his hands. "It does my heart good to see that look of sadness gone from your eyes. I am glad you want to be involved again and solve this case. But I'd only remind you that sometimes you tend to be a little too keen. You take risks. You should remember—we should both remember—that someone in this house is capable of murder."

We looked up as Bridie came out of the bedroom.

"Liam is asleep," she said. She gave us a questioning look. "What are you doing? Did you come up to check that Liam was sleeping properly?"

I shook my head. "No, we just happened to meet up here and had some things that needed to be said in private. Captain Sullivan is going to be telegraphing the police to see if we can find the people who held Charlotte captive all these years."

"Poor Charlotte," she said. "I feel so sorry for her. All these years away from her family." Then she grinned. "But I suppose I've been away from my family for a long time and I've loved every minute. But then I wasn't shut away in a room."

"I suspect Mrs. Van Aiken will make it up to her." I put my arm around Bridie's shoulder, noticing how tall she was becoming.

When we returned to the company we found that sherry and cheese straws were being served. Then the gong sounded for luncheon, or rather the Christmas feast. We went through to a beautifully decorated dining room. There were poinsettias and freesias the whole length of the table and their sweet smell hung in the air. Candles had been lit on this dark and gloomy day and their light sparkled onto china and silver. We sat at our appointed places and the first course was served. It was a clear consommé with tiny herbed croutons in it. Then the goose was carried out, its skin brown and crisp, surrounded by baked apples. And not only the goose. On another platter was a chicken, and on the third a large ham. Clearly we were not going to starve. Cedric stood up to carve the goose, then the chicken, and we were served by a footman and a maid. A sweet potato casserole, red cabbage, and onion sauce were the accompaniments, and a crisp white Riesling was poured into our glasses. Toasts were drunk. Silence reigned as we attacked mounds of food. Then the plates were cleared and the pies were brought in: apple and pumpkin and pecan. And the thick Jersey cream from the farm along with homemade ice cream.

At last, stuffed and replete, we left the table. My mother-in-law and Aunt Florence declared they were going for a rest. I went up to check on Liam and found him awake and playing with his toys. Suddenly I felt a shiver of alarm at leaving him alone up here. What if he had managed to open the door, or, God forbid, the window? What if he had wandered out into the snow, just like Charlotte did, and had simply vanished from the face of the Earth? I resolved to ask Bridie to stay with him when he slept from now on, until we could go home—which could not be too soon for me.

Twenty-three

Everyone seemed to have revived by the time coffee and cake were served. Daniel produced his new camera and posed us for photographs outside the front door, where there was enough light. Darkness fell early and Cedric had the candles on the tree lit again, as well as candles in each of the windows. The flickering flames from the fire and the glowing candlelight created a festive scene. A steaming punch bowl was carried in, and there were dates and figs and nuts to eat. We were about to play some parlor games when Sid and Gus arrived.

"I hope you were sincere in your invitation to join you, Mr. Van Aiken," Sid said as he came forward to greet them. "But we simply had to come over to wish Molly and her family a merry Christmas and to see how Liam is enjoying his presents."

"Of course. Do come and join us." It was hard to tell from Cedric's tone whether he was pleased to see them or not.

"You are indeed most welcome." Winnie stood up and held out a hand. "I am Mrs. Van Aiken and we are delighted to have Captain and Mrs. Sullivan as our guests here. And also glad that you are able to celebrate with us, because a miracle has occurred and our daughter has come home."

Sid shot me an astonished look.

"Your daughter?" Gus asked. "The one who . . ." She couldn't finish it.

Winnie finished it for her. "Yes, the one who vanished. She appeared on our doorstep last night and here she is, my darling Charlotte, now all grown-up and come home to me."

Charlotte smiled shyly as Winnie stroked her hair.

"Isn't she lovely?" Winnie said. "I couldn't be more happy. Cedric, pour these ladies some punch."

We drank a toast.

"Ah-Sid?" Liam tugged at her skirt, wanting attention.

Sid knelt down beside him. "Did Santa Claus bring you some good things?" she asked.

"Horsey." He pointed to the horse and cart.

"Oh, and a bear. What's his name?"

"He doesn't have one yet," I said. "He was a gift from Mrs. Van Aiken."

"He's adorable. He has such a wise face. You should call him something wise, like Solomon," Sid said.

"Copernicus," Gus suggested.

"Gus, have a heart." I laughed. "He can barely say 'horsey.'"

"Bear." Liam held it up, giving us a disparaging look that it should be called anything different.

"And what did he think of our gift?" Sid asked.

"We didn't open gifts from you yet," I said. "We thought it would be more fun to let you watch Liam opening them when we were all back in New York. He has plenty to keep him occupied at the moment."

"Good idea," Gus said. She drew me aside. "I'm dying to see his face, however, because we bought him a wind-up bear from Germany and it turns somersaults."

I laughed with her. "He'll now wonder why this bear doesn't do the same," I replied. Then, realizing we were sufficiently apart from the others not to be overheard, I said, "There's something I want you to do for me."

"Yes?"

"Mr. Van Aiken isn't convinced that this girl is his daughter. She claims she was held in a room in Boston and only came here when the woman who was looking after her was dying and told her the truth about herself. You're from Boston. Could you find a way to chat with her and see if what she says rings true?"

Gus looked confused. "They think the girl might be an impostor?"

"He does. She doesn't. As you can see, she is ecstatic."

"So would it be wise to discover the truth, only to disappoint her again?"

"My thought exactly." I glanced around, but everyone seemed to be watching Liam while Sid did silly stunts with the bear and he laughed. "I have to think she is genuine. She does resemble Winnie."

"Yes. I think she does," Gus said. "So why is the husband so keen not to believe she's his long-lost child?"

"I don't know," I said. "There is a piece of this puzzle that I don't understand. Something that doesn't quite fit. I wish I knew what it was."

We rejoined the others and soon Sid and Gus were chatting with Aunt Florence and Daniel's mother while the girls sat on the rug with Liam, continuing the game with the bear. I joined Daniel and Mr. Carmichael over by the punch bowl, trying to half listen to the conversation by the fire.

"You lived in Boston, did you not, Miss Lind?" Gus asked. "What part of Boston?"

"Actually across the river in Cambridge," Aunt Florence replied. "Such a lively area with all the students. Do you know it well?"

"I'm from Boston. Beacon Hill," Gus said. "Boston Brahmin country, you know. I haven't been back for a while."

"You'll find it changed and not for the better," Aunt Florence said. "Some of the grand old houses have seen better days, and immigrants are pouring in by the thousand, from Italy and Poland and Russia—just like New York. The city is now no longer safe in all neighborhoods, although Cambridge still remains a pleasant spot."

"That is indeed a pity," Gus said. She looked down at the rug, where Charlotte had been listening in on the conversation. "And Charlotte, I'm told that you were in Boston too. What part of the city?"

"I'm afraid I can't tell you that," Charlotte said quietly. "I was hardly allowed out."

"You didn't go to school?"

"No. The lady taught me at home. There were books. I read a lot."

"You poor little thing. A virtual prisoner. Where did you go when you were allowed out?"

"Nowhere really. We walked down to the river a couple of times on hot days."

"The Charles River? Or Mystic River? Or Boston Harbor?"

Charlotte's face was red. "I'm afraid I don't know. When I was out I was not allowed to loiter or speak to anyone."

"So did it have wharves or a park beside it?"

"Oh, wharves, I think. Yes, there were ships tied up there."

"It was probably Boston Harbor then, my dear," Aunt Florence said. "Did you see any big ships?"

"Not really. In fact I don't remember much about the ships."

"What about smells?" I chimed in. "Smells are usually evocative, aren't they? I know in New York there was that coffee importer down by the docks and one could have located them blindfolded."

Charlotte wrinkled her nose. "The harbor smelled bad. That's why we didn't stay out long."

"So what was the street name where you lived?" Gus asked.

"I don't know."

"Now I'm really curious," Gus said, squatting down beside her. "Let me see if I can figure it out. So what sort of street was it? Wide, narrow? What kind of houses?"

"Just ordinary houses with fire escapes and basements. We were in the basement. It was damp and there were rats."

"How awful for you," Gus said. "You must have been so glad to escape at last."

"Yes." Charlotte nodded, but I thought she did not look

glad. Perhaps she was finding this new life overwhelming. Perhaps she had really become attached to the woman she called Mother and was missing her.

"And what kind of people lived around you?" Gus continued. "Americans? Immigrants?"

"Irish, I think. I never met any of them, but I heard people laughing and drinking and shouting sometimes."

"Did you hear anything else? Church bells? Tugboats on the river?"

"Oh, we were close to the water. There were seagulls and you could hear the boats," Charlotte agreed readily.

"Well, that's something to go on. Near the center of the city or out in one of the suburbs, do you think?"

"In the middle of the city, I'm sure."

"Could you see the gold dome of the State House?" Gus asked.

Charlotte shook her head. "I never saw a golden dome."

"A church spire?"

"We were in a basement. What I saw mostly was feet going past."

I moved away, not wanting the girl to feel she was being quizzed. Gus's face was friendly and she was apparently telling Charlotte about outings she made as a girl; picnics at the beach, walks across Boston Common. I watched Charlotte's face. It was wary, as if she was forcing herself to smile.

"We should be getting back," Sid said, interrupting Gus. "We must not overstay our welcome, and our friends will be missing us."

"You didn't walk across the grounds, did you?" Winnie asked.

"Oh, no. The Briarcliff Lodge has a sleigh at the disposal of the guests." Sid chuckled. "We didn't think wet feet would be appreciated, either by you or by us. It's waiting outside for us. Thank you again for your hospitality and merry Christmas to all. I'm glad it comes with such good news for your family."

"I'll see you to the front door," I said. "And we look forward to exchanging gifts with you when we all return home in a few days."

As we entered the foyer Gus moved closer to me. "I'm not sure that she really was in Boston," she said. "How did she not know the name of her street when she went out? Streets are well labeled in the city, and the wharves all have names and there are shops on every corner with their names on them. Anyway, I asked her about the railway station she left from, and then I threw in a couple of landmarks and asked if she spotted them and weren't they lovely. She agreed readily that she did, but neither would have been visible from the New York depot."

"Interesting," I said. "This gets more complicated by the second. Why say she was in Boston if she wasn't? Why not truthfully say where she really had been? It would have been equally hard to trace her in New York City."

"There had to be a good reason," Sid said. "Perhaps it was important to somebody that she had been in Boston. Something that would verify her credibility."

"Yes," I said. "Daniel is supposed to telegraph police headquarters tomorrow. Perhaps we'll learn more, although I doubt it."

"How old is she supposed to be?" Sid asked.

"Thirteen."

"She looks older than that. Compare her to Bridie and the little companion. They are still children."

"Girls mature at different rates," I said. "We can't go on that. And she did seem to remember things about the house. And she thought her father used to be clean-shaven and now he has a mustache. How would she know those things?"

Sid put a hand on my shoulder. "You're the detective," she said. "We leave it to you."

They put on their coats and scarves and went out to the waiting sleigh.

Liam was fed and went to bed willingly. I think he was exhausted from all the attention. We were summoned to a simple supper, which was a good thing after the afternoon's feast. Hot vegetable soup, cold chicken and ham, jellies and relishes, served with crusty bread. Nobody felt like eating much and I was glad when Cedric suggested that we should assemble around the Christmas tree and sing carols, since our session had been interrupted the night before. Chairs were brought into the foyer and the piano was wheeled into the doorway, where Cedric could see us. As we started singing all the good old favorites, I realized that we had not been to church; we had not really celebrated the true meaning of the feast at all. Maybe that was the Protestant way of doing things, but it was the first time in my life that I had not gone to mass on Christmas Day.

"We always sing some old European carols from my childhood," Cedric said. "Do you know 'Silent Night'?"

I'd heard Sid and Gus sing it and joined in the English version. Then Cedric and Winnie sang it in German. They both had good voices and it sounded so pure and evocative in the original language.

"And this is another old German carol, but we always sang it in Dutch," Cedric said, looking up from the piano. "My childhood favorite. It's a simple tune with simple words, so do join in." He started to sing "Kling Klokjee Klingelingeling." It had an appealing tune and we tried to sing along. Cedric alone sang the Dutch words of the verse, but as he came to the last line a little voice added, *"Kling klojkle kling,"* finishing off the phrase for him.

It was Ivy. Cedric stopped and stared at her. "How do you know that song?" he asked.

"I don't know." Ivy went bright red.

"Perhaps she learned it from the nuns at the orphanage," my mother-in-law said, smiling down at the embarrassed girl. "I know they have German nuns there. They probably sang it in German to the children."

"Yes," Ivy agreed. "That must have been it."

"Well, I'm glad I have someone to sing it with me," Cedric said. "Come and stand by the piano and you can join me."

"Oh, no, please. I don't remember. . . ." Ivy stammered.

"You're making the child uncomfortable, Cedric," Daniel's mother said. "Let's sing something we all know. How about 'We Wish You a Merry Christmas'? We can all sing along to that one."

And we did.

Twenty-four

The next morning Daniel took the carriage and went into Scarborough. He had been planning to telegraph police headquarters, but at the last moment he changed his mind. "I think I'll go in myself," he said. "There are certain parties at headquarters who would not exactly put themselves out for me. I, on the other hand, can get things done." He put a hand on my shoulder. "You'll be all right here?"

"Of course," I said. "It's a fine day. The children can play outside."

The grip on my shoulder tightened. "Just don't . . ." he started to say. I understood him all too well. Don't poke my nose where it wasn't wanted. And be careful.

"You won't forget to ask about Henry Wheaton, will you?" I said.

"I've not much else to go on," Daniel said. "Ada Smith, who lived in a basement room somewhere near the harbor in an Irish neighborhood. That could account for half of Boston. If only the girl could have given me the name of a particular store or business. Surely there were advertisements all over the wharf."

"You know, Gus was not sure she came from Boston. She asked her a few questions and apparently Charlotte didn't get the answers right."

"Interesting," he said. "But if she didn't really come from Boston then where the devil do we start looking? And why would the girl lie to us?"

"Because she doesn't want Ada Smith to be found and to get into trouble?" I suggested.

He frowned. "Maybe. Or maybe she's part of a criminal gang and is pulling the wool over everyone's eyes."

"One thing that might be useful: Ada Smith told Charlotte she was dying and she didn't want Charlotte to watch her die. It's quite possible she has checked herself into a hospital now that Charlotte has gone."

"Good point," Daniel said. "I'll definitely try the hospitals."

He kissed me and off he went. For us it was a somber morning. Cedric had telephoned the doctor, who came to write a death certificate for Great-Aunt Clara. I was tempted to share my suspicions with him, but he seemed to be an old friend of Cedric's family, and frankly I didn't see what could be achieved at this moment by suggesting that foul play might have been involved. The certificate was signed in two seconds and he left, commenting that she had lived a good, long life, and what better than to go up to heaven on the birthday of Our Lord.

He must have then dispatched the undertaker, who

arrived in a black draped carriage and carried out the body in a coffin. Funeral arrangements were discussed. I made sure I kept the children out of the way. The weather held up, allowing the younger generation to play outside, taking turns with skis and snowshoes and enjoying a snowball fight. By luncheon time the body had gone, and we enjoyed a good meal of leftover cold meats, chicken soup, and baked potatoes. I tried to observe the members of the household one by one to see if they were relieved that Aunt Clara's death certificate had been signed with no problems, but they were all talking about her freely, discussing her favorite hymns for the funeral and the fact that she would be buried in the family vault that had such a fine view across the Tappan Zee.

After the meal Liam fell asleep with no problem. The jigsaw puzzle was finished in the afternoon and we were playing charades before the evening meal when Daniel returned. He looked quite weary, as I suppose one does after a train ride to the city and back. He accepted a glass of whiskey from Cedric.

"Any luck?" Cedric asked.

"I have put in a request to the Boston police to follow up on Ada Smith, including women recently admitted to the hospitals. We'll have to wait and see. Oh, but I did find out something interesting. My wife suggested I look into Henry Wheaton."

"Why would she do that?" Cedric demanded.

"Because his name had come up, when your poor great-aunt confused him with me. And your aunt said he used to come to visit all the time and then he stopped. So I wondered if he could have anything at all to do with the kidnapping."

"Absolute rubbish," Cedric said angrily. "Henry Wheaton was just a friend from my youth. He and I grew apart years ago. Nothing to do with this at all."

"So did you find out anything about him?" Aunt Florence asked.

"I did," Daniel said. "He's dead. At least a man with the same name is dead."

I heard a little intake of breath from someone in the room.

"Do we know how he died?" Cedric asked, his voice taut now.

Daniel nodded. "His body was found in the Hudson, downstream from here after the ice melt in the spring. Naturally his face was quite unrecognizable, because presumably he'd been in the water for quite a while, but they were able to identify him by his tailor's label in his suit jacket and the laundry mark on his shirt."

"How long ago was this?" Aunt Florence asked.

"It was the spring of 1897," Daniel said. "Rather significant, don't you think?"

"I'm sure there are several fellows with the same name," Cedric said. "Not necessarily my old pal. As I remember it he was going back to Buffalo, where he came from. We could check. . . ."

I had been watching faces and I saw that Winnie had turned quite pale. Now she was looking down at her hands in her lap, her fingers plucking nervously at the silk.

Aunt Florence sighed. "Well, it looks as if we'll never

come to the truth now. And I suppose we should ask ourselves why we should try. We have our dear girl back with us. Do we need to cause ourselves more grief by digging up unpleasant memories?"

"You may be right, Aunt Florence," Cedric said. "And I don't see how my poor pal Henry winding up in the Hudson could have anything at all to do with this."

"I could think of several reasons," I said. Heads turned sharply toward me. I saw Daniel frown at me, but I continued, "Perhaps your friend happened to stumble upon the kidnappers. He recognized your daughter. He tried to intervene and save her and was knocked out and thrown into the frigid water for his bravery."

"Yes," Cedric said. "That would be the way Henry behaved. He would have risked his life for Charlotte."

"We should drink a toast to honor his memory," Aunt Florence said.

Cedric filled glasses with sherry or whiskey. He raised his. "To my good friend Henry. May he rest in peace."

We drank, silently. Then the dinner gong roused us from the somber mood. We went in to a magnificent rib roast of beef with all the trimmings, and by the time we reassembled around the fire we were chatting pleasantly again, the gloom of Daniel's news forgotten. Or was it? I noticed that Winnie hardly said a word. The fire burned low. We went up to bed.

"You seem to have hit the nail on the head somehow with Henry Wheaton," Daniel commented as he unhooked the back of my dress for me. "The news of his death clearly rattled them. And then your explanation of his sacrifice and act of bravery was well accepted."

"Too well," I said. "I think at least some of them know more than they want to share."

"You still think that this Henry fellow took the child?"

"Had something to do with her kidnapping," I said. "And not as the hero."

"It's unlikely we'll ever find out now," Daniel said. "I wonder if Cedric still wants me to dig deeper, to find the truth about Ada Smith and proof that this girl is his daughter?"

"We'll have to see. I don't know about you, but I would like to go home as soon as possible. I've found this whole experience unsettling." I put on my robe and went down the hall to the bathroom. As I approached the landing I heard footsteps coming up the stairs. I didn't want to be seen in my bathrobe so I shrank back into the shadow between lamps. I saw Winnie come up the stairs and turn toward her side of the house, then Cedric appeared behind her and grabbed her arm.

"You say anything and you know what can happen, don't you?" he whispered to her. "I can easily do it and I will, if necessary."

Winnie shook her arm free. "You caused all of this," she said. "It's about time you took your share of the blame."

Then she stalked ahead of him down the hall and into darkness.

Twenty-five

The next morning we awoke to dreadful weather. The snow had turned to driving sleet, washing away much of the white covering from the gardens and peppering the windows. I had secretly been hoping that we could leave and go home, but there was no way I'd want to travel in this weather. And I realized I did want to get to the truth. The detective in me could not just leave things as they were and walk away.

I washed and dressed Liam and went down to breakfast. No sign of Winnie or Cedric, but Daniel's mother and Aunt Florence were eating a hearty meal, chattering away and enjoying each other's company. Ivy sat at the other end of the table next to Charlotte, neither of them talking. Bridie went immediately to join them.

"I'm afraid we're all stuck indoors today," I said. "I wonder if there are any board games or drawing materials to keep you occupied?"

"There were games and things in the old nursery," Bridie said.

"Have you been there yet, Charlotte?" I asked. "Have you seen your old nursery?"

"Yes. Mother showed me yesterday. I'm afraid I didn't remember a thing."

"You were probably so shocked and terrified by what happened to you that you blotted everything from your memory," I said.

"Can we go up there and play?" Bridie asked. "Liam loved riding the horse."

"We should probably ask Mrs. Van Aiken first," I said. "She might want to keep everything as it was. Go and amuse yourselves in the big room by the fire first and we'll wait until Mrs. Van Aiken comes down."

We finished breakfast. Liam was settled on the rug with his horse and cart and the bear, and the girls set up various shops selling nuts for him to deliver in his cart. I smiled as I watched them all engrossed in the game, the big ones enjoying it as much as my two-year-old. *He needs brothers and sisters to play with,* I thought. *Maybe next year I'll be lucky and we'll have another child.*

When the clock struck ten and there was no sign of Winnie a shiver of alarm went through me. I couldn't help thinking of two days ago when Great-Aunt Clara hadn't appeared and Aunt Florence went up to find she had died. And Cedric's threatening behavior from the night before worried me. I had to go up and see for myself. I left the children and crept up the stairs. I turned left instead of right and made my way down the hall to the very end. I tapped on the door, suddenly realizing that I'd feel really foolish if it opened. What could I say to Winnie? That I wanted to know if she was all right? She had a houseful of servants she could summon if she wanted anything, as well as an efficient aunt.

There was no sound. I opened the door cautiously. The room was empty. The bed was made as if it hadn't been slept in. Was it possible that Winnie had run away? Surely not when her beloved daughter had just been found. Or had she been taken away? A flash of conversation came back to me: Cedric had hinted that his wife might be losing her sanity. I knew all too well how easy it was to have a woman committed to an insane asylum on the word of a husband. But surely Cedric would not do something like that, especially not now with guests in his house?

As I came out of the room I met a maid carrying a jug of water.

"Have you seen your mistress this morning?" I asked.

She nodded shyly. "Yes, ma'am. I brought up her breakfast, a while ago. She didn't feel like coming down. She had one of her headaches. So I took her up a boiled egg and some coffee. And when I came up to get the dirty dishes she was already up and dressed. So I made the bed."

I was going to go back downstairs to see whether Winnie might be in one of the other rooms, the library maybe, or writing letters in a quiet sitting room, but on the landing I paused. At that moment Cedric passed below me. I saw him enter the gallery, asking in jovial tones, "And how is everyone this morning? No snowball fights today, I'm afraid."

This somewhat reassured me and I realized that I had not yet seen the famous nursery. I went up one more flight.

The first door was to a simple bedroom where Ivy had been sleeping. I saw her snow globe on the bedside table and smiled at the joy such a small thing had given her. Then I went on down the hall until I opened a door and stepped into a big, beautiful nursery. It had tall windows and on a fine day the sun must have flooded the room with light. The rocking horse was indeed magnificent and had pride of place in the window. There was a child-sized table and chairs painted white with flowers on them. There was a doll buggy and a wooden doll bed, and a row of china dolls and stuffed animals sat on a daybed. There were books on shelves and even a child's piano. Everything a little girl could dream of. My eyes scanned the room and then I started, almost letting out a cry. Winnie stood in the far corner, holding a big rag doll in her arms, tears running down her cheeks.

I went over to her. "Winnie, my dear. What is wrong?" I asked gently.

She shook her head, unable to talk. "It's nothing," she said when she could compose herself.

"Of course it's more than nothing." I touched her arm gently. "Would it help to tell me about it? Is there anything I can do?"

She shook her head. "I can't tell you. I can't tell anyone. I made a promise."

My grip on her arm tightened. "Winnie, do you think you might be in danger?"

She looked up sharply. "Because you might feel safer if somebody else knew what is troubling you. And my husband is a respected police captain."

She shook her head again. "I can't."

"It's not my business to pry," I said, "but I could tell you were upset by Henry Wheaton's death."

"Yes," she said. "I was. I am."

"I thought he might be somehow involved in Charlotte's disappearance," I said. "In fact I suspect that he and your sister . . ."

"My sister?" she stared at me incredulously. "What has my sister to do with it? My sister was gone long before I married."

I saw then that I might have gotten it wrong. I led her across the room and seated her on one of the small chairs; then I knelt on the carpet beside her. "You were in love with Henry Wheaton?"

"Yes," she said.

"But you think he took your child? He kidnapped Charlotte?"

"I know he did," she said.

"You know he took her?" It was my turn to sound incredulous.

She nodded. "I took her out to him. He was waiting for her in the garden and I sent her to him."

"Why?" I had not imagined this.

"Because he was her father," she said.

"Henry Wheaton was Charlotte's father?"

She nodded. "I suppose I can tell you the truth. Nothing matters now. I kept quiet all these years because I feared for his life when all this time he was dead." Tears rolled down her cheeks again.

"You feared for his life?"

She nodded. "Cedric told me that if I ever tried to contact Henry, he'd accuse him of being the kidnapper and he'd make sure that Henry was hanged."

"But why did you give your child to Henry? It's clear that you adored her."

"Two reasons," she said. "One was that I was beginning to fear for her safety, and another that I wanted to be with him. I wanted us to be together and happy."

"So your husband knew that he wasn't the child's father?" I asked.

She gave a brittle laugh. "It was his idea. He arranged the whole thing." She paused, took a deep breath, and went on, "I suppose I should explain. I was eighteen when I married Cedric. I had no mother. I had been sent to the seminary because my father disliked my aunt's influence on us. So I knew nothing of the world, or of men. My father and Cedric arranged the match between them. I didn't object. He was a handsome man with a fine estate and a position in society. It was only after I married him that I discovered he was . . . that he couldn't . . ." Her face flushed bright red and she couldn't say the words.

"That he could not perform the usual husband's duties?" I finished for her.

She nodded. "I was so naïve at that time. I didn't even know what a man and a woman are supposed to do together, so it didn't worry me to start with."

"But then?"

"Cedric wanted a son," she said. "His family name was very important to him. He wanted an heir to carry on the line."

I said nothing, but waited for her to continue. I could tell how hard she was finding it. She was staring down at her hands. Not meeting my gaze.

"So he asked his best friend to take his place?" I said for her.

She nodded. "He asked Henry to provide the heir. Henry didn't want to. Of course he didn't. He was a decent man. But Cedric begged him and I wasn't against it. I had little affection from my husband. I wanted a child. I did not want to spend my days alone in a completely loveless home."

"So you made love with Henry?"

She nodded. "It was wonderful. I had no idea what I'd been missing. He was so gentle. So tender . . . And I did get pregnant, but I had a girl. Cedric was furious. He refused to allow a second time, because I think he could tell that Henry and I were falling in love. Henry was warm and funny and we joked together. He was everything that Cedric wasn't. He came often to see his daughter. Cedric couldn't really stop him, but he became horribly jealous. Then he started to resent Charlotte. She had some unexplained falls and I began to think that her life might be in danger." She paused again, staring at the pattern on the carpet as if she was speaking to herself. "Henry and I had talked for some time about running away together, taking Charlotte to safety. We set up the perfect plan. The servants' Christmas party. Charlotte's nursemaid would be there with all the other servants. I'd slip out of the ballroom, get her dressed, and send her out to Henry, who would be waiting at the creek. I'd tell her it was a special

Christmas game. He'd take her into town on snowshoes down the frozen creek. Then later that evening I'd complain of a headache, put on my own coat, and follow him."

"You were going to walk into town?"

She shook her head. "I'd been practicing on skis. It's all downhill. It wouldn't take long at all. Then we were going to take the train to Canada and start a new life there."

"So what happened?" I asked.

"When I went upstairs to change, Cedric appeared behind me and locked the bedroom door. He had been spying, reading my letters, and he knew all along what we'd been planning. He kept me a prisoner in that room, never letting me out of his sight for a second. He told me he'd name Henry as the kidnapper if I tried to contact him, and I knew what happened to kidnappers. It was the hangman's noose."

"So you never found out what happened to your child?"

"Never. We had a backup plan of a place to meet if by any chance I couldn't get away that evening. But I knew he couldn't wait there indefinitely, not after the newspapers had reported her missing. I thought he must have taken her to Canada and would be waiting for me to join them. Of course we had to alert people and have the grounds searched, knowing she wouldn't be found. And all the time I expected him to find a way to contact me. When he didn't, I had to face the truth: He thought I had changed my mind and didn't want to join him. I had elected to stay with my husband. All this time I pictured him having a lovely life with our daughter, missing me, but still happy. How wrong can you be?"

"It seems clear now that somebody intercepted them quite near here," I said. "Someone took the little girl and killed Henry."

"Yes," she said. "That is what I think now."

"Do you suspect your husband?" I asked.

"I'm not sure I would believe him capable of such an atrocity," she said. "But he was here, with me. He never left me alone for a minute for several days after Charlotte disappeared."

Cedric was clever, I thought. *He could have paid someone else.* And I thought of Harris the gardener, whose body wound up in a snowdrift. Had he been hired to kill Henry, to take Charlotte, and deliver her to someone? In which case, had Cedric known who Ada Smith was all this time?

"At least I have my daughter back now," she said. "That is something to be grateful for."

"It seems to me that your husband is not overjoyed to see Charlotte back here."

"Why would he be? He never wanted a girl and her presence will remind him, every single day, of what happened."

"Perhaps you should take her away," I suggested.

"Where could I go? I have nowhere, no money." Her expression was bleak.

"I understood that your family was rich."

"Yes, we are rich, and my father has been more than generous to us since my marriage. But not one penny is in my name. It is in Cedric's bank account."

"Could you not talk to your father? If you told him the truth about Cedric and Charlotte's birth, would he not want to help you?"

She gave a derisive snort. "I rather suspect that my father knew quite well about Cedric's impediment when we married. He was still furious that his older daughter had disgraced him and desperate to make a good match for me. He might even have been told about Henry. No, I don't think you'd find that my father was on my side."

I wanted desperately to do something for her. I had felt uneasy since I entered this house. More than uneasy, actually. A growing feeling of danger. Now I was sure of it. There was danger lurking in this house. I wondered if I should tell her that we suspected her great-aunt had been suffocated. Was it Cedric, or her father? I suspected the former, but I realized we could never prove it. I would have to enlist Daniel's help. We were still sitting together as I pondered these things when we heard the sound of young voices, and Charlotte, Bridie, and Ivy burst into the room. Bridie was carrying Liam on her hip. He wriggled to get down as soon as he saw the horse.

"Horsey," he said. "Ride horsey."

"Just a minute, girls," I said, scrambling to my feet.

They reacted as I had done at finding someone in what they had taken for an empty room, backing away, clearly embarrassed.

"Oh, I'm sorry, Mama," Charlotte said. "We didn't think anyone would be here and Bridie and Ivy wanted to explore my old nursery with me."

"Of course, my darling." Winnie stood up, stiffly. "Do you remember it? You used to love your dolls and your horse." She went over to it and ran her hand through its mane as if it was alive. "You used to say it was a flying horse and Uncle Henry called it Pegasus. But you couldn't say the word and you called it Pegadus."

Bridie looked first at Ivy, then at me. "That's what Ivy called it," she said. "I teased her about it and Molly said it wasn't nice because Ivy had been raised in an orphanage and she hadn't read many books."

I was staring at Ivy as if seeing her for the first time. So many things that we had taken as clumsy or odd now began to make sense to me. She had walked into a wall where there had once been a door. She had mistaken where the Van Aikens' bedroom was, because it used to be where we were now sleeping. She had known the last words of the Dutch carol. And she had remembered touching the Christmas tree through the bars of the stair rail, not over it, because that was how a three-year-old would have reached out to the tree. So many strange little incidents. Too many to be purely coincidental.

"Ivy," I said. "Were you in the orphanage your whole life?"

"No, ma'am," she said. "The nuns told me my father dropped me off there when I was little because my mother had died and he couldn't take care of me anymore."

"Do you remember your father?"

She shook her head. "I don't remember anything, except the bird. I do remember the bird."

"Which bird is that?" Winnie asked, staring at her intently.

"The one in the golden cage that you gave Charlotte," she said. "I remember that my mother used to have one just like it and I'd sit on her lap and she'd wind it up for me.

And we'd sing a song about 'little bird, little bird, what a merry song you sing . . .'" She started to sing. Her voice was high and clear and beautiful. Then she realized we were watching her and froze into embarrassed silence.

"'Soaring high, through the sky, on your tiny wing,'" Winnie finished for her.

The silence in the room was so thick it was overpowering.

"Was Ivy always your name?" Winnie asked her.

"No, that was what the nuns named me. I told you we were all named after flowers of some sort."

"Do you remember your name before you went to the orphanage?"

"Not my real name. Only a baby name. I remember I was called Tottie."

Winnie gave a gasp. "Charlotte used to get her letters mixed up. We called her Lottie, but she called herself Tottie. But how can it be? Is it possible that you are my daughter?"

"Your daughter?" Ivy stared at her. She shook her head. "No. No. It's not possible. But the moment I came into this house I felt I'd been here before, and you look like the lady in my dreams. But that can't be right, because Charlotte is your daughter."

We turned to stare at Charlotte, who was looking terrified.

"Is that right?" Winnie asked her. "If Ivy is my real daughter, then who are you?"

Charlotte put her hand up to her mouth and fled from the room.

Twenty-six

Winnie and Ivy continued to stare at each other.

"I think I knew it right away," Winnie said. She turned to Ivy and put out a tentative hand to stroke her hair. "The moment I saw you I remember thinking that if my daughter had grown up, she'd look just like you. And I never had that feeling with Charlotte—or whoever she is. Oh God. Cedric was right this time. She is an impostor." She held out her hands. "But you—look at you. My little girl. My own precious Tottie."

"Mama?" Ivy said in a quivering voice. "Is it really true?" And she flung herself into Winnie's embrace. They stood, locked together while tears streamed down both their cheeks.

Then Winnie seemed to come to her senses. "You must find your husband, Molly. The girl must be arrested. Clearly she's part of some criminal gang, sent to steal our money. We'd better find her before she escapes."

She took Ivy by the hand and led her out of the room.

I followed. I was curious to know who the girl was, but I couldn't picture her as a budding criminal. She was awfully young, for one thing. And she seemed so vulnerable. Had she, as Cedric suspected, been schooled and placed here by a gang? In which case, was it the same gang that originally kidnapped little Charlotte and killed Henry Wheaton? There was so much still to be found out. . . .

We went downstairs and found a surprising scene. The girl we had called Charlotte was now in the gallery beside the fire, sitting on the sofa beside Aunt Florence, who held her in an embrace while her body shook with sobs.

Aunt Florence looked up at us. "What is this all about, Winnie? You've suddenly rejected this poor girl and decided she isn't your daughter after all? How could you do that?"

"Because I've found my real daughter. She was here, under our noses, all the time." She took Ivy by the hand.

"Ivy?" Mrs. Sullivan exclaimed. "Ivy is your daughter? What makes you come to that conclusion?"

"I think I was the one who came to the conclusion," I confessed. "I've wondered about Ivy for some time. Remember when she ran into the wall and was so embarrassed? She was never clumsy at your house. And do you know why? There used to be a door there. And she knew the ending to the Dutch carol."

"And she called the horse Pegadus, which was what my little girl used to call it. And she said her baby name used to be Tottie. My daughter always called herself that, because she couldn't say Lottie," Winnie said. "What more proof do you need?"

"Well, I never," Mrs. Sullivan said. "Then who is this child?"

The girl they had called Charlotte was still sobbing in Aunt Florence's arms. "They'll send me away and I'll have nowhere to go," she gasped between sobs. "Please don't let them send me away."

"What is this, Aunt?" Winnie demanded. "You were party to this deception? You knew all along that this wasn't my long-lost daughter? How could you?"

Aunt Florence looked up. "I only did it for the best, Winnie. I wanted to make everything right."

"Make everything right, by sending an impostor into my home? How could that possibly make everything right? Who is this girl?"

The girl forced herself to turn around and face Winnie. She took a deep breath, swallowing back tears. "Aunt Florence suggested that I come here and say I was your daughter because you were so sad, and because my mother was dying and I'd have nobody to take care of me."

"Your mother? You mean Ada Smith?"

She shook her head. "That was just a name she used. Her real name was Lizzie Carmichael."

Winnie stared at her. "You're Lizzie's daughter? My sister's child?"

The girl nodded. "My name really is Amy."

"And my sister really is dying?"

Amy nodded again. "The doctor said she only had a few weeks at the most. She has a tumor on her brain."

It was Winnie's turn to put her hand up to her mouth. "My poor Lizzie, dying. I've wondered about her all these years. I've hoped she's been happy."

"Not very happy," Aunt Florence said. "She's had a difficult life. It's almost impossible to raise an illegitimate child alone."

"But she ran off with a young man," Winnie said. "We assumed she had married him."

"That's what you were told by your father to save his face, to save the family reputation," Aunt Florence said. "In reality she went to him and told him she was with child. He told her it was up to the man who had done this to her to take care of her from now on. She was no longer his daughter. Then he showed her the door."

"But the man did not do the right thing and marry her?" Winnie asked in a trembling voice.

"The man could not do the right thing. He was already married, with a family."

"Oh. The older uncle who used to visit you," Winnie said. "Now I see." The girl nodded.

"Did you know he was your father?"

The girl nodded again. "I guessed it. My mother never actually admitted it, but he was always so nice to me. And the way he looked at me—as if he really cared. I think he loved us both."

"He paid Lizzie's rent and supported them while he was alive," Aunt Florence said. "Then he died of a heart attack two years ago and there was no more support coming. I did what I could, but my own funds are limited. And then this diagnosis for dear Lizzie. I saw this as the only hope for Amy. I realized how much she bore the family resemblance and I prayed you'd accept her as your daughter. It would have worked perfectly if Mrs. Sullivan had not rescued Ivy from the orphanage."

Ivy tugged at her mother's sleeve. "Do we have to throw out Amy because of me? I could go back to working for Mrs. Sullivan if you like. She's really nice."

Winnie looked at her in amazement. "What a sweet child you are. You always were, of course. You had the kindest nature. You'd rescue a butterfly with a broken wing. Even an ant." She smiled. "Of course we can't throw your cousin out. There is plenty of room for her here, and she'll be a companion for you in your lessons. We'll hire a good governess. . . ."

"What about Mr. Van Aiken?" Amy asked. "He won't want me here. He'll be furious that I tried to trick him. He may not even believe that Ivy is his daughter."

Winnie took a deep breath. "Nothing is going to separate me from my daughter a second time. I will remind him that the money to run this establishment comes from my family. And I wish to have my family around me. Which includes my sister's child." She stopped, looking at Aunt Florence. "And my poor sister. Is there anything that can be done for her at this late stage?"

"I don't think there is much anyone can do," Aunt Florence said.

"We'll go and find her immediately," Winnie said, sticking her chin out resolutely. "At least we can bring her here to die in comfort and peace. It's the very least we can do. Does she live in Boston?"

Amy shook her head. "No, we have been living in New York all this time. In Brooklyn, actually. Aunt Florence suggested I claim I was from Boston because she didn't want anyone searching for us in New York."

"I'm afraid you failed that test," I said. "My friends were convinced you had never been to Boston."

"I know. It was horrible," Amy said. "I was so embarrassed."

"But that makes it easier. We can send the carriage down to Brooklyn for her," Winnie said.

"Your father will probably not allow her into the house," Aunt Florence pointed out.

Winnie tossed her head defiantly. "It's my house, not his. He has caused enough grief."

I almost applauded. Winnie's recovery of her daughter had given her the backbone she had lacked all these years. I realized that she had lived in fear of Henry Wheaton being arrested and hanged for kidnapping. Now she had nothing more to fear.

"Will you go and tell Cedric?" Aunt Florence asked.

"No. Let's bring everyone together in this room. I'd rather have you here for support, just in case." She rang for a servant. "Go and find Mr. Van Aiken and Mr. Carmichael and Captain Sullivan and tell them they are all wanted in the gallery immediately," she said.

"Yes, ma'am." The maid looked at her in wonder, hearing the new authority in her voice. We didn't have to wait long. Daniel entered first, then Winnie's father.

"What's this about, Winnie?" he asked.

"Please take a seat. All will be made clear," she said.

"Is this a parlor game?" he asked.

"No game. Deadly serious," she said, then held up her hand as he went to ask more questions.

A silence fell over the group. Then we heard the brisk

tap-tap of Cedric's shoes. He entered the room, giving us a questioning look.

"Has something happened? You've found out more information for us, Sullivan?"

"Not Captain Sullivan," Winnie said. "I finally have proof for you that we have found our daughter."

"Proof? What sort of proof? Can a child change her coloring? I don't think so."

"I don't think so either," Winnie said. "That was what made me slightly hesitant before. But you see, she hasn't changed a bit. I think I recognized her the moment she came into our house, but I wouldn't let myself admit it. Come over here to me, darling."

Cedric stared as Ivy took her mother's hand.

"Are you quite mad?" he demanded. "Are you so desperate for your lost child that you are now embracing a servant girl? An orphanage brat?"

"She's my daughter, Cedric. I can give you plenty of irrefutable proof if you like, but I think you have to admit that she looks exactly as Lottie would look today. And she remembered her name. She said she used to be Tottie."

"Good God." Cedric stared at her. "Yes, I suppose she does have the look." He walked around the girl, then took her face in his hands. "The eyes. She has the eyes. Then who is this? Didn't I suspect she was an impostor?"

Aunt Florence tightened her grip around Amy. "This is Winnie's niece, Amy. Lizzie's child. Her mother is dying. I brought her here because I thought it might be a solution that made everything right for both parties. Winnie was still grieving for her child and Lizzie was desperate that her daughter be taken care of after her death."

"There was no husband?" Cedric asked sharply.

"Amy's father could never marry her mother. He was already married—as I think you always knew, Jacob." She turned and glared at Winnie's father. "You drove your daughter out to ruin and shame and you didn't care what happened to her."

"I told her she had made her own bed and now she must lie in it," Mr. Carmichael said gruffly.

"Fortunately the man took care of them until he died. After that they would have starved if I hadn't helped out."

"You see yourself as the great do-gooder, don't you?" Mr. Carmichael said angrily. "Interfering in other people's lives because you don't have a life of your own."

"I think I have a remarkably good life," Aunt Florence said. "I have enough money to live on. I have plenty of friends. I only came here because I wanted to make sure that Amy was accepted and settled in properly."

"And now you can leave again, and take the girl with you," Cedric said.

"They will both be staying here with me," Winnie said. "Amy will be the perfect companion for our daughter."

"That is for me to decide," Cedric said. "I am the master of this house."

"No, Cedric. This time I am telling you how things will be," Winnie said.

"You dare to dictate to your husband?" Cedric demanded. His face had flushed bright red.

"Yes, I do," she said. "For too long I've been dictated to

by you. I've been at your mercy. You have held our secrets over me. Now, the tables are turned. If you don't want the whole truth to be made public, if you don't want to find yourself a public laughingstock, you'll do what I say."

There was a horrified silence in the room. Personally, I wanted to applaud.

"Winnie, what has gotten into you?" her father said angrily. "It's that woman. She's put these ridiculous suffragist ideas into your head."

"And you think I should listen to wise and good men like you and Cedric?" Winnie demanded. "You, who wrecked my sister's life and then wrecked mine, all for the sake of your own social-climbing ambition?"

"Enough," Mr. Carmichael snapped. "If I were your husband, I'd put you over my knee and give you a good spanking. It's what you deserve."

"Fortunately I have the Sullivans and Aunt Florence here, who are quite aware of what has happened in this family and will make sure of my well-being." Winnie gave him a long, hard stare.

"We'll discuss this later in private, Winnie," Cedric said, standing in front of her in a manner that could be described as threatening. "We will not air dirty linen in the presence of others. People of my class and status in life do not do that."

"What do they do, Cedric?" she demanded. "How low do they stoop?"

He refused to answer that one, but turned on his heel and stalked out of the room. We heard a door slam across the hallway.

I glanced across at Daniel. "We should leave, I think," he said. "This is a family matter for them to sort out."

Winnie came over to me. "Don't go," she said. "Not yet, please." And I saw fear again in her eyes.

As you can imagine, the rest of the day was not the most pleasant. Winnie focused her attention on her daughter and niece, showing them around, deciding on which rooms they should have and how they wanted them to be decorated. It was all rather heady for both girls, who had grown up in poverty, but I could see that they were glad to be companions in this house.

"You took an awful risk bringing Lizzie's daughter into the house and trying to pass her off as Charlotte," Daniel's mother said, as we sat together with Aunt Florence in an otherwise empty gallery.

Aunt Florence nodded. "You are well aware that I've always been known for my impetuous nature. I just thought that . . ." The rest of the sentence was left hanging.

"I understand it well," I said. "You are like me. You want to make everything right for everybody."

"I do. I knew I had to do something to save Lizzie's child and frankly I didn't mind if that meant Winnie became aware of her sister's plight."

"And if you hadn't taken in little Ivy, it would have worked." I turned to Daniel's mother.

"It seems I am destined never to keep a trainee maid for two minutes," Daniel's mother said with a wry smile. "First Bridie and now Ivy. How extraordinary that the very house we are invited to turns out to be her home. How did she come to the orphanage, do you think?"

"I think the kidnapper must have claimed to be her father and the poor little thing was so traumatized that she couldn't deny it," I suggested.

As I said this I put events into place. And it all came back to Cedric. He had not followed Henry and Charlotte himself, because he had guarded Winnie to prevent her escape. But he must have paid Harris the gardener to follow them, to kill Henry or knock him out and throw him into the frigid waters of the Hudson, then to take the child to New York City and drop her at an orphanage two days before she was reported missing to the world. And when Harris returned to collect the large amount of money he had been promised, he met his own fate.

Then I took things one step further. Great-Aunt Clara, who sat at her window and watched things going on in the stableyard, had possibly witnessed money being exchanged between Cedric and Harris, and had put two and two together. And when her mind started to go and she rambled about old events, there was a danger she'd blurt out the truth. So Cedric stifled her. I wondered what we could do. Presumably there was no way of proving any of this. The main participants were now all dead, except for Cedric. And he was a respected man in the community. I wondered whether Winnie and the girls might now be in any danger or whether Cedric would accept his newfound family rather than create a scandal. I wondered if I should approach Winnie's father. He had betrayed both his daughters before, but surely he would put Winnie's safety and happiness first now? And the fortune had been his. Presumably he still controlled the purse strings, something that clearly mattered to Cedric. *The ultimate bargaining tool,* I thought.

I went to find Daniel and talked this through with him. Daniel was not so sure. "You think the threat of withdrawing his allowance will make Cedric Van Aiken turn into a loving husband and father?" he asked. "Should a family be bound together by veiled threats and not by love?"

"If it were up to me, I'd remove Winnie from this place and set her up in a comfortable home with her new daughters and Miss Lind to keep an eye on her," I said. "But it's not up to me. I just want to keep her safe."

"Do you think she won't be safe?" he asked.

"You heard Cedric talking about her mental instability, didn't you? I'd wager he was planning to have her committed to an insane asylum," I said. "You know how easy it is to get rid of an inconvenient wife. Then he would have her money, and I suspect an unfortunate accident might befall his daughter."

"You really believe he is as evil as that?" Daniel asked.

I nodded. "Yes, I do. Any man who can calmly have his best friend killed and his daughter sent to an orphanage has no heart. I consider him capable of any kind of evil."

"Then what do you suggest?"

"That you use your power as a police captain," I said. "You tell him that we know exactly what happened ten years ago and that he will be watched. If anything happens to his wife or daughter, you will have him arrested, and the NYPD is very capable of making charges stick."

He had to smile at that. "You realize that the New York Police Department has no power out here."

"I do, but Cedric might not."

"I'm glad you are not on the force yourself," he said. "I think you'd be among the most crooked of them."

"No, I just want justice to be served," I said. "Like Miss Lind, I want to make everything right for everyone."

He crossed the room and stared out of the window. It was snowing again, swirling white flakes blotting out the landscape. "I'll have a word with him," he said. "Not threaten him, but just let him know what we now know." He turned back to me. "Then, for God's sake, let's get out of here. I can't wait to be home."

"Neither can I," I said.

Twenty-seven

I was dreaming I was back home in Ireland. Our cottage was cozy and snug while a gale blustered at the windows. The fire crackled and glowed and the sweet smell of peat smoke hung in the air. I opened my eyes, savoring the memory, until I realized that the smoke had not been in my dream. It still tickled my nostrils. *The fire is smoking,* I thought. *I should get up and poke it. Maybe the wind is coming down the chimney, and . . .*

That's when I realized that there were no fires in the bedrooms. The house was equipped with central heating. I got out of bed and opened the bedroom door. Smoke was curling toward me down the hallway and in the haze beyond I could hear a crackling sound.

"Daniel!" I shouted, running over to wake him. "Bridie!"

Bridie appeared, rubbing her eyes. "What's the matter?" she asked.

"Fire!" I screamed. "The house is on fire. Daniel, grab Liam. Bridie, give me your hand. We have to get out now."

Daniel scooped up our son, covering his head in a

blanket. We made our way to the stairs, only to find the staircase engulfed in flames.

"What are we going to do?" Bridie gasped, grabbing at my sleeve.

"There must be a servants' stair somewhere," I said. "There usually is in these big houses."

"You look for a way out. I'm going to get a pitcher and see if I can put out the flames," Daniel said.

"I'll help you. Bridie can take Liam."

"No. You take them down. Take Liam and get out now." He almost shoved me away from the glowing hallway.

"But I don't want to leave you here alone," I protested.

"Molly. Get them out."

"Well, don't you try to be too heroic" was my parting shot as I took my son. I heard Daniel going down the hallway, banging on doors and yelling, "Fire!"

We tried the doors, one by one, until at last a door opened into darkness and a waft of cold air rushed into my face. "This must be a servants' passage," I said. "Quick. This way."

I held Liam tightly to me, and Bridie grasped at my nightgown as we felt our way into darkness. We walked along a hall and then my foot reached into nothingness. Stairs going down. We felt our way, one by one. Down and down. The staircase seemed to go on forever. Then at last we were in another cold passage. I fumbled around on the wall and eventually located an electric light switch. The passage was flooded with the light from a bare bulb, revealing that it led directly into the servants' dining room and then the kitchen.

"Fire!" I yelled in case any of the servants slept down here. "Fire! Get out!" There was no reaction so I guessed that the servants slept on the top floor.

I handed the still-groggy Liam over to Bridie. "Take Liam outside. Go around to the front of the house and wait for me," I said.

"Don't go back up there again," Bridie begged. "It might all be on fire by now."

"I have to," I said. "The way the fire was racing up the stairwell it could have reached Ivy's room by now. She's on the top floor. I have to get her out, and to make sure Captain Sullivan doesn't try to be too brave and stupid!"

I pushed her in the direction of the back door, then went back up the stairs, my task now a little easier because I had light. As I reached the top of that first flight of stairs smoke swirled toward me, stinging my eyes and making me cough. I peered out into the hallway, but I could no longer see Daniel because the smoke was now so thick.

"Daniel?" I shouted, my voice harsh. I immediately started coughing again. "Daniel? Are you there?" I screamed it this time.

"I thought you'd gone," he shouted back. "Get out of here now."

"You get out too. I'm at the servants' staircase. It leads to the back of the house. Come on. Let's go. You can't do anything to stop the flames now."

I was relieved when a dark shape came toward me. I watched him emerge from the smoke, his face and night-shirt now dirt-streaked. "I have to agree with you," he said, wiping his face. "It's raging right up the stairwell. Maybe we can get to the telephone and call the local fire brigade, although I doubt that they'll have anything powerful enough to stop this. It's an inferno back there."

We entered the servants' passage.

"Where are you going now?" he shouted to me as he saw me head away from the staircase.

"Ivy. She's still sleeping in that little room next to the nursery," I shouted back.

"Are you mad? You're not going up there alone." He changed direction and followed me. I found the stair that led up and emerged onto the third-floor hallway. Smoke licked along it and at the far end was a red glow and the sound of roaring. I ran down the hall, banging on doors. "Fire! Get out!" I shouted, and got an immediate reaction. Doors opened and terrified maids emerged, wide-eyed, clutching each other.

"Down the stairs," Daniel shouted to them. "No, don't go back to get anything."

Only Ivy had not emerged at the sound of my voice. The flames were already licking at the ceiling and curling into the passage. I could feel the heat as I tried to open her door. It wouldn't budge.

"Daniel!" I screamed. He ran to me and flung his shoulder at the door. It burst open. I could make out Ivy's slender form asleep on the bed.

"Ivy, wake up." I tried to rouse her. She moaned and turned over in sleep.

"Grab one of her arms," Daniel commanded. Between us we hoisted her from the bed, dragged her down the hall, and then carried her down the stairs. Fortunately she weighed almost nothing, but I was glad he had come with me. I don't think I could have negotiated two flights of stairs alone with her. It wasn't until we were outside in the freezing night air that she started coughing and sat up, gasping for air.

"She was already overcome by smoke," Daniel said. "If we hadn't reached her soon, it would have been too late."

But my mind was moving along a different track. The girl that couldn't be roused. The door that wouldn't open. It seemed to me all too possible that Cedric had decided to get rid of an unwanted daughter by starting a fire that would impact her room before all others.

At the front of the house we found a huddled knot of people standing together. I spotted Daniel's mother, with her arm around Amy, the girl we had known as Charlotte, who was shivering in a cotton nightgown. I rushed to take Liam from Bridie. He was howling and screaming, "Mama! I want Mama."

"Thank God." Daniel's mother moved toward us as I took Liam into my arms. "And you have Ivy. Is she all right?"

"Smoke inhalation, I think," Daniel said as Bridie helped lead her to sit on the front steps. "She'll soon be fine in the fresh air."

Amy rushed over to her cousin. "Poor Ivy. Is she going to be all right?"

"I think so," I said.

Amy sat beside her. "Bridie and I will take care of her."

"Where is Winnie?" I asked, checking around me. "And Miss Lind?"

"I don't know," Daniel's mother said. "Mr. Carmichael led us out. He's gone to rouse the grounds staff."

"And Cedric? Where is he?"

"He was here," Daniel's mother said. "He went to try and reach the telephone."

"How did you get out?" I asked. "Is there a back stair to your side of the building?"

"There is. Across from the kitchen there is a passage past the butler's pantry and the closets," she said.

I glanced at Daniel. "We should go and see if they need help."

"You're not coming," Daniel said. "You stay here with your son."

"No, I want to help."

He put a firm hand on my shoulder. "I can handle it. You stay here."

"Be careful, Daniel," I called after him.

Liam was clinging like a limpet to my neck as Daniel took off back toward the house. "It's all right, my darling. We're safe. We're all safe," I told him. But I kept staring up at the house, that awful red glow between the drapes and the fire now licking at the top-floor windows. Where were Winnie and Florence? Where was Cedric?

Mr. Carmichael had rounded up grounds workers and grooms and they had started a bucket chain from the stream. It seemed like a waste of effort when one could hear the roar of the fire and watch top-floor drapes go up in flames. I found I was holding my breath. It was all I could do to stop myself from rushing after Daniel. Then to my intense relief I saw figures emerging from the darkness. Daniel and Aunt Florence were carrying Winnie between them.

"Winnie. Oh my God. Is she going to be all right?" Her father ran to meet them.

"We couldn't wake her," Aunt Florence said as they set Winnie down beside Ivy. "Thank heavens Captain Sullivan arrived, because I couldn't carry her by myself. She must have taken one of her sleeping powders. She's out to the world."

"Thank God." Mr. Carmichael kissed Winnie's unresponsive cheek. "My darling girl. I couldn't bear it if . . ."

It was the first time I had seen him show any affection toward his daughter. Perhaps he had just realized how his actions had affected lives and what he had put his daughters through. I watched Winnie's white face. She looked so peaceful, breathing rhythmically. *But one of her sleeping powders?* I asked myself. And Ivy was also conveniently deep asleep. Had Cedric wanted to get rid of his wife and a daughter at once? Where was he?

At that moment he appeared, running toward us across the grounds, dressed in his dressing gown and slippers. This alone was suspicious to me. None of us had had time to find our robes. I was already shivering in the bitter night air.

"Oh, you're all safe," Cedric said. "Thank God. I've just run over to the Briarcliff Lodge. They are sending men to help fight the fire and they have telephoned for the village fire brigade. But it's no use. They'll be too late to stop it, won't they?"

But men arrived quickly from the Briarcliff Lodge, carrying pumps and hoses. They were directed around to the back door and attacked the fire from the kitchens. Then we heard the clanging of a bell and the village fire brigade arrived, horses galloping madly as they pulled the engine up the driveway. With the combined efforts the fire was out within an hour. The stairwell and adjoining rooms were destroyed, but much of the house was unscathed. The gallery had been scorched, the grand piano eaten by the fire, and the other drawing room was now smoky and soggy, but the fire had not reached the servants' quarters or the back part of the house. So we sat in the servants' dining room while the cook made us hot milk with brandy in it for shock.

Winnie was finally revived and was fed hot milk by her father.

"It's all right, my little girl. You're going to be fine." He spoke to her as if she was three years old.

"My house. My family home." Cedric was near to tears. "Can it ever be rebuilt? Where shall we live?"

"I don't think it's too bad at all," Mr. Carmichael said. "Could have been much worse. It's mainly the foyer and the stairs. The flames shot straight upward. It must have been the candles on the Christmas tree that caught the tree on fire. You know how fiercely a dead tree burns."

"I blame myself," Cedric said. "I meant to make sure all the candles were out before I went to bed. I've done it all the other nights. But I was tired and we'd had quite a lot to drink, so I completely forgot."

I have been known to take risks in my life before. My husband and friends have told me I take too many. But I decided to take a huge risk now. I had no proof. It was only instinct; call it my Celtic sixth sense.

"The candles were all out when we went up to bed," I said. "I double-checked."

Cedric stared at me. I felt eyes on me and a silent sense of expectancy around the table. I plunged on, knowing what dangerous territory I was sailing into. "But later I was on my way to the bathroom and I heard footsteps and I watched you go down again, Cedric. And I saw you arranging the candles so that one was directly beneath a branch. And I think I heard the sound of you striking a match at you relit them."

"What?" Winnie's father stood up.

"That's a lie," Cedric shouted. "You couldn't possibly have seen me. I made sure that everyone . . ."

There was silence.

"You made sure that what, Cedric?" Aunt Florence asked. "That everyone was safely in their rooms?"

"Before you administered the sleeping draught to Ivy and Winnie?" I looked across at Winnie's white and dazed face. "You must really have wanted your wife and daughter out of the way to have risked burning down your beloved home."

Cedric was standing facing us. His eyes were blazing. "You can prove nothing of this. One hysterical woman's testimony doesn't count. An elderly spinster aunt. Who would believe a meddling, stupid old woman who brought a brat into my house and convinced my wife it was her long-lost daughter?"

"But I remember you, Papa," Ivy said. "Now I do remember you. It's coming back, little bits of memory. You didn't want me then, did you? That pony you put me on and then you hit it and made it run off with me."

"Cedric?" Winnie demanded. "Then my suspicions were right in those days. You were trying to get rid of her. I always thought that Lottie was too accident-prone. I didn't want to suspect . . ."

"Stupid women. A bunch of meddling, interfering women," he shouted. He lunged at Aunt Florence, who was standing behind him. "And you are the worst. Get out of my sight."

Aunt Florence reeled backward and was caught by Mr. Carmichael. "Steady on," he said. "Cedric, have you gone mad?"

"Get out of my house, all of you!" Cedric screamed. "Do you hear me? Get out."

Daniel moved quietly over to Cedric. "Cedric Van Aiken, I am arresting you for the attempted murder of your wife and daughter," he said. "And for the murder of Clara Van Aiken."

"Aunt Clara? You killed Aunt Clara?" Winnie demanded. "No, that can't be true."

"I'm afraid it is," I said. "She was suffocated. Daniel and I both saw the signs."

"You'll not lay a finger on me." Cedric fought Daniel off and rushed from the room. Daniel chased after him. I followed. Cedric rushed up the servants' stair with Daniel in hot pursuit behind him. Their footsteps echoed from the bare walls and linoleum-covered floors. I couldn't keep up, wearing my dainty slippers, now wet and soggy with snow. And I was finding it hard to breathe in the lingering smell of smoke. I heard Daniel shout as they went up the second flight.

"It's no use. You can't get away," he shouted.

And then I heard no more. No more footsteps. Nothing. I came out onto the upper hallway. The acrid smell of burning still stung my eyes and nose. It was pitch dark up there. My heart was thudding. I had no idea where they were or what kind of cat-and-mouse game they were playing. I didn't want to call Daniel and put him in any more danger. *An electric light switch,* I thought. *There must be a switch on the wall.* I started groping around me and then I heard the scream. And then the sickening thud.

"Not Daniel," I whispered to myself. "Daniel!" I shouted.

He came toward me, grim-faced. "Cedric Van Aiken just threw himself down the stairwell," he said.

He took my hand and led me back down. We found the others clustered around the servants' stair. When Daniel delivered the news to them, Winnie gasped and put her hand up to her mouth. Ivy rushed over to her. "Don't cry, Mama. I'm here. I'll look after you."

"We'll all look after you," Aunt Florence said.

I helped lead Winnie back to a chair. She sat down, staring in front of her. "I can't believe it," she said. "The nightmare is finally over."

Twenty-eight

Later that night Daniel and I were safely back in our room. The local police had been called, and the doctor. The verdict was given as death by misadventure. I could see it was better if it was left that way. But as I snuggled up to Daniel in bed I whispered, "Daniel, you didn't actually push him over the edge, did you?"

His grip around my shoulder tightened. "What an awful thing to think about your husband. Much as I would have liked to push Cedric Van Aiken off the nearest cliff, I did not touch him. He waited until I closed in on him and then he jumped." He paused, then added, "I am one of the few straight police officers in New York City, remember. I swore to uphold the law and save lives and that's what I've tried to do."

"I'm sorry," I said. "I might have pushed him if I had been up there."

He chuckled. "You certainly might have. So let me ask you something: Did you really see him going down again to light the candles on the tree?"

"Between ourselves, no," I said. "But I guessed that was

what must have happened, and I wanted to see how he'd behave if he was cornered."

Daniel shook his head. "Just when I think you have settled down to being a model wife and mother, you go back to your old ways and act without thinking."

"It worked though, didn't it?" I said. "Just think, if I hadn't made him more or less confess, we'd have considered the fire an accident. We'd have gone home and sooner or later something horrible would have happened to Ivy and to Winnie."

"Quite possibly," he said.

"I wonder what will happen now," I said.

"I've no doubt Miss Lind will have everything organized and back to normal in days," Daniel said dryly.

And, for the first time in ages, I laughed.

The next morning we examined the sorry remains of the center of the house.

"It's clear we can't live here for a while," Mr. Carmichael said. "We'll move to the Briarcliff Lodge while I find a place to rent nearby."

"Oh, no," Daniel's mother said. "I have a better idea. Why don't you all come and stay with me until you find a more permanent solution? I have enough rooms if the girls don't mind sharing."

"We don't mind." Ivy grinned at her cousin, Amy. It seemed that the fire had turned them into instant friends.

"But what about my sister?" Winnie asked. "What about Lizzie? We can't leave her to die in some hospital ward."

"You and I can share, Winnie dear," Florence said. "We'll

make room for Lizzie if Mrs. Sullivan agrees." And she looked first at Daniel's mother and then at Mr. Carmichael.

The latter cleared his throat. "I will be happy to pay for the best nursing home. . . ."

"No, not necessary," Daniel's mother said. "She must come to us. She must be with her family. I'm delighted to do anything to help." And I could see that she was. It felt good to be needed.

And so it was arranged. I went upstairs to pack up our belongings. I was in the midst of rounding up Liam's blocks when I heard the sound of agitated voices and feet running down the hall. Sid and Gus came bursting into my room.

"Thank God, thank God." Sid rushed over to me. "We knew nothing about the fire until we came down to breakfast this morning. How terrible for you. How terrible for the Van Aikens."

"Is everyone all right?" Gus asked.

"Everyone except Mr. Van Aiken," I said. I paused, forming a sentence in my head. "Unfortunately he fell from the top-floor landing."

"How terrible. Poor Mrs. Van Aiken."

I wondered if I would ever tell them the truth. Probably not. Winnie was now free. She had her daughter back and her aunt to look after her. I wondered if she would ever return to live at Greenbriars.

Our bags were carried down to the waiting carriage. Sid and Gus stood outside, waiting to wave to us as we departed. "We'll be home in a couple of days," Sid said. "The others wanted to stay over the New Year, but we find we've done enough celebrating. Now we want to get back to our boring old routine."

"Boring? You?" I laughed. "Who else turns their living room into a Mongolian yurt and cooks Peking duck?"

As we walked out into the cold, crisp day, Winnie drew me aside. "I want to thank you," she said quietly. "You have given me my life. Anything I can do for you in return, please ask. And if I hire a tutor for my girls when I am settled in a new place, maybe Bridie would like to come and join them. They have become so fond of her."

And of course then it came back to me. Bridie was leaving. Our stay at Greenbriars, and all the drama, had pushed that worrying thought from my mind.

"That is very kind of you," I said. I couldn't form the words to say any more.

And so we departed. We arrived home on a gray, dreary day, with the wind from the Hudson blowing sleet into our faces. Our little house seemed small and shabby after all that luxury, but I can't tell you how glad I was to be home. Liam also seemed happy to be back in his usual surroundings, immediately transporting his toys one by one in the wagon all over the downstairs floor. Bridie, I noticed, had become awfully quiet.

"You must miss Ivy and Amy," I said.

"Yes." She nodded.

I knew what she was thinking, but I couldn't find any words to comfort her. To take her mind off things we decided to open Sid and Gus's big pile of presents. Liam unwrapped his mechanical bear. Daniel wound it up for him. The bear immediately turned a somersault toward

Liam. Liam gave a frightened cry and rushed over to me, pawing at my skirt. "Up," he said. "Up."

"It's a friendly bear," I said. "It won't hurt you. See, it wants to be friends with your other new bear."

I put them together. Liam eyed them suspiciously. Luckily Sid and Gus had a second gift for him, some wooden soldiers. These were an instant success as they could be transported into battle in the horse and cart. Daniel and I were given a carved spice rack, stocked with jars of spices. *To take your cuisine into other realms,* Sid had written.

"Personally I'm quite happy with my Irish stew," Daniel commented.

I could see Bridie looking around for her gift. Surely they hadn't forgotten her? Then I saw the slim envelope with her name on it. She opened it, stared at the piece of paper inside, and then smiled.

"What is it?" I asked.

"They want me to choose any books I want from their library. They will pay to have them shipped to Ireland. It's so kind of them." And she burst into tears.

I put my arms around her. "It will be all right, I promise you," I said.

"How can it?" she said.

I couldn't answer that.

We had been home for two days when we received a letter from Daniel's mother. It was just a line to let us know that they had all settled in happily at her home. They were a little cramped, but everyone seemed to have accepted the situation well. Ivy, now Lottie, was blossoming by the minute and she and Amy were as thick as thieves. But the main news was that Winnie's sister, Lizzie, had been found and brought to the house with a nurse. She was very weak and not expected to live long, but at least she would be surrounded by those she loved.

I thought of how hard it must have been for her all these years, living in secrecy under an assumed name. The world is not kind to mothers of illegitimate children. And how unfair it was that the man who caused this shame went on living his own life, with his own family, with no censure at all. I wondered if things would ever change. Not until we had the vote; that was for sure.

Sid and Gus arrived home and told me they had decided to throw a big New Year's Eve party. They quizzed me about themes. Maharaja's palace? Turkish harem? The North Pole? I knew they were working hard to cheer me up, but I could not get into the spirit of celebration and fun. The depression I had held at bay over the excitement of the Christmas holiday now threatened to creep back and overwhelm me as I thought of losing Bridie. I tried to keep myself as busy as possible. I swept; I dusted; I polished and cleaned. Anything to make myself so tired that I fell asleep.

New Year's Eve approached. I went over to help Sid and Gus decorate. They had settled on the harem theme because, as Gus put it, "Sid has always wanted to wear a diamond in her belly button."

She took me aside as we started decorating. "We want to do something that's fun for Bridie. And there's something else, Molly. Sid and I have been talking about it. Do you not think that one of us could adopt her? You know we would love to, but you might also want to."

"It would be up to her father, Gus," I said. "She does have a parent who apparently wants to have her with him and take care of her."

"But surely he can't give her what we can."

"We don't know that," I said. "If he has indeed made a fortune, then she'll have a good life. Dublin and Belfast are fine cities."

"I dare say." She sighed. "But I don't want to give her up without a fight."

We draped the house with bright fabrics, bronze lamps, Oriental statues. Sid brought joss sticks from Chinatown and falafel and hummus from a deli. Then we threaded lamb onto skewers to grill kebabs with a yogurt dip. It was all incredibly exotic for me. They made a wicked-looking punch, even though I pointed out to them that those women in harems were Moslem and thus didn't drink.

"We don't need to be too accurate," Gus said. "And we do want everyone to enjoy themselves."

When the time came Daniel didn't want to attend. "Half-naked women and their perverted friends?" he said.

"Don't be such a spoilsport," I retorted. "We don't have to expose our belly buttons."

"You go, then," he said. "I'll stay home and look after Liam."

"Are you sure?"

"You and Bridie go and enjoy," he said. "It will give her something to remember."

"A party with my half-naked women and their perverted friends?" I asked, giving him a sarcastic smile.

"Well, maybe they are not as bad as all that," he said, smiling back at me. "And the two women are awfully fond of her."

So Bridie and I draped ourselves with fabric and tulle veils and off we went. It was tremendous fun. Sid and Gus's friends were an interesting mixture of earnest suffragists and writers as well as flamboyant artists and playwrights. They all seemed to have an equally good time and Bridie and I stayed to toast the New Year. As we crossed Patchin Place to come home Bridie said to me, "This will have been the best New Year's of my life."

Twenty-nine

On the second of January, Daniel went to meet the new commissioner. I felt as nervous for him as he was. After all, his whole career, our whole future, hung in the balance. If he felt he was no longer welcomed and respected in the New York police force, he would have to go elsewhere. Either he'd apply for the chief of police position in White Plains or choose to work full-time for Mr. John Wilkie in Washington. And we'd move away from our dear little house. I didn't like to think of either possibility.

Bridie asked whether she should go back to school. "I've already said good-bye to everyone," she said. "I don't want to go through that again."

So I let her stay home. We were both bundles of nerves, pacing and waiting. Seamus's letter had only said the new year, not an actual day. That could have meant anytime in January or February, I supposed. Poor Bridie could not be going through this torture for days or even months.

"If he doesn't come tomorrow, go back to school," I said. "At least you'll be kept busy there."

"Perhaps he has changed his mind," she said hopefully.

I took her little face in my hands. "Bridie, he is your father and he does love you," I said. "Do you really not want to be with him again?"

"I suppose it's terrible to say it, but I want to be with you. You and the ladies across the street and Captain Sullivan's mother. You are my family now. I don't feel Irish and I don't want to live in Ireland."

"I'm sure you'll feel differently when you see him again and he takes you to a fine new house," I said, but I couldn't sound convincing.

Daniel was gone all day and didn't arrive home until darkness had fallen. He stepped into the front hall, unwinding the scarf from around his face. "My, but it's bitter out there tonight," he said.

I came to help him off with his coat. "What news?" I asked. "You've been gone all day."

"Yes," he said. "And I don't want to speak too soon, but the news is all good, I think. The new commissioner knew my father. He remembered him well. Thought he was a fine man. A man whose word he could rely on. And he looked forward to having me to rely on too. He said he'd heard rumors, and heard that I was thinking of leaving. He hoped that wasn't the case."

My eyes didn't leave his face. "So I told him as long as I had his confidence I'd give it another chance. And yes, he could count on me to be perfectly straight, to do the right thing."

"So you're going to stay?" I tried to keep my voice even.

He put his hands on my shoulders. "Look, I know how

unsettling this last year has been for you. I dragged you into danger in San Francisco. You never knew whether I was alive or not when I was working in Washington. I can't put you through that anymore. I want you to be safe and happy and with your friends. I want us to settle down and have more children."

"I do too," I said.

"You wait. We'll have another baby this year, I promise you." He drew me to him, slipped his arms around my waist, and kissed me.

Our love tryst in the front hall was interrupted by a knock on the door.

"Probably Sid and Gus wanting to know what has happened," I said. "They must have spotted you coming home."

"Talk about no peace for the wicked." Daniel gave me a wry smile as he went to open the door. Then I heard him say, "Oh! Can I help you?"

"We're looking for Bridie O'Connor," a boy's voice said, with a hint of aggression to his tone.

Curious, I joined Daniel at the door. Standing in front of me was a boy I recognized, although he had grown considerably since I saw him last: It was James, one of Seamus's cousin's sons. I had stayed with that family when I first arrived in New York. Hovel would have been a polite term for their terrible tenement home. And my memories of the family had not been more favorable. But James had been an appealing little boy in those days. He was now a scruffy and disreputable-looking adolescent.

"James, isn't it?" I said. "How good to see you again. Bridie's in the kitchen. Come on in."

"I've brought Cousin Seamus with me," the boy said, glancing back into the street nervously. "He's come looking for Bridie."

The dark shape in the swirling snowflakes revealed itself to be Seamus, all bundled up. He stepped forward, holding out a big, meaty hand. "It's good to see you again, Molly Murphy. You're looking grand. All grown-up and settled as a married woman now." He gave me a firm handshake. "And you remember my boy, Shamey."

Another shape revealed itself through the swirling snow.

"I do. Come in, out of the cold." I ushered them into my narrow hallway.

Shamey had been a skinny little scrap of a lad when I had first brought him from Ireland six years ago. Now he looked like a man; big, strapping, and with the first sprouts of hair growing above his lip.

"How are you, Miss Molly?" he said in a deep man's voice. "Or should I say Mrs. Sullivan?"

"You've certainly grown up." I shook his hand. "I'd never have recognized you."

"Well, I've been doing a man's work so now I have a man's body," he said.

We stood in the front hall, their breath coming out like steam. "And this is my husband, Captain Sullivan," I said. "No doubt you remember him."

Hands were shaken. I noticed James was glancing across at Daniel and edging toward the front door. If he was anything like his brother, he had become a Junior Eastman, a member of one of the city's most notorious gangs.

"I'll be leaving you then," he said. "You can find your own way back, I've no doubt."

And he ran off into the night.

I went to close the front door. "Bridie. Come and see who is here," I shouted, although I was sure she could have heard everything we had said from the kitchen.

"Just a minute," Seamus said. "I've brought someone else with me I want you all to meet." He turned back to the alley. "Come on in, my love."

"I thought you were going to keep me standing out here freezing forever, Seamus," said a female voice, and a large woman stepped over the threshold. She was olive-skinned with flashing dark eyes. Her hat was decorated liberally with feathers and fruit and the whole effect was exotic looking. She stared at me and then at Daniel. "Well, here's a warm welcome, I must say."

Seamus cleared his throat. "I'd like you to meet my new wife, Lola," he said. Then his face lit up as he saw his daughter coming down the hall toward him. "Well, if it isn't my little Bridie, all grown-up." He opened his arms wide. "Come and give your old dad a hug."

Bridie came to him, slowly. He went to embrace her. She pushed him away. "Da, you're all wet," she said.

He laughed. "So I am."

"Here, let me take your coats," Daniel said.

We helped them out of their outer garments.

"And please come through to the back parlor," I said. "We've no fire alight in the front parlor tonight, but the back is snug enough." I led them through and went to retrieve Liam from the kitchen.

"You've a little one of your own. He's a strapping fine boy," Seamus said as I carried him through and handed him to Daniel.

"Yes. We're very proud of him," Daniel replied, still stiffly formal. "Won't you take a seat?"

"Thank you kindly," Seamus said. "But first Bridie can now give her daddy a hug and a kiss."

Bridie stood like a statue while he embraced her. "And here's your big brother, dying to see you again. You don't know how he's talked about you, all this time away. Wondering how you were and what was happening to you."

"Bridie?" Young Shamey took a tentative step toward her. "You're looking grand. All grown-up like a lady." And he hugged her, tentatively, as if she was made of porcelain.

"It's good to see you too, Shamey," she said.

"Would you listen to her?" Shamey laughed. "She sounds like a Yankee, doesn't she?"

Seamus took Bridie's hand. "And this, my darling, is your new mother. Come and say hello to her. I've told her all about you."

Lola pushed Shamey aside and went up to Bridie. "Well, aren't you a pretty little slip of a thing," she said. "I know we're going to get along just famously." She took Bridie's face in her hands and planted a kiss on both of Bridie's cheeks.

"When did you get married again, Da?" Bridie asked him.

"In the fall. I'd had my eye on Lola for some time. She was the barmaid in my favorite tavern in New Orleans. All the fellas liked her and I don't know why she favored a lump of lard like me, but she did. I asked and she said yes."

"Don't put yourself down, Seamus," Lola said. "You treated me like a lady, which is more than I can say for some of them."

"Are you from New Orleans, Mrs. O'Connor?" I asked.

"Lola, please. We don't stand on formality here. No, I'm not from New Orleans. I'm a little nomad. No real home ever. My mother was of Spanish origin. She was a dancer, and my father was a no-good sailor. We lived all over the place. I was orphaned young and have had to make my own way in the world. And finally I've landed on my feet with this fine man and we're looking forward to settling down and having a lovely life together."

Seamus was beaming. "I've saved a tidy sum and I'm going to provide the best for my family."

Lola slipped her arm through Seamus's. "We're going to buy land, near where his family came from, but near enough to Belfast so that I can go shopping and we can visit the theater if we've a mind to. And we're going to raise chickens. I've always wanted to raise chickens."

"And pigs too. Remember we talked about pigs," Seamus said. "Plenty of profit in pigs."

"What about you, Shamey?" I asked.

"I'm going to help them get the farm going," Shamey said. "And then Da has promised me land of my own. We'll be the big land-owning family and have people working for us, instead of the English foreigners owning everything. And when Ireland is finally independent, then we'll be leaders. You wait and see."

"So you see, Bridie, you won't want for anything," Seamus said. "And another piece of news for you. You're going to be a big sister. Lola is expecting a little one this summer. How about that, eh?"

"I bet she'll be a splendid little nursemaid and mother's helper," Lola said.

"But what about school, Da?" Bridie said. "Where will I go to school if we live out on the land?"

"School?" Lola let out a loud laugh. "Aren't you done with school yet? How old are you?"

"Almost thirteen," Bridie said.

"Well, there you are then." Lola was still chuckling. "Most people have all the schooling they want by twelve, don't they? You know how to read and write, don't you? What more do you need?"

"I want to go on studying," Bridie said. "I want to go to a college like the ladies across the street. I might want to be a teacher or a writer."

"Would you hark at her?" Lola said, digging Seamus in the ribs. "She's certainly picked up airs and graces since you left her here."

"We can see about a school for you, if that's what you want, Bridie," Seamus said. "Now go up and pack up your things. We're staying at a hotel near the docks and I've passage booked for us on the *Majestic,* sailing in two days for Liverpool. You remember the *Majestic,* don't you? It was the ship you came on, only this time we'll be in a good cabin, not down below." He gave her an encouraging smile.

"I'm not coming with you," Bridie said.

There was a sudden silence.

"What did you say?" Seamus demanded.

Bridie stood staring defiantly at him. "I said I'm not coming. I don't want your kind of life. I want to stay here."

"But I'm your father," Seamus said. "You're my child and you do what I say. And I say I want you home in Ireland with me."

"You don't care about me at all." Bridie's voice was now raised. "You left me to be a servant. If it weren't for Molly and Captain Sullivan's mother, I'd be scrubbing floors today. Maybe getting beaten and sleeping in a cellar with rats. They saved me. They have educated me and they have loved me. You couldn't love me or you wouldn't have abandoned me."

"I did what I had to so I could make money," he said gruffly. "Make a decent life for us. That's what I wanted. We both went through a lot down there in Panama. We both nearly died of sickness. And then I worked my way home; hard manual work on the docks, Bridie. All so that I could finally provide for my family. I'm grateful for what these people have done for you, but now I want you back again."

Bridie shook her head. Her cheeks were flushed and her eyes very bright. "You might want me for myself, but she wants an unpaid nursemaid for your new child. And that's not what I want. If you really loved me, you'd want what was best for me."

"Of course I love you and I want you back where you belong. We're not fancy folk. I want you home with me. Back in Ireland."

"You can't make me come," Bridie said. I was watching her with amazement. She had always been such a quiet and compliant little thing before now. Never fighting to get her own way.

"Oh, yes, I can. I can go to the police and have you brought to the ship, if I've a mind to."

"Captain Sullivan is one of the most important policemen in New York City and he would stop you," Bridie said. "He wouldn't want me to go where I'd just be an unpaid servant."

"Don't say that. You wouldn't be treated like a servant."

"Yes, I would." She turned to glare at Lola. "You heard what she said. I'd be a grand little mother's helper. And she thinks I have all the schooling I need. And there is no way I could go to a proper school out on a farm."

"But, Bridie, my darling girl." Seamus stepped forward and stroked her cheek. "I'm awful fond of you. You remind me of my dear dead Kathleen."

"I love you too, Da." Bridie was crying now. "But you have to see that's not the life for me. I love books and studying and the ladies across the street have promised to send me to their college one day. To Vassar, Da. Can you imagine that? I could be anything I wanted to be."

Lola grabbed Seamus's arm and dragged him away from his daughter. "Oh, let her go, Seamus. Who'd want a surly-faced, ungrateful kid like that round the place? You can see right now she'd be more trouble than she was worth."

"But she's all I've got to remind me of my Kathleen," he said.

"Kathleen's dead and buried. You've got me now." Lola

put her hand on his shoulder. "And I can give you any number of daughters, I promise you. I can fill the house with daughters. Forget about this one. If she wants to stay here, I say good luck to her. Come on, let's leave this poky little place and get back to the hotel."

Seamus shook her off and stood facing Bridie. "If you're sure that's what you want?"

"It is, Da."

"And how do you know these people are going to want to keep you?" he said. "What if this lady has daughters of her own someday and doesn't have a place for you anymore? What then, eh? Thrown out on the streets?"

I went over to Bridie and put an arm around her shoulder. "First of all I would never throw her out, whatever happened. I've loved her like my own daughter since I brought her across to Ellis Island as a terrified little scrap. But if I couldn't take care of her for any reason, she has more homes in New York. Plenty of people who love her would welcome her into their homes. My neighbors across the street also wanted to adopt her, and my husband's mother would certainly welcome her back. So you see, Seamus, Bridie is loved and wanted here."

"Well, that's that then." Lola brushed off her hands, then grabbed at Seamus's arm. "We'll be getting back to the hotel. I'm expecting a decent dinner tonight. A good steak."

Seamus was still looking at his daughter. "Will you at least come and wave good-bye to your old da?" he said. "Wave when the ship sails?"

"If you want me to."

"I do. I do want you to."

She nodded solemnly and I could tell that she was now torn. "Then I'll come. And maybe I'll come and visit you in Ireland someday, when I'm a college student or when I'm a writer."

"Lovely." He beamed at her. "I'd like that. Come and meet your new brothers and sisters. That will be grand."

He hugged her then, fiercely, and I realized the sacrifice he was making. *Would I give up Liam so that he had the chance for a better future?* I wondered. If Lola hadn't been in the picture, I believe I would have let her go without a fight. But I simply couldn't have sent her to live on a pig farm being bossed around by that self-centered, brash, and uneducated woman.

We walked them to the front door. They stepped out into the chill night air. We watched them walk down Patchin Place. Daniel closed the door and we stood there in the hallway. Bridie was in such a state of shock that she kept staring at the closed door. I put my arm around her shoulder. "Come on in by the fire, my love. You're shivering."

"I did the right thing, didn't I?" she said. Her voice quivered. "I mean, my poor da. He has been through a lot and he was always kind. It's just that . . ."

"I understand perfectly," I said. "You've changed. You've become a New Yorker. You've learned to love books. You should have every opportunity possible."

"And I certainly wouldn't get it on a pig farm looking after chickens and babies, would I?" she said, making me burst out laughing.

"No, you wouldn't." I led her back into the parlor. "You should go across the street and tell Sid and Gus," I said.

"They will be so happy. They wanted to adopt you, you know. But I'd never let that happen. You're my little girl. You always have been. In fact, why don't you start calling us Mom and Pop?"

"Really?" She looked across at Daniel.

"Why not?" Daniel said. "You've called me Captain Sullivan for years and it's far too formal."

Her eyes were sparkling. "All right. I will. And can I go over to the ladies now?"

"I've got a better idea," I said. "Come and help me in the kitchen, and we'll make a hot punch and warm up some of that gingerbread and we'll invite them for a celebration."

"Oh, yes. A celebration." Without warning she wrapped her arms around me. "You're the only mother I remember," she said.

We stood there, while tears of relief and happiness flowed down both our cheeks. The year had started off as one of losses, but it had ended with many things being found again. I looked around at my family with satisfaction and it came to me that I could look forward to the future with hope.